A Tangled Weave

BY MICHAEL SKEET

FIVE RIVERS PUBLISHING

WWW.FIVERIVERSPUBLISHING.COM

Five Rivers Publishing, 704 Queen Street, P.O. Box 293, Neustadt, ON N0G 2M0, Canada.

www.fiveriverspublishing.com

A Tangled Weave, Copyright © 2019 by Michael Skeet.

Edited by Lorina Stephens.

Cover Copyright © 2019 Jeff Minkevics.

Interior design and layout by Éric Desmarais.

Titles set in Chopin Script Font designed by Dieter Steffmann as an airy homage to the formal writing of early nineteenth century France.

Text set in Tinos designed by Steve Matteson as an innovative, refreshing serif design that is metrically compatible with Times New Roman™. Tinos offers improved on-screen readability characteristics and the pan-European WGL character set and solves the needs of developers looking for width-compatible fonts to address document portability across platforms.

Published in Canada

Library and Archives Canada Cataloguing in Publication

Title: A tangled weave / by Michael Skeet.

Names: Skeet, Michael, 1955- author.

Canadiana (print) 20189067438

Canadiana (ebook) 20189067446

ISBN (Print) 9781988274591

ISBN (EPUB) 9781988274607

For Lorna, always.
And in loving memory of Sara Simmons, who brought
Rat-Boy to life.

Contents

Chapter One

Blue Elephants

ROBERT, CHEVALIER DE Vimoutiers, hefted the purse he had hung from his belt and exhaled his relief at having escaped unscathed. His skill as a card-player—or, more likely, his luck—seemed to continue to improve and he wondered how much longer it would be before his luck ran out or his friends realized how often he won lately. *Perhaps the two are really the same thing,* he thought, letting the purse hang back down again. Its weight was a pleasant balance to the weight of the épée he wore on his left side.

He was still going to tell Maman that he was out of funds, though he might wait until just a few days before his allowance was due. It wouldn't be fair to her to make her think he was becoming independent of her, poor woman.

"Which way did he go?"

The voice was familiar, and came from the front door of Respire's gaming house. That didn't make it any less unpleasant to hear, and Robert stepped sideways into the deeper shadows of the port-cochère. "Vimoutiers!" the voice shouted. "You won't get away easily, you know." Laughter burst out around the declaration, and a cat-call or two. "It's not fair, you lucky ass—you have to give us a fair chance to win our money back."

I suppose they've realized it now, he thought. Striding into the street he began to look for a locked door—or gateway deep enough in which to hide from over-eager friends.

Victoire breathed a soft prayer, and the intensity of her God-light dropped until she could hardly see Hachette on the other side of the stable. The gaps in the door- and window-frames meant that more than the faintest light would be visible from the street outside, and she didn't want to attract attention to what she and the boy were doing here in the middle of the night.

The dense, sweet smell of hay and manure was at once strange and reassuring, triggering a faint memory of the crude pleasures of the trip she had once made over the Alps, to and back from the Italian lands of the Holy Roman Emperor. And the feel of the cloth under her fingers was exciting, promising wealth that would bring intense pleasure even if past experience argued that pleasure wouldn't last long.

"Thank God for Luc and his Apostles," she said. "They've delivered right on schedule, and I count twelve bundles including this one." She looked up at Hachette. "Sometimes there *is* honesty among thieves." Hachette grinned.

"Let's start breaking up these bundles," she told him. This stable, north of the Palais Cardinal on the Right Bank, had proved itself a safe enough temporary hiding place for the smuggled cloth she dealt in, but she always moved the bundles on as quickly as she could to the old house she had bought for her gang. The house was safer if only because there was always somebody there. Most loads—she ordered two a year—she had moved out of the stable within two nights of arrival. This time she was a day late in starting, but that was the fault of the weather, which had been hot, humid, and oppressive even at night.

"Show me what we got this time," Hachette said. "Please?" Hachette was twelve years old, going on thirty; this was his twelve-year-old side.

She smiled, nodded, and knelt down to cut open a bundle. Inside were bolts of painted Indian cotton, wrapped in wax-coated linen to protect them from moisture; she unwrapped one of the bolts and increased the light around them so Hachette could see.

"What are those?"

"Elephants," she told him. "Giant creatures that could squash you the way you'd squash a beetle."

"Wonderful." He almost sounded wistful. "What colour do you think that is?"

"Really hard to tell right now, Hachette, but I think it's blue."

"Do elephants come in blue in real life?"

"Do humans?" She smiled.

"They might." He knelt down, facing her. "Show me what you're going to do with them."

"Can't you wait until we start doing the work? I can't really show you until Catherine has worked her thread into the cloth."

"I want to see it first. And you don't have to wait for Catherine. I've seen you make the cloth dance, to show Catherine what she has to do before she even picks up a needle."

"Good God but you can be stubborn, Hachette." Well, a quick dance wouldn't take too long. She bent her head, closed her eyes, and began to pray, wrapping wisps of prayer around the image of the dancing beast in her mind.

After a moment she heard him giggle. Opening her eyes

7

again she saw one of the elephants—or the shadow of the beast on the cloth—dancing on its hind legs. *That's a nice effect,* she thought. *Must tell Catherine about it.* "There," she said as the dancing elephant faded into the dark. "Satisfied? Now will you start moving these bolts into hiding?"

He nodded. "That was good, Victoire. Thank you." Evidently satisfied, he set to work. As Victoire opened each bundle he helped her pull it apart into its component linen-wrapped bolts of cloth, each small enough for even Victoire to carry. As each bolt came free from a bundle, Victoire muttered over it a brief prayer to protect it from the smells emanating from the stable's regular inhabitants. Then Hachette dragged it across the stable, wooden sabots occasionally thumping when they encountered wood or stone set into the stable's floor of packed earth. Victoire worked to the rhythm of Hachette's steps and the sounds of him tucking bolts in hiding places built into the dark end of each stall.

"That's everything stowed away except these elephants," Hachette said as he knelt beside the first bolt they'd opened. "Is it all elephants?"

"No. Where's the fun in having it all the same?" *Fun.* She sometimes wondered if she found this work more exciting than was healthy. "Though I do think my favourite cloth is—" She stiffened, then looked to the door. "What was that?"

She was on her feet before she'd finished the question, and Hachette was right behind her.

"Shit," Hachette said. He'd dropped to his knees and was looking through one of the bigger gaps between door and frame. "There's someone out there. And he's waving to someone. God, it's Inspector Grenier."

Victoire didn't think; she had prepared herself for this

even though she'd hoped she would never need it. Grabbing the bolt of cloth, she ran back to the far end of the stable. She threw open the hidden rear door.

"Run," she told Hachette.

Blue elephants. I am going to the Bastille for the sake of blue elephants.

Victoire felt the soles of her boots skip and slide across the cobbles as she turned the corner, and for a horrifying moment the glamour that made them appear as sabots shimmered with threatened failure. "There! Up that way!" someone shouted, and she realized that she had never considered the need to disguise the chance that a hobnail might strike a spark on the cobbles, something no sabot could ever do. *Make a note of that for next time,* she thought to herself. *If there is a next time.*

She ducked down the first street she came to. It wasn't on her planned escape route, but right now taking a direct route mattered less than confusing the policemen chasing her. Besides, she knew where she was going and there were eight different routes to that doorway. When she had first contemplated this enterprise, Victoire had spent weeks analyzing every step of the routes she might need to take though night-time Paris. She could find her way to that door blindfolded if she had to.

Victoire paused in an alleyway just a stone's throw from the Tuilleries Palace, listening for sounds of pursuit. Steadying herself, getting her breathing back under control, she fixed in her mind her location, and the various routes to her intended hiding-place. The night air was warm and damp, and the city stank of a summer that had outlived its welcome. She was, she knew, contributing to the stink; running on such a warm, humid night had made her sweat like a blacksmith. At least she seemed to be safe now: the bulk of the palace was nearly as dark as the sky behind it with the emperor and his family not yet returned from climates cooler than this. Though it was now September it remained as hot as August had been, and anyone who could afford to was still well north of Paris.

She thought she might be safe for at least a few minutes, which would be enough time to hide the cotton she'd been carrying when she and Hachette fled the stable. Spotting a small gap between two buildings, she set the bundle into it. Then she prayed, weaving a glamour that would prevent anyone from seeing anything other than an extension of one of the walls. The prayer was stubborn, taking much longer to come together than it should have. She was, she knew, tired, but it shouldn't have been this hard. *This has never happened to you before,* she reminded herself as she resumed her journey.

The shouts of her pursuers seemed to be fainter. It was a good thing the archers of the Paris police were more enthusiastic than professional; smarter policemen would have kept silent as they searched, rather than betray their positions in this way. Smarter policemen wouldn't have given her even the small opportunity she'd had to escape the stable before they reached it. Still, Victoire decided it wasn't safe enough to risk a main street. She continued to use alleys and small, dirt-paved side streets as she made her way east, in the direction of the Place Imperial, toward the aristocratic neighbourhood called The Swamp—the *Marais*—and her intended hiding-place. The eastern edge of the city was far away from her true destination; the houses in the Marais were rich and large; and nobody would think of looking in one of them for the hard-bitten street tough she had prayed herself into resembling. One of them had a courtyard gate whose lock was surprisingly easy to pick, and lackeys behind it who were prone to drink and sleep.

She nearly tripped over the archer before she saw him. *Shit*, she thought, and the prayer was on her lips before she had to think it. She swung her fist in the general direction of the archer's jaw, but it was magic that slammed him backward and into the filth of the street.

Not before he had shouted the alarm.

No need to be careful now, she thought, and ran. If she managed to avoid obstacles or cramps in her side, she would be safely inside that ill-guarded courtyard before any of his fellows had caught up with the archer she'd just stunned. Ahead she could hear voices, but these weren't official; from the laughter she guessed they belonged to young aristos on their way home from a night in a tavern or gaming-house. She spared a small blasphemy for younger sons who never had to give a thought about where the money came from.

Finally, she was at the rue des Francs Bourgeois, and the glow from the occasional lantern provided enough light for her to spot the desired indent in the street, and then she was darting past the empty guard-house and into the alcove of the port-cochère.

And colliding with the other person hiding there.

"Get the hell out of my way," she gasped, wriggling back and out of his grasp. "What are you doing here?"

"I might ask you the same," someone asked, a young man judging from the voice. "After all, I was here first."

Oh, Lord. An aristo on a spree. "Why don't you go rejoin your friends? Surely they're looking for you."

"Of course they're looking for me. Why do you think I'm

here?" Then the idiot kindled a flame of God-light. "Who are you?"

"Put out that light, you horse's ass! Are you trying to bring the archers?" A horse's ass he doubtless was, but he could follow orders: the light vanished as quickly as it had appeared.

The impression she got before darkness wrapped him again was of someone young and fashionable, curls cascading from the top of his head over his shoulders and down his back. No doubt he was the sort who thought the emperor's court a place to be avoided at all costs. There wouldn't be an intelligent vapour in his head.

"Now that you mention it, perhaps I ought to call the archers," he said. "After all, you're quite a dodgy looking sort, for all that you don't precisely sound as if you're street-born and bred. And you've come charging in here, smashing into me and rumpling my suit and implying you somehow have a right to this spot that I don't."

"No, don't do that. It wouldn't—it wouldn't be wise." She felt sick. *I ran too far, too fast. I have to get inside there, even if I have to drag this clod in with me.* She found herself bending over, trying to fill her lungs and not quite succeeding. *I could probably manoeuvre him into leaving me, if I didn't look like someone who'd rather cut his throat than talk to him.* "Could I persuade you to at least look the other way for a moment?" It was a stupid idea; it was also the only one she had.

"I rather suspect it's too late for that," he said, and Victoire heard the shouting from the direction of the river. They were coming closer.

So. The Bastille it is, then. "Temple-cursed stupid blue elephants." She sighed and began to straighten.

"No, bend back over again like you were," he said.

"Whatever prayer you cast is starting to fail, and you're beginning to look as wobbly as"—he paused, and she could almost hear his smile—"as wobbly as we want them to think you're feeling." He was silent again, for a moment that was too long for comfort. Victoire, concerned, turned and looked up to find him staring at her, eyes widening. And then he said something extremely odd. "Oh, no. Not again."

Before she could ask what in God's heaven he had meant, he had edged between her and the street—in the process pushing her closer to the door and preventing her from standing upright. "Think wobbly thoughts," he said in a voice that suddenly sounded deeper, more thick. Then he thumped her, hard, in the middle of her back. Victoire began to cough.

"Hi, you!" a voice shouted from the street. Then it was closer, and more apologetic. "Sorry, monsieur. Thought you was someone else, there."

"That's surely not him," a second voice said. "Come on."

"No, there's someone else in there," said the first voice.

"My friend," said the young aristo. "A bad night at Respire's, I'm afraid, made worse by drinking as badly as he was playing."

"Did you see someone go by here a minute ago? Short little rat, long hair tied back. He came up this street, we know."

"Sorry, my good men, but I didn't see anything." A pause, then: "Oh, I heard something, all right. A God-awful clatter, going up that way. Probably heading to Les Halles, I should think."

"But you didn't—"

"No, I was too busy taking care of my friend here. As I said, a bit the worse for wine tonight."

"Let's have a look at your friend, then," said the second archer. "Right, sergeant? We're supposed to ask everyone, that's what the inspector said." The first archer—the sergeant, Victoire supposed—sighed the eternal disgust that experience felt for uninformed enthusiasm.

"I'll see if I can make him presentable," said the aristo. Victoire heard him turning around—was he really turning his back on policemen? She took a deep breath—it didn't hurt so much to breathe now—and resumed her straightening up.

Then she heard the aristo's muttered prayer, and the smell of vomit filled her nose. Horrible, bad-wine vomit. The smell was so strong, the suggestion so urgent that her exhausted stomach put up no fight whatever. She sank back to her knees, retching.

"Um," the archer said. "Maybe we don't have to intrude, eh, sergeant?"

"You're damned right we don't have to. That's nasty. And don't think I won't remember this, you clot." Victoire heard the slap of the back of the sergeant's hand connecting with his subordinate's head, followed by the clack of boot-nails on cobble-stones. The sergeant said, "Sorry to intrude, monsieur. Don't want to be rude, but I sort of feel an obligation to point out that you and your friend there is out after curfew."

"Never fear, sergeant. I intend to get my friend home and safely into bed just as soon as I can."

Victoire threw up again. With the last strength remaining to her, she tried to aim for the aristo's high-heeled shoes.

"They're gone," the aristo said, once she had finished spewing. "You can get up now. My name is—"

"No," she said, and tried to spit some of the foulness out of her mouth. "I don't want to know. I am nobody *you* need to know. And if you are still here when I am able to get up," Victoire said, gasping for breath and spitting some more, "I am going to gut you like a fish."

"What? I just saved you." The aristo sounded like a little boy arguing that he'd been punished unfairly.

"There was no need for you to be so thrice-damned realistic about it!" She sat back on her haunches, willing her stomach to stop clenching.

"I told you: your prayer was fading. If they'd got a good look at you I don't know what, exactly, they'd have seen, but I'm pretty sure they wouldn't have liked it. And I happen to know that prayer I used pretty well, so I knew it would work. My friends, ah, think it's an amusing way to end an evening's sport."

"I'll just bet they do," Victoire muttered. "Well, my good Monsieur, if what you say is true then I'm going to ask you to be on your way before I get up and go on mine. Believe me, you don't want to see anything that you didn't want the archers to see. It'll be safer for you. Trust me."

"Oh, that's just what I want," the aristo said. "To be safe is so much fun."

Robert tried to follow the mysterious—woman? He was pretty sure it had been a woman, her boyish glamour notwithstanding—but was forced to give up almost immediately. For one, she was just too good at not being followed. For another, there really were far too many archers out and about tonight, and it wouldn't be fair if his efforts accomplished nothing more than to help them find and arrest her. Whatever she had done, he decided, he wanted her to get away with it

"Oh mademoiselle, no!" Marie-Louise fluttered her hands, clearly wanting to hug Victoire and yet repulsed by the stained coat and shirt facing her. "What happened to you tonight? And where is the cloth?"

"Where is Hachette?" Catherine asked, coming up behind Marie-Louise with her eyes wide with fear.

"I have no idea where Hachette is, but I'm sure he's safe." Victoire felt herself smiling, despite her fear and anger, at the thought of the boy leading the archers on a chase that doubtless ended with him laughing and them plunging into the river. The boy could look after himself, no matter what the city or the authorities threw at him. And he, too, knew innumerable ways of making his way back to this tiny old house, on a rudely named side-street near l'hôpital de la Trinité, in which Victoire hid her enterprise amongst the prostitutes and beggars.

"As for what happened tonight, plenty happened and all of it bad. I'll tell you everything, Marie-Louise, but only after I've got out of these clothes and washed myself." She stripped off the coat. "You should probably burn these."

"Not until I've done everything in my power to clean them," Marie-Louise said. "Fabric this good should not be burnt, mademoiselle." Scurrying to the fireplace, she swung the big iron pot, on its hook, over the flames. "Catherine, don't just stand there gawking! Help her out of those clothes. We can brush the coat, but that shirt and trousers will have to be boiled."

Before the watch called out the next hour Victoire was in the small garden behind the house, cleaned up and as cool and comfortable as the weather allowed, wearing the lightest shift Catherine could find for her and sipping a cup of the half-sour wine that was the best they could currently afford. The house officially belonged to

Catherine, but it was Victoire who had bought it, to serve as the shop through which they sold their enchanted cloth to aristocratic women and bourgeois dressmakers. On the eastern edge of a small slum—a *cour des miracles*—north of the Halles marketplace and south-east of the greater slums near the Filles-Dieux convent, the house was old and decrepit enough to resist official notice, but close enough to rue St-Martin to allow Victoire and her employees—co-conspirators—easy access to the aristocratic houses of her customers.

Marie-Louise topped up the wine in Victoire's cup while Catherine twisted her arthritic fingers around one another, and both of them stared at her with nervous, unhappy faces.

"Grenier knew where the cloth was," she began, "and he knew we were coming to collect it." Victoire told them as much of the tale of their discovery and her escape as they had to hear. "The good news is, he doesn't really know much more about who we are than he did yesterday. The bad news is, we had to leave the cloth behind. It's hidden," she added as the others voiced their dismay. "But I don't know how dangerous it will be for us to try collecting it again." She relaxed her shoulders and slumped in the chair.

"It's hard to imagine him not finding the cloth, if he does any sort of search at all. His master de La Reynie will be pleased. And we are out several tens of gold Louis." She couldn't muster up the energy to be as angry as she ought to be, but she cursed anyway.

"What do we do now, Mademoiselle Victoire?" Catherine was brilliant where cloth and clothing were concerned, but in every other respect she might as well have been seven years old. That unworldliness made it all the more cruel that Victoire's mother had cast her away when arthritis attacked those talented fingers, crippling her usefulness as a seamstress and dressmaker.

"I don't know yet, Catherine. Well, I suppose we can pick up my hidden bundle, at first light tomorrow. Then we could walk to the stable. If we're very lucky the cloth will still be where we left it; it does look like cheap linen, after all. And Hachette and I got out before the archers came in, so perhaps they were too busy chasing us to do a proper search." She didn't really believe it would end so well, but she knew it wouldn't do Catherine and Marie-Louise any good to know that.

Had it been coincidence that had brought those archers to the livery at the precise moment she and Hachette were opening the smuggled bundles? Had Inspector Grenier finally learned to predict her movements? Or had she been betrayed? If so, by whom? Victoire closed her eyes, beginning to feel sick again.

Marie-Louise stood and said, "So let's not worry about anything tonight beyond getting some sleep. Plenty of time tomorrow to worry about the future, if God wills it." Marie-Louise was a weaver's widow. In Victoire's employ she had travelled further, and more frequently, than even the most exalted of aristocratic women. The men who actually brought the cloth over the mountains and into France for Victoire weren't allowed to buy even an ell of it from the Italian traders; it was Marie-Louise's eye that determined what would be purchased, and her sharp tongue that obtained the best terms.

"You're right, Marie-Louise." Victoire got to her feet. "I'm going home now." It wasn't always easy for her to decide which of the two buildings was her real home in Paris, but for now *home* was her soft bed in her parents' hôtel. "I'll come by tomorrow morning in my usual disguise; we'll discuss what's to be done then."

Her first thought, when she saw the lights through the small ground- and first-floor windows of the house, was that Inspector Grenier had somehow intuited her role in tonight's adventure and had arrived to arrest her. Then she saw the shadowed bulk of the travelling coach and the twist of tension unravelled.

Her parents were home.

Papa, of course, was still awake when she went upstairs, having entered the house through the kitchen door. "You are very late, my dear," he said as she passed the open door of his bedroom. His voice, soft and distracted, passed no judgments but she felt a flush nonetheless; she had never quite accustomed herself to the amount of lying she did to him.

"I was too involved in a conversation with Jeanette," she said, "and didn't notice the time."

"Jeanette—"

"Jeanette Desmarais," Victoire told him.

"Ah. The poor cousin of the de Beaune woman. A nonentity to be certain."

"But a friend for all that," Victoire told him, apologizing silently to Jeanette for the lie the poor woman was unknowingly supporting.

"Not everyone can have our pedigree," Papa said, and she heard the smile in his voice. "So I can't criticize you for your friends, any more than you should criticize me for the company I'm forced to keep at court."

I wish we had half our pedigree and twice our fortune, Victoire thought. But of course Papa would never agree, and so she never spoke in this way to him. Once upon a time she had been able to speak that way with Maman, but not for some time now.

"I feel somewhat guilty that I let you out of the hôtel on

your own so much, my dear. I trust you had a proper escort home?"

Victoire giggled, thinking of her current glamour's appearance. "A most thorough ruffian and street-rat," she said. "I felt completely safe, Papa. How was the north?"

"A bore, as it always is. But as Saint-Simon couldn't be with the emperor for the whole of the summer someone had to watch him, and that someone was me."

"Surely the duc de Saint-Simon doesn't believe the emperor would try to take away your ancient rights and privileges while he was away from Paris, Papa."

"These Burgundians are a crafty dynasty," Papa said, and for a moment Victoire wasn't completely certain he was joking. "It wasn't a complete waste, though. Tomorrow when I wake remind me to show you the latest addition to my library."

As Papa's library mostly consisted of books and manuscripts supporting the ancient pedigree of the comtes de Berenguer, Victoire felt no urgency to see his latest treasure. "I have to go out in the morning," she said, "but I will try to be back home by the time you awake." Which, she knew, would be well past mid-day.

"Don't forget to say hello to your mother before you leave."

And her damned priest, too, I suppose, she thought. "Good night, Papa."

He was staring at the cup in which his breakfast chocolate cooled when Robert de Vimoutiers realized today no longer had to be like yesterday or the day before. Or the day before that.

I believe I'm going to find out this morning who she is. Or at least I'm going to start finding her out.

That the person he'd met and helped last night was a young woman was by now nearly a certainty to him. He didn't know why he was certain, just that he was. Something in the eyes, perhaps. Mind, the eyes were really all he'd had a good look at before she'd made him douse his God-light. He felt the corners of his mouth tugged upward as he recalled the prayer he'd made to drive away the archers. *She didn't find it so funny,* the voice of his conscience reminded him. He decided she'd be less angry once she knew him a little better.

"You're suspiciously quiet this morning," Maman said. "And I don't like that grin either. What were you up to last night?"

"What am I up to every night?" There was a pretty good chance Maman knew the young woman, or at least her mother. But it was too soon to get Maman involved. And anyway, where was the fun in the discovery if all he had to do was ask over the breakfast table? "I was just remembering a joke I played on a chap after the party broke up."

"Very well. I certainly don't need—or want—to know about the sort of joke you find amusing." The duchesse de Vimoutiers sipped her chocolate. "You won't forget we are both expected at the Saint-Simon event tonight." Maman didn't seem to be looking forward to the event any more than Robert was, but he kept silent. There was nothing to be gained by reminding her of the rarity of such invitations lately.

"I won't forget."

"And you won't disappear fifteen minutes after you've greeted the hostess this time either."

"No, Maman. If you insist." He ventured a smile. It fell on salted ground.

Then an idea struck him, and he felt the smile broaden. "Lise is in the city now, isn't she?"

The name succeeded where smiles and raillery had failed. "She is," Maman said. "I had her to dinner last night and found her very well. I admit I would not have credited it, but marriage to that scoundrel has made her thrive." A pause for effect. "You could have talked with her if you had been able to keep yourself away from Respire's for one night." The look she gave him was far softer than her words had been.

"I will rectify my error this morning, Maman, if you'll tell me where I am most likely to find her."

Golden sparks flitted from side to side behind her closed eyelids, and up and down. Victoire, praying, corralled the sparks into lines without reducing their tendency to curl and curve. Once she felt her control of the sparks lock in, she built another layer of image in her mind, this one occupied by the pale grey thread Marie-Louise had placed beside Catherine's embroidery frame. Taking care, Victoire looped the prayer-sparks around, and bound them to the thread. It was a slow and tiring process, but doing it correctly was what made the cloth she sold so valuable.

She was sweating when she opened her eyes again. Catherine, Marie-Louise and Hachette sat in a row, watching her like cats staring at a fish-monger's inventory. "I think that's done it," she told them. "Catherine, it's over to you. Let me know when you've finished the first couple of elephants and we'll put my prayer to the test."

Catherine nodded, picked up a fine needle and leaned over the cloth stretched on the frame. Victoire turned away; she didn't like having to see reminders of Catherine's growing rheumatism. "Hachette, tell me what happened to you last night. How many archers were there?"

"Oh, dozens," he said. "Most of them went after you, and I didn't think that was fair. So I ducked back into the stable, grabbed some horse-shit and threw it at Grenier and their officer." He laughed. "That did the trick; I wound up with most of them chasing me. That was good with me—I know this city. Most of those asses are just a few months off the farm. They didn't stand a chance, you know. Not a chance, not with me."

"Oh, you're a clever rat-boy, you are," Marie-Louise muttered.

"Hey! You know you're not supposed to call me that."

"Well, you do have a ratty sort of face," Victoire said, unable to suppress a giggle. It was a relief to have the magic done with, at least for now.

Hachette sucked his prominent front teeth at her. "You can call me anything you like, mademoiselle Victoire. I just don't have to put up with it from the likes of them."

"You're prepared to cook for yourself, then?" Marie-Louise asked.

"Stop it, you two. You're disturbing Catherine," Victoire said. "Did you put the archers into the river again, Hachette?"

He smiled, toothily. "You should have seen it. It was absolutely splendid."

"I'm sure it was wonderful," she said. "Though I wish it hadn't been necessary at all." She watched Catherine embroidering for a moment. "I still don't understand how the cloth disappeared that way." Besides the bolt she had rescued they had recovered only one other—and that one Hachette had taken with him when he'd fled the stable.

"It doesn't make any sense to me either, Mademoiselle Victoire." He paused a moment. "Didn't make sense to the archers either."

Victoire, who had been watching Catherine embroider the cloth, turned back to Hachette. "To the archers?"

"Well, to their officers, anyway. I thought I'd sneak back to the stable once I'd dropped the archers in the river. Just as I get there, I see two officers coming out. One says to the other, 'I can't guess how they got it out of here. There were only two of them and I swear they didn't come back here.' And the other one says, 'And where could they take it?' I didn't understand what they was talking about until I went back inside."

"And found the cloth was all gone."

"Every last damned bolt and bundle," he grumbled.

"But if the archers didn't take the cloth," Marie-Louise began.

"Then who did?" Victoire finished for them all.

Chapter Two
Customer Dissatisfaction

THE MARQUISE DE Réalmont kept a very fashionable salon at her townhouse in the north-east corner of the Place Imperial. At one time no self-respecting person went there; it was frequented by nouveau-riches, nobles of the robe and even actresses and women authors. But some of the more salacious incidents of the Affair of the d'Audemars had taken place in the marquise's drawing room, and the resultant scandals had made her salon a much more attractive place in the following months. Even now, two years after the scandal, madame de Réalmont remained a popular hostess and Victoire was a regular visitor. The sort of woman who frequented the marquise's salon was exactly the sort who was prepared to pay good money to violate one of the emperor's more pointless laws, and look good while doing it.

Some of them already had, in fact, and it was to meet two of those women that she had come to the salon earlier today than usual. At first she could spot neither of them. Then she saw the next best thing: her friend Jeanette Desmarais, downtrodden cousin of the duchesse de Beaune and the friend who provided alibis when Victoire had to be out at night moving smuggled cloth.

"Good morning, Nicolette. Is your cousin here yet?"

"Oh, yes. And she's in a right mood, too. Better you have to talk with her, Victoire, than I."

"Oh, that will make of this the perfect week." Victoire looked around the room. "I don't see her."

"She's in the small salon. I'll walk with you."

"Thank you. You probably shouldn't come in with me, though." *I don't want this to be a public humiliation.*

Nicolette de Perusse, duchesse de Beaune, was a remarkably beautiful woman, and always dressed with an easy sort of sophistication Victoire understood well and matched whenever she could afford to. Today she wore one of the new light-weight dresses—it was of cotton, of course—and reclined on one of the marquise's new sofas, laid back far enough that her carefully crossed ankles were exposed. *It's a pity,* Victoire thought, *that she's not as pretty as she looks.*

"Madame," she said, curtsying deeply.

Before she could continue, the duchesse said, "I hear the most disturbing news this morning, Mademoiselle de Berenguer. Is it possible that it can be true?" The duchesse's eyes sparkled like so much ice.

Victoire set the purse down on the table beside the sofa. "My apologies, madame. I have, indeed, had some... difficulty with my latest shipment. Until the rest of it arrives, I think it best I return your deposit to you, less the price we agreed for the one bolt of cloth I was able to send to you this morning. I regret this inconvenience, I assure you."

"I don't care about your regrets," the duchesse said, "or your excuses. What I care about, mademoiselle, is the rest of the cloth that you promised would be delivered to my woman today. I have been waiting, mademoiselle, for months."

As have I, and at considerably more risk. "And I appreciate your patience, madame. There are some risks, however, that cannot be entirely avoided. The police do not have the same appreciation for fashion as we, I'm afraid."

"Don't try to make a joke of this, girl. I pay you well enough for those risks you run—and it's only your word that they're as bad as you say they are. I pay you—and my friends do."

Well, at least she's not trying to be subtle. "I understand, madame, and if you choose to take your business elsewhere there isn't much I can do about it."

"At least you have the wit to recognize that. Now: when will my cloth arrive?"

"Alas, madame, I cannot say. I have to find it first. I am still investigating the, ah, incident."

"I don't want investigations. I want my cotton!" The duchesse actually stamped her foot as she said this, and Victoire decided that even if she were able to complete this arrangement she would never again deal with the duchesse de Beaune. "My friends and I can make life difficult for you, mademoiselle, if this problem is not solved to my satisfaction." There was a stupid viciousness in her smile that left Victoire unable to respond. She had to concentrate on not shaking as she turned her back on her wealthiest customer and left the small salon.

A newcomer was in the large salon. He was very well-dressed, Victoire saw, and though it would be easy to dismiss the flamboyance of his costume, a closer look— and her own experience with matters of fashion—revealed that in fact he showed considerable style, and the purple of his coat set off perfectly both the silver of a long, double-pointed waistcoat and the light brown of his carefully curled hair. There were women amongst her customers who could take lessons in style from that young man.

He was speaking, with enthusiasm, to the marquise de Réalmont; the animation made his face look rather handsome, she thought, though her assessment argued he wasn't, really. Nor was he tall, nor especially well-built about the shoulders. But there was something about his eyes, she decided.

Then he noticed her. At first his smile was as vacant as it was genial, and Victoire began to regret her assessment of him as good-looking. Then his gaze reached her eyes, and his mouth fell open. She heard him speak—and felt her own jaw drop. It was only with an effort that she prevented herself from fleeing the house.

The good-looking young man was her clumsy saviour of the other night. *I'd rather be looking at Nicolas de La Reynie,* she thought; at least the lieutenant-general of police knew what he was about.

He surprised her, though, recovering faster than Victoire had. She was still trying to understand what in the world that man would even be doing here when he approached, the marquise in tow. "Would you believe it, my dear? The gentleman comes up to me and says he's absolutely smitten and simply must be introduced to you right away. Is it not remarkable?"

"That is a word for it, yes," Victoire said, utterly trapped.

"Robert, chevalier de Vimoutiers," the marquise said, simpering, "please allow me to present mademoiselle Victoire de Berenguer." Victoire curtsied as clumsily as she felt. "You two have so much in common," the marquise

28

said, "as your families are amongst the oldest and most noble in the empire—and since before the empire, too!"

"I'm sure monsieur le chevalier will enjoy discussing genealogy with my father," Victoire said as the marquise retreated. "It's a hobby of his."

"The only hobbies I'm interested in are yours," de Vimoutiers said, bowing with a grace that made her curtsy look even worse. "But first allow me to congratulate you on your dress, mademoiselle. This look suits you much better, I think."

"I don't care what you think," she said—though she had, in fact, taken considerable care in dressing today. "I don't want to talk to you about—about that night. In fact, I don't want to talk to you about anything at all. I think it would be best for both of us if we forgot that night, and this introduction, ever happened."

"Too late for that," he said. "Can't undo what's already happened. And in this case I'm glad. Mademoiselle de Berenguer, you really have to meet my cousin, Lise. That's her over there—duchesse de Bellevasse, at the centre of that crowd. You and she have a lot in common, you know."

"Oh, I doubt that," she said, looking at the tall, elegant brunette de Vimoutiers had pointed out. Even her father would have to admit the primacy of the Bellevasse family, even before you took the duc's immense wealth into consideration. Lise de Bellevasse's eyes sparkled the way the duchesse de Beaune's had so completely failed to do, with a light of joy and happiness that left Victoire feeling small and sour. "I *really* doubt it," she added for emphasis.

"You'd be surprised," de Vimoutiers said. He was smiling in that idiotic way he had on seeing her a moment ago, but the bland vacancy had been driven from his eyes, to be replaced with something Victoire didn't understand and that made her feel uncomfortably small. "Don't go away," he said.

Victoire did precisely that, as soon as he'd crossed the salon to grab for his cousin. She was nearly at the door of the grand salon when she saw the other person she had come here to speak with. With a smile made more genuine by the relief she felt, Victoire steered the woman through the crowded salon and into the smaller room recently occupied by the duchesse de Beaune.

"It's as insulting as it is self-interested," said Marguerite, the baronne de Geoffroy. "And it's an abrogation of our rights as nobles."

"You'll get no disagreement from me," Victoire told her. Marguerite had taken the bad news with far more grace— good humour, even—than had Nicolette.

"Honestly, do they think we're dim?" the comtesse said. "They claim their infringement of our right to wear what we wish is to prevent the weavers of the country from being put out of work. As if they care about weavers. As if we don't *know* it's the emperor himself whose patronage supports the weaving factories."

"I am most grateful, madame," said Victoire, smiling without pleasure, "that you understand the situation in which I find myself."

"The law may be insulting and unfair," the baronne said, "but to break it carries as much risk as would be the case of a just law. How could I not understand?"

"Would that everybody had your understanding." Victoire looked through the open door, seeing the duchesse de Beaune in flirtatious conversation with Robert de Vimoutiers. Flirtatious but brittle, Victoire decided. *Serves you right*, she thought at de Vimoutiers.

"Do you have any idea now of how long it will be before you can fill my order?"

"I'm afraid not," Victoire had to admit. "My—my enterprise—does not yet have any provision for this sort of emergency."

"Please don't be insulted," said the baronne, "but wasn't that a dangerous oversight on your part?"

"Oh, yes," Victoire said with a sigh, getting up to leave the room. "I am well aware of that, madame."

At the foot of the stairs she paused just long enough to summon the glamour-prayer she had spent so much time developing, and it was a liveried servant of the Bellevasse family who stepped out in to the heat of the afternoon.

The baronne is right, she thought. *And it's an oversight I'll have to correct right away. If I can't find that cotton, and soon, my reputation—and maybe even my safety—is going to be pretty much worthless.*

She had to learn what had happened to that cotton. If she couldn't sell the missing shipment she wouldn't have enough money to maintain her position at court, and court returned to Paris in just a few days. If she couldn't recover the cotton before the duchesse de Beaune permanently blackened her name, she would lose the one source of money on which she had been dependent these past two years. God knew her father had nothing to give her.

It was the threatened end of her life at court that upset her most. Forget the threat posed by Inspector Grenier and his chief, de La Reynie: being shut out of court was the real punishment. Not just because she'd lose activities she truly enjoyed, either. A place at court was a strategic asset for Victoire and her family, one that could convert friendship with a princess into a patronage relationship, or could even somehow improve her family's estate. To say nothing of the advantageous marriage it could promote.

She's as quick on her feet as she is with a glamour prayer, Robert thought. For a moment he stood at the bottom of the stairs, wondering if there was any point in jumping out into the traffic on the Place Imperial. But of course there wasn't: outside the marquise's house Victoire de Berenguer could look like anyone. *For all I know she's able to disguise herself as a carthorse.*

Taking his time, he climbed back up to the marquise's salon. At least there was Lise to talk to: that was an unexpected benefit to what had always promised to be an unpleasant errand. Odd how often the word *unpleasant* attached itself to anything to do with Nicolette de Beaune lately. *And yet here you are,* he thought, feeling the smile tugging at the corners of his mouth. *As you are so often.*

Lise pounced on him as he re-entered the large salon. "Robert!" She grabbed his shoulders and spun him around, laughing with obvious delight. "What are you doing here? Why are you even in the city?"

"Might ask you the same thing," he said. "I thought you were up at Bellevasse where it's at least a little bit cool."

"We got back yesterday. I have to meet with—well, you know who —" that would be de La Reynie, lieutenant-general of police, for whom Lise occasionally worked, "and I just stopped by to see who was back in the city ahead of court." She frowned. "And as usual you've evaded my question: what *are* you doing here? You're not the salon type."

"Not as such, no," he said. "But I'm following orders. Nicolette asked me to meet her here."

"Oh, Robert, you're still not paying court to that offensively self-regarding woman, are you?"

"Shout it a touch more loudly, would you, Lise? She may not have heard you." Feeling himself flush despite his intentions, Robert scanned the salon. But though her companion was there, sitting in the corner trying to be invisible as always, Nicolette had apparently disappeared when he had raced downstairs. Turning back to his cousin he said, "She's beautiful and she can be very pleasant when she wants to be. I've had worse mistresses."

"Now that is the sort of compliment all women wait for. You're a born romantic, Robert." Lise shook her head. "How is your mother? Has she stayed in the city as well?"

"I suppose it's a sign of how sick she became of the countryside while she was—away from court—that even now she declines any invitations she may receive to leave Paris." Not that there had been many of those. The duchesse de Vimoutiers had been absolved of any blame in the Affair of the d'Audemars, but that didn't mean that she hadn't suffered ostracism. Two years on, things were finally beginning to improve—Robert knew Lise and her husband had taken special care to be seen to approve of her, and the emperor had done what small things protocol had allowed—but his mother was not yet fully back to the self-assured state of command she had enjoyed before the Affair. "Enough of me, Lise. How are the boys? And what are you investigating for de La Reynie?"

Her face took on that soft, slightly silly look that new parents always seemed to wear. "We had to leave Raf and Dom with their grandmother, because they're still too young for travel. And you should know better than to be asking about my work." She stopped abruptly and stared at him; he could practically see the calculation going on. *Like clockworks moving,* he thought. Leaning in closer to him she said, "Though perhaps you might know something helpful."

"Not to hear m' mother say it," he said, grinning. Then: "Know something about what?"

"People who suddenly seem to have an improved station in life," she said, almost whispering. He must have seemed startled because she hastily added, "Nothing big or impressive. Just—better than before."

"Someone I know?"

"Someone you *might* know. A younger son or minor noble, maybe. If you can think of anyone who was in financial trouble and now suddenly isn't, please consider telling me about them."

Robert, remembering what had happened to him the last time he allowed himself to be talked into helping his cousin, grabbed with both hands the opportunity to change the subject. "What do you know of the Berenguer family, cousin? They haven't turned up in your, um, occasional work for you know who, have they?"

She stepped back, frowning. "I hope, Robert, that you aren't developing the impression that every noble family in this empire is utterly depraved. Or that I'm on a first-name basis with all their depravities." She couldn't maintain the facade, though, and soon was laughing again. "I almost certainly know less about them than you. The father's something of a snob—I'm sure he thinks of me as an *arriviste*—and the mother is, well, on the religious side and never crosses my path. There's a daughter, isn't there? About my age?"

"Or perhaps a year younger. I suppose I'll have to ask Maman about them, then."

"You've developed an interest in the daughter?" Lise clapped her hands onto his shoulders. This was easily done:

she was nearly Robert's height. "I heartily approve. Shall I intercede with her on your behalf?"

"Good God, no!" As usual, Lise had completely misunderstood him. "Just—well, met her under interesting circumstances. Thought you and she had some things in common." *You both like to present yourselves as men and get other people into trouble.* "She was here a moment ago; was trying to introduce you."

"Oh, is that the attractive little girl who was running away from you?" Lise smiled sweetly, showing far too many teeth. "I begin to think that intercession might not be enough to help."

Robert was on the verge of pointing out that Victoire was only *little* in the sense that few women were as tall as Lise when he saw Lise step back and drop into a carefully casual curtsy. Turning, he saw Nicolette rising from her own, smiling at Robert. "I'm so sorry for interrupting," Nicolette said, "but I wonder, Robert, if you could do that one small favour I asked for?"

"I take it you have no objections yourself to setting foot inside a shop." Robert smiled at the woman he was escorting. "For myself, I don't understand Nicolette's objections at all. I find the bourgeois infinitely fascinating. I could watch them work all day long."

Jeanette Desmarais was a cousin of Nicolette's, from a branch of the family that hadn't held a title in some generations. She had that decaying *vieille-fille* look Robert recognized from his own extended family: an unmarried and unmarriagable female employed to provide at least the pretense of rectitude to a more fortunate cousin-about-town. "You need not worry on my account," she said, though without returning the smile. "I am very much accustomed to performing errands on my cousin's behalf." She turned to look at him now, and while Robert still saw no hint of a smile, he did see plenty of careful assessment—*Analysis, I'd call it.* "I do wonder, in fact, that she sent you with me in the first place."

"Shouldn't doubt it was to get me out of her way," Robert said, happier at that thought than he supposed he ought to be. It wouldn't be a bad thing at all if Nicolette threw him over, in fact. The club of men she had done this to was not small, however exclusive its members might consider it. "This way I'm not only not with her, she knows precisely where in fact I am."

"You don't seem too upset about it." Jeanette's face made it clear that, in his place, she certainly would be.

"Oh, not much point to that," Robert said. *It's not as if I really cared about her, is it?* "I'll survive."

Jeanette muttered something he was evidently not meant to hear; it was probably along the lines of *Easy for you to say.* More clearly she said, "The shop is on the rue des Francs Bourgeois, so we just go straight ahead across the rue de la Couture here."

A bourgeois Fortune Vidal might have been, but he hadn't suffered much because of it. His shop, while not large, had numerous windows to let in daylight, and a sign consisting of a huge, white-painted diamond whose facets were outlined in brilliant gold leaf. When Robert stepped inside, following Jeanette, he smelled spice and an underlying hint of soap. Monsieur Vidal knew his customers' expectations.

In this case he apparently knew his customer as well. "Is that Mademoiselle Desmarais?" he heard a voice call from the back of the shop. The young man behind the counter answered in the affirmative, and no sooner had the young man closed his mouth again but his place was taken by a slender, grey-haired man whose age could be anywhere from thirty to fifty. "It is so good to see you again, mademoiselle!" Monsieur Vidal said, and with a huge grin set about flirting outrageously with Jeanette.

Who, to Robert's considerable surprise, flowered under the jeweller's flatteries, in the process apparently losing half of her years. Viewed in the light of Vidal's attentions, Jeanette was revealed to Robert as being not much older than he himself was; what he'd thought was age was, rather, a symptom of stress. Which made sense, given how tired he often felt when waiting upon Nicolette's pleasure.

"It will not take very long to fix this setting," Vidal told Jeanette. "This is a piece of yours?" Jeanette shook her head vigorously, and Robert guessed that no such baubles graced this lady's life. "In that case," Vidal said, "my nephew can take care of it. It's not as if your cousin is going to pay my bill anytime soon—if at all." He said this in a mock-conspiratorial tone that, to Robert's bemused pleasure, made Jeanette laugh like a porcelain bell. As she turned her head away, perhaps shocked at the liberties she had taken with her superior cousin's good name, Vidal looked over at Robert. Robert, to his surprise liking the man, favoured him with a smile and a wink.

"If you would care to come upstairs," Vidal said to them, "I have some new stones and some new gold-work you might like to see while your piece is being done."

"Oh, I wouldn't think of bothering you," Jeanette said, but with an automatic quality that made Robert want to look around, expecting to find Nicolette disapproving from the doorway. "I could never justify taking up your time, monsieur."

Robert was on the point of protesting, but Vidal got to the point first. "You wouldn't be taking up my time, mademoiselle. You would be entertaining me, by allowing me to entertain you."

"He's absolutely right, you know," Robert said. "I think we should do our bit to help the man, don't you?" Faced with two males sharing the opinion opposed to her, Jeanette had no option but to yield. Robert noted, though, she was smiling as she climbed the stairs ahead of them.

Chapter Three

A Fishing Expedition

"**I AM NOT** letting them win," Victoire said to the three employees of her enterprise. They had gathered in the front parlour—the shop portion—of Catherine's house. "We may not know—yet—who it was stole our cloth. But I swear whoever it is will not keep it. There are things I can do to help us find it." *I think there are, anyway.*

"I bet it's magical things."

"How would you know, Hachette?" Marie-Louise asked, wiping her hands on her apron.

"As it happens," said Victoire, "he's right. The first thing we'll try is prayer."

"See?" Hachette said, thrusting out his scrawny chest. "I know things."

"You'll be helping me, too," Victoire added.

"Huh?" Hachette's proud expression faltered. "Please, mademoiselle—"

"I'm sorry, Hachette. I know how you all feel about magic, and I can't say you're wrong to avoid it. But I need your help if I'm going to make the Finding prayer work for us."

"I can't do anything with magic. It would mean the stake for me if the Inquisition found out."

"You won't be doing anything with magic," Victoire said. "I just need you to hold my hands and think."

"Don't be so sure he can do that either," Marie-Louise muttered. Catherine shushed her before Hachette could explode.

"Let's sit down together," Victoire told Hachette, "you and I. Catherine, please watch the door and see we aren't disturbed."

"Mademoiselle—"

"Hachette, there's nothing to worry about." Victoire pulled the shop's one chair alongside an old chest. Sitting in the chair, she pointed to the chest. "Down," she said. When Hachette had—however slowly—complied, she held out a hand to him.

"All you have to do, Hachette, is to think back to the stable the other night. I want you to remember everything you can about the cloth."

"Like what? It was just cloth."

"Think about how it felt, when you opened up the bundles. Remember what it was like to see the elephants on the cloth I showed you."

"What's he supposed to be doing, mademoiselle?" Catherine asked.

"The Finding prayer is supposed to let me find missing things of mine. I'm not entirely sure how it works, but I do know the more I've held and used a thing the easier it is for the prayer to show me where it's got to." Victoire grabbed Hachette's hand and squeezed. "I didn't have much of a chance to do much with the cloth, so I'm hoping the prayer will be able to work better if I'm also absorbing Hachette's memories of it."

"If we had been able to do the embroidery," Catherine began.

"Yes," Victoire said, smiling and nodding. "My prayer of animation on your embroidery would work like a bell or a beacon-fire to call the Finding prayer. But I'm not going to waste time worrying about things I can't do anything about. Hachette, start thinking."

Victoire closed her eyes and began to pray.

It did not come easily. Building the image of the missing cloth stretched her power of prayer beyond comfort, and even so what she was able to visualize was a child's sketch of the thing rather than a true image. Pulling in Hachette's memories wasn't any easier, not least because his mind seemed to fight her every attempt to touch it. *Can't say I blame him,* she thought. Soon she realized she would have to work with what she had; if she didn't start the actual Finding soon she would be too tired to extend the search beyond the neighbourhood.

She was faintly aware of the others' nervous fidgeting but did not let it intrude on the prayer. A heavenly touch seemed to guide her soul along a gentle, spiral path outward from the old house; she was aware of the river, and then a spark lit up and an elephant danced—

—Alongside *fish?*

Paris is really a rather interesting city, Robert told himself, *if you can just get most of the people out of it.* Well, not the poor; you were never going to get rid of the poor, apparently. He'd heard a sermon to that effect, once. But with most of the well-born—to say nothing of the emperor himself—still out of town avoiding the last of the summer's heat, Paris was pleasant, if over-fragrant. It was much easier to move around when one wasn't constantly dodging chairs and carriages.

And the population of the city was about to drop further,

knowledge of which had Robert humming something sprightly as he walked homeward from the Île de la Cité. From the way Nicolette had evaded his questions during the visit just concluded, he was no longer in any doubt concerning the guess he'd made to the duchesse's unhappy cousin Jeanette. Nicolette was definitely on the verge of being finished with him; no doubt the only reason she hadn't actually told him so this evening was that she hadn't fixed her interest yet with whomever was to be her next *amour.*

Better you than me, he said in silent salute to the unknown victim. For a moment he wondered just what it was about women like Nicolette, or Denise de L'Este, that attracted fools such as he. Then he decided that it was too nice an evening to waste time on that sort of thinking, and began to think about what to do tonight. Paris was quiet, but it wasn't completely deserted; no doubt somebody would have something going on. *You could always have stayed with Maman at the duc de Saint-Simon's party,* he reminded himself. He hoped he had dallied long enough that his mother wouldn't condemn him for rudeness. God knew it had felt enough like forever.

He was so caught up in planning his approach to the remains of the evening that at first he didn't recognize the voice asking: "Are you sure we're supposed to cross the river?" When he did make the connection, he was nearly too late: the speaker was turning the corner and was on the verge of coming face-to-face with him, if not running him down. Heedless of the risk, Robert dashed into the street, and ran to the opposite side. *Good thing it hasn't rained today,* he thought; he never would have got across without falling if he'd been running across wet cobblestones.

She was in the same glamour she'd worn the night he met her, but this time Victoire de Berenguer was accompanied by the most appalling urchin Robert had ever seen. A long, narrow nose, pronounced front teeth and receding chin gave the boy an astonishing appearance; he resembled nothing so much as a large, bipedal rat and Robert found himself looking behind the boy for evidence of a tail. Then he looked again, and realized that Victoire had modelled her glamour on the boy: her magically disguised features were like the rat-boy's, but with the sharp edges and pointy bits chipped away and smoothed out.

"If I'm right about what you saw, Mademoi—I mean, that is, if I'm right then we have to cross the river. You'll understand when we get there."

They'll be taking the Pont Neuf *then,* Robert said to himself, just as Victoire said, "Well, we're going to take the *Pont Neuf,* then. I am not risking my life with any boatman on the Seine."

Robert had already decided to follow her when he heard her say, "I just hope we really do find our cloth in this fish-place of yours."

"Just how well do you know this neighbourhood?" Victoire asked, as Hachette turned into a street so narrow no woman wearing a proper dress could turn around in it. Of course, no woman would dare to venture down such a street in the first place; she was beginning to have second thoughts herself. *A good thing I left Catherine and Marie-Louise at home,* she thought. *Poor Catherine would have fallen into a dead faint as soon as we reached the left bank of the river.*

"I know it better than you do. Stop worrying."

Poor Hachette. He's frightened too, and doesn't dare show it. At least I can admit it. Sort of. "I'm not worried," she lied. "I just want to be sure we can find our way out again. I have never had a client in the Latin Quarter, and I have no idea where you're taking us." *You and the prayer,* she added to herself. God was still leading her here, she felt.

"This street is called la rue de la Chat Qui Pêche," he said. "The *fishing cat.* That's why I think your prayer showed you fish. There's a thief lives here, a very big one."

"And that's why the prayer has brought us here. He has the cloth."

"He might. I don't know magic the way I know the city."

Hachette stopped at a low, crumbling building that, on the evidence of the sign hanging by a single hinge, had once been a wine-shop. Perhaps it still was. This place was on the fringe of the university district, meaning a student clientele. Since students would rather riot than pay a bill, anyone selling to them had to cut costs not only to the bone but into it.

"Down there," he whispered. "The cellar has its own entrance."

Victoire repeated the Finding prayer one last time, and now the response was a bright light shining in her mind: the cloth was definitely here. Pressing her lips together she reinforced the glamour's hold on her appearance. She had decided to strengthen the similarity to Hachette, turning her into his older brother. Somewhat to her surprise, not only had he not been offended by this change, he seemed pleased with it. Proud, even. What a life the boy must have led before they'd found each other.

The cellar was larger than it had appeared to be from the outside, and she and Hachette were well inside it before she realized how deeply and far into the earth it went. By that time a pair of skinny but mean-looking young men had placed themselves between her and the steps up to freedom.

I'm not worried, she told herself. *I was expecting this.* "I'm here to see Clopard," she said, deepening her voice and making it more husky. "He has information my master is seeking." Now that her eyes were becoming accustomed to the weak light she could see tiny points of light further in, evidence Clopard was using candles somewhere in there.

"That Hachette?" The voice was dry, and thin as paper. Victoire fought against the instinct to call up God-light in order to see the voice's owner. *You're not a noble here,* she reminded herself. *You're Rat-boy's older brother.*

"A brace of Hachettes," she said.

"You never told me you had an older brother, boy. And what do you mean by barging in on me this way?"

"You never asked," Hachette replied, his twelve-year-old bravado in full cry. "And you should know why I'm here. You have some cloth of ours. We want it back."

"Some what?" The voice was coming closer, and then she could see him. Clopard was huge, almost grossly fat, with a wiry, foul-smelling beard, and there was a black void where one of his eyes ought to have been. "I think your master may be mistaken about something. Why should I care about what *you* think?"

"Maybe we don't matter," Victoire said, "but my master definitely—"she fumbled inwardly to call up the Finding prayer again. *What?* She repeated the prayer. *It's not in here. Then how—?*

"Perhaps we should go back and ask Master to consider again," she said.

"Perhaps your master should consider the cost." Clopard's grin was broad and insulting.

"The cost of what?" This had all gone very wrong, and with surprising speed.

"Of your return," Clopard said. He wrapped a massive,

soft arm around her. The strength in that limb was distressing. "What kind of businessman just lets anyone come and go without so much as an *excuse me*? If your master thinks you two are important enough, he'll be happy to pay me the few coins I'll request in exchange for you." He applied a bit more pressure to her. "Just you tell me where to send for him, and we'll have this settled in no time."

"Bastard!" Hachette was on Clopard before anyone could react. *I had no idea he was so quick,* thought Victoire, who had seen him in action plenty of times. She ducked out of the big man's grasp when he yowled, and when she was able to see again she saw that Hachette had Clopard's beard in both fists and was pulling with all his strength.

It was an unequal fight, though, because Clopard didn't seem to care too much about having his beard pulled, and his two guards were on Hachette within seconds. She couldn't see what they did to him, but he screamed and let go and fell to the rough limestone floor of the cellar, becoming an indistinct whimpering shape in the darkness. "Whatever you did to him, you'll pay," she said thinking through her options. If Hachette was seriously hurt, it would be harder to get the two of them out of here.

"Tell me again when you're able to collect," Clopard said. "Now, why don't you tell me where I can find your master, and I'll send one of my boys out to deliver a message to him."

"Oh, I'm supposed to just hand over a secret to you?" *Keep him from thinking too much,* she told herself. "I don't know anyone says you can be trusted." She still had one solid advantage over Clopard: he had no idea she was noble, and capable of magic. *A blinding spell,* she thought, *while my own eyes are closed. I can have Hachette out of here before the rest of them have recovered their sight.*

"You don't know enough people, then. I always play straight with aristos and bourgeois. They're the ones with the money. And your master'll think nothing of paying a livre or two for your return; aristos never think twice about dropping a coin here and there."

"We don't all have the sort of money you think," said a voice from the bottom of the steps, and Victoire stiffened, appalled. *What in the name of heaven and hell is Robert de Vimoutiers doing here?*

"You're master of these boys?" Clopard rubbed his chin; evidently Hachette had inflicted some pain after all. "I was just telling them: Not polite to just drop in unannounced."

"I would have knocked," de Vimoutiers said, "but you appeared to be busy and I didn't want to disturb you."

You utter idiot, Victoire shouted to herself. It would be tricky enough getting herself and Hachette out of here. How in the world would she rescue de Vimoutiers as well?

"Well, thank you for saving me the trouble of tracking you down," Clopard said. "I'm always happy when negotiations go quickly."

"I don't think you should be negotiating with this fellow," Victoire began.

"Shut up, boy." Clopard raised a huge hand; in the near-darkness it loomed like a boulder about to fall down a mountainside. Somewhere in the darkness Hachette still whimpered, trying to recover from whatever those two thugs had done to him.

"I'll take care of any discipline needed," de Vimoutiers said, and Victoire heard the distinctive click of an épée being loosened in its scabbard.

"Take care, aristo," said the thief-master, and a scuffling suggested the two thugs were reaching for weapons of their own.

"Oh, I'm very good at taking care. Please allow me to take care of you, monsieur…."

"My name doesn't matter to you."

"It's Clopard," Hachette squeaked from the darkness, "and I hope you drive that blade through his throat."

"All in good time," de Vimoutiers said, as cheery as if he was ordering another round. "For now, I believe you were looking for payment."

"It's only what's due me."

"You should certainly get what's due you," Victoire said. Clopard growled but she ignored him, shifting until she found Hachette. She helped him to his feet. "Can you run?" she asked him, voice pitched to below a whisper. He squeezed her hand in affirmation. "Good," she said. "On my signal. If anything goes really wrong, you get out and head straight home. I'll follow." *Once I've done what I can to help this poor fool who thinks he's helping me.*

"I think I've got something you'll like here," de Vimoutiers said. "It's not coin, I'm afraid—I wasn't expecting to need any tonight—but it will likely bring you more than any purse I would have been carrying." Victoire turned in time to see faint candlelight glinting on gold. He tugged at his belt with his other hand, and Victoire heard a stiffening from Clopard and his boys as a dagger glinted in the faint light. "Oh, don't be such old women," de Vimoutiers said.

He muttered a moment, and God-light sprang into being, showing Victoire even more of Clopard's disgusting face—he'd survived an encounter with the pox relatively recently—and revealing to everyone that de Vimoutiers was using his dagger to pry a large stone from the ring he'd shown Clopard. In the God-light the stone appeared to be the dark green of deep water. *He's not giving up an emerald, is he? Idiot!*

"Thank you for your time, monsieur," de Vimoutiers said, and he flipped the emerald further into the cellar.

With a shout, both of Clopard's boys vanished into the darkness behind him. "No!" Clopard shouted. "Not yet—not until we have all of them!"

"Now," she said to Hachette, shutting her eyes—just as de Vimoutiers said the same to her.

The cellar exploded into light; for Clopard it must have been like staring directly into the sun. Victoire could only hope that Hachette had closed his own eyes. Then de Vimoutiers grabbed at her left hand as she was grabbing at Hachette with her right, and the three of them ran up the rickety steps to the cellar entrance and so out into the street.

In the God-light he carried with him she could see a smile of blissful, idiotic delight on Robert de Vimoutiers's face. "I suggest," he said, "that we get to a bridge and cross the river as soon as we can. Right now."

"I agree," said Hachette. "Thanks, monsieur whoever-you-are."

"No," said Victoire, leaning back against Clopard's door. *Not until I work out what went wrong here.* "Just give me a moment." She closed her eyes, ignoring Hachette's protest, and cast the Finding prayer again. The dancing elephant flared up in her mind again.

If it seemed to be in the cellar from here in the street, but the same prayer got a muffled response inside, then—*I have been tricked. By somebody who knew I'd be looking.* "Hachette, take a quick look around this door. There should be a piece of cloth hidden somewhere. Probably a small piece."

He dropped to his knees, and in the space of a couple of breaths he was back up again. "Here you go." In the darkness the design was impossible to make out, but it didn't matter: the cloth he'd given her wouldn't have made a handkerchief.

"Now can we run for our lives?" de Vimoutiers asked.

"How is it," Victoire demanded when they reached the end of the narrow street, "that you couldn't have just tossed him a couple of silver Louis?" A gust of wind whispered the length of the street; back where they'd come from, bits of cloth circled in the air, mocking her flight. "If you wanted to throw away a stone the size of my thumb I can think of better things to do with it!"

"You would be wrong no matter what you proposed. Why do you think we're running?" de Vimoutiers asked. He said nothing more until they'd reached the bridge. Then he slowed to a brisk walk, saying, "I think we're far enough away now."

"In that case," she said, "I want to catch my breath." She stopped, leaning against the stonework. "Hachette, did he hurt you?"

"Of course not. I just wanted him to think he did. Make him careless. So, I don't see why we had to run away from him like we were scared!"

"I'm glad you weren't scared," de Vimoutiers said. "I certainly was. And still am, a little." He urged them back into motion. "We want to be well away from Monsieur Clopard," he said, "before he gets a chance to hold that *emerald* up to the light. I bought it five minutes before I came down into that cellar, from an old woman who swore to me it was genuine. Since it cost me all of five sous I'm reasonably certain the old woman was stretching the truth a wee bit, but I'd rather we were on the other side of the river before Clopard has a chance to confirm my suspicions."

"I don't see why we had to sneak away from that chevalier," Hachette said as Victoire, after a careful look both ways down the street, closed and locked the front door of her little old house near l'hôpital de la Trinité. "He seemed like a good sort to me. I'll bet he has money, too."

"Yes, his family's very rich and very powerful," Victoire told him. "We don't want to be coming to the notice of that sort of people, remember? In fact, I think we've already been noticed too much. And in the wrong way."

"I don't understand," Catherine said from the back of the shop-cum-parlour.

"Clopard's place was a trap," Victoire told them. "Our cloth wasn't there tonight, and I don't think it was ever there."

"But your prayer, mademoiselle," said Marie-Louise.

"Found something, yes." Victoire produced the piece of cloth Hachette had uncovered. "Something placed at the entrance to Clopard's cellar, for the sole purpose of being found by my prayer."

"Somebody knew you'd be using the Finding prayer?" Marie-Louise scowled.

"But that cloth is so tiny," Catherine said, confused. "Could your prayer have found something that small?"

"It was cursed," Hachette said, "wasn't it?"

"Somebody applied some sort of prayer to it, yes." Victoire pulled the chair toward herself and slumped down into it, wanting to be rid of the boots and the coarse trousers and shirt she wore, but knowing she had to return to the family hôtel before she could allow herself that luxury. "Knowing how I would be searching."

"But only aristos can do that," Hachette began. "Oh."

"Yes," Victoire said. "It seems to me that one of my customers has decided to go into business for herself. I can't think of anyone else who could know enough to try and trap me this way."

"What about Inspector Grenier?" Marie-Louise asked.

"He's a bourgeois," Victoire said. "He couldn't have done this."

"But what about the man he works for? The *intendant* of customs is a nobleman, yes? Or maybe he's hired himself a wicked monk. No shortage of them about."

Damn. I can think of one right now—one in my father's house. More possibilities, more complications. "I hadn't thought of that, Marie-Louise. We'll have to consider both of those, I suppose." She gestured towards Catherine. "Pour us all some wine, please, and we'll discuss what we're going to do next."

She could have kindled some God-light to brighten the room—in August there was no question of having a fire except to cook—but for reasons they had never been able to explain to her, neither Catherine nor Marie-Louise was comfortable with the expenditure of Victoire's blessing on their behalf. So, she made do with the odoriferous tallow candles that were the best she could afford, and contented herself with the thought that at least the capricious yellow light wouldn't fatigue her the way magic would.

"We are all going to have to investigate this," she said once Marie-Louise had handed around the wine Catherine had poured. "But we shouldn't have to consider absolutely everybody a suspect, though."

"Not all of our customers have anything to gain by betraying us," said Marie-Louise.

"Exactly. I will think about them overnight and see how many we can eliminate. Meanwhile, Marie-Louise, you and Catherine still have friends in the cloth and clothing trades. I want you to ask them for any information they can give about any new sources of printed cotton."

"And me?" Hachette's eyes glowed and he grinned broadly.

"*If* you can do it without getting yourself killed, Hachette, I want you to find out if our friend Clopard knows more than he was letting on tonight. Something he said at the end there worries me." The thief had apparently intended to capture de Vimoutiers as well as herself and Hachette. But why?

"I can do it right now." He drained his cup and scrambled to the front door. "Night-time is the right time for asking."

"I think we've all had enough excitement for tonight," Victoire told him. "Even if you say Clopard didn't hurt you as badly as I think he did."

"Mademoiselle makes a very good point," Marie-Louise said. "And you should take it seriously yourself, mademoiselle." When Catherine looked puzzled, Marie-Louise told her, "It will be difficult for us to investigate inside a criminal activity, Catherine. Difficult and dangerous: thieves won't be any more likely to help us than we would be to help them to learn about what we do. And those people who might be reluctant to strike back at the police or any emperor's man won't hesitate to attack or even kill any of us. Even you, mademoiselle."

Hachette opened his mouth to retort but was stopped by the sudden rattle of the front door. The boy froze, his hand on the latch.

"Damn it," Victoire muttered, getting to her feet. There were only two likely causes of that noise, and she didn't want to deal with either of them. To Hachette she said, "Get your club, Rat-boy." To a whimpering Catherine she said, in as soothing a tone as her anger allowed, "It's nothing to worry about. Even if it's the watch they're not getting in here."

"Who could it be if not the watch?" Marie-Louise asked.

"Who indeed?" Victoire replied, unbolting the door. She pulled it open and said, "I thought as much."

"You should probably let me in and shut the door," Robert de Vimoutiers told her. "I'm pretty sure the watch is following me."

Chapter Four
Close to Home

"**If you've led** the watch to my door I'll kill you before they can arrest me!" Realizing that de Vimoutiers could do much more damage to her outside the door than inside it, Victoire grabbed him by his embroidered lapels and pulled him inside the house. "Shut the damned door," she told Hachette, who appeared sufficiently upset at what had happened that he didn't even question the order. Nor did he say anything when she ordered him out the back door to observe and warn her if the watch approached the house.

She was so angry at what de Vimoutiers might have brought upon her that it was only once he was inside the house and the door safely bolted that Victoire realized that his presence here meant something even more ominous than the watch. "How did you find us?" she said, hating the fact that she had to look up at him to say it.

"It's a funny thing," he said, grinning in that annoying unconcerned way, "but do you know? I have no idea. At first I thought I was trying to follow you, because, well, it seemed to me the decent thing to do to make certain you got home safely. But then I realized that you weren't going to where I thought you'd be going, and then I got very confused about what you were up to, and then damned if a watchman didn't start eyeing me with that look they get. You know the look, I presume."

"I do not. I make a point of not coming to the notice of the watch."

"Really? Curious. Though I suppose it makes sense, given what I've learned about you so far."

"I don't care about your speculations," she said. "Though that doesn't mean I'm anxious for you to tell all and sundry—or, for that matter, anyone at all—what you think you've learned about me." She paused for a moment. "I note that you have not actually answered my question."

"But I did! I don't know how I found you. I was just sort of wandering around and I realized that I was somewhere between your family home and mine, and then that watchman started giving me the You're-In-Trouble-Now eye, and so I thought I'd best leave him alone with his malign thoughts, and then somehow I was in front of this house and I just knew you were inside. Maybe I was fated to find you."

Or maybe I just didn't do a good enough job of evading you and you don't want me to realize that. No sooner had she thought this than she shook her head: whatever he was, Robert de Vimoutiers was nowhere nearly clever enough to play that sort of game with her.

"You don't believe in fate?" Again, the tone was of unconcerned, blissful ignorance.

"I don't believe in this one, no." *Nor in younger sons with no money and less sense.*

Whatever he had intended to reply was forestalled by Hachette's return through the kitchen door. "Nobody out there now," he said.

"Good," Victoire said.

"That's a relief," said de Vimoutiers.

"Not as much a relief as the feeling I'm looking forward to," Victoire said. "Monsieur de Vimoutiers, I believe it's time you left us."

"What, with the watch still out there?"

"Weren't you listening? They're gone," Victoire said. *If they were ever here, which I sincerely hope they were not.* She pointed to the kitchen door. "Hachette, can you please guide the gentleman away from here and back into a neighbourhood more suited to his sense of fashion?"

"You can trust me, monsieur," Hachette said, nodding. "If I don't want anyone to see you, nobody will see you."

"Actually," Victoire said to him, keeping her voice low, "it wouldn't bother me at all if the watch caught a glimpse of him once you're well away from here."

When he woke the next morning, Robert realized he was smiling. It took him several minutes of determined recollection, and two cups of chocolate, before he could make himself realize that his encounter with Victoire de Berenguer and her astonishing friends had made up only a small portion of the previous night. In his mind the event had taken on a sort of defining nature.

Poor Respire, he thought, feeling the smile broaden. *He may be on the verge of losing one of his best customers.*

He avoided his mother on his way out of the house; he didn't feel much like lying to her this morning, and that was certainly what he would have to do if she asked about his evening. And she would ask; she invariably did. He was, he realized, going to have to develop the sort of expression that good gamblers had—the sort that gave away nothing of what he was thinking—if he intended to pursue this new acquaintance.

He had never been that good a gambler.

Robert was in the vicinity of the market-place at Les Halles, still working on different approaches to a stone face, when a recently familiar voice intruded. "A word with you, sire, if you please."

Robert spun around, his right hand automatically going to the hilt of his épée. He was on the verge of regretting the impulse—Clopard was a big man, and Robert made a policy of avoiding confrontations with big men—when he realized that Clopard was moving away from him. At some speed. He had thrust his hands out in front of him, as if somehow they could protect him from a sword-thrust.

"No need to be hasty, sire. No need at all." Clopard wiped his forehead with a grimy fist, leaving a dirty streak behind. "I just wanted to say something. Won't bother you for more than a moment, I promise."

"About a certain gem, I take it?" Robert kept his hand on the épée's hilt; if the mere sight of a sword was enough to make Clopard think twice about grievous assault, he was more than happy to continue the display.

"Oh, that." Clopard laughed, with about as much real amusement as a Jesuit tutor would show. "You fooled me good with that. But no, that's not why I want to talk to you. We'll just leave the gem as our little joke. You paying me back for what my boys done to you, eh?"

What? I took great care last night to see that your boys did nothing *to me.*

The confusion must have been obvious—he really would have to work on his facial expressions—because Clopard said "I understand you don't want that discussed in the street. Good thinking on your part, sire. So let's just leave it at that. What's done can't be undone, after all." *Especially when one of us hasn't a clue as to what's been done.* "But

58

we—my chief and me—we thought you might be desirous of not having it happen again. That thing we can't undo."

"Go on." *Eventually you might start to make sense.*

"So instead of dealing with that person you was used to deal with, why don't you come in with us?" He smiled, but the gap-toothed cavern thus displayed was not ingratiating. "We can promise you as good a price as you've been getting. And you'll run less risk. A lot less."

"Well," Robert said. After a moment, realizing that Clopard expected more, he added, "You've certainly given me something to think about." *And a headache. I hate having to think.*

"I'm glad you seen it that way," Clopard told him. He walked away, but slowly because he was walking backward, evidently unwilling to risk his considerable bulk to Robert's skill with the épée. "You should take up the offer, though. Might get dangerous for you if you didn't." He waited, presumably for Robert to absorb the threat. "Someone will come for your answer soon. Unless you want to send it to me." He smiled, more broadly and hence more disgustingly. "You know where I am, after all."

"Indeed I do," Robert told him with what he hoped was menace.

At these words Clopard turned and sped into the crowd. Without hesitation, Robert followed him. It appeared Clopard wasn't expecting this, because neither he nor the two gutter-rats who joined him made even one look backward as they waded into the crowd of shopping women.

"Why didn't you thump him?" one of the rats asked. "I'd of thumped him a good one. Especially if I had hands like yours, boss."

"And that's why I'm the boss and you're an idiot. Do you

have any idea how much trouble we could get into if we messed too much with that family?"

"Nobody gives you trouble, boss."

"Because I don't make it worth it to them, idiot." Clopard cuffed the boy on the back of the head, with more force than Robert thought strictly necessary. "You don't know how powerful that family is, boy. That de Vimoutiers may look like a fool, but he's on a first-name basis with the emperor *and* with de La Reynie." At the name of the lieutenant-general of the Paris police both gutter-rats spat in disgust. "Plus," Clopard added, "his cousin is married to de Bellevasse, who does black magic—and *she* does black magic for the police." Robert let them vanish into the crowd; the last words he heard from Clopard were, "I only talked to that man because the chief ordered me to."

Well, Robert said to himself. *Somebody is giving me credit for far more enterprise than I deserve.* The question was, who was making this mistake? He was already pretty certain he knew who deserved the real credit.

There were few townhouses in Paris as old as the Hôtel Berenguer. But the reason for this, Victoire reminded herself as she pulled back the heavy bed-curtains, was that most of the noble families who lived in Paris had rebuilt their houses a century or more ago. Some had rebuilt several times over the past hundred years. Because of her father, though, she had to make do with a pile of stone whose walls still had *turrets*, for God's sake. Victoire half-believed the Valois kings were still on the throne when the hôtel was built.

The house's age pleased her father, she knew, and she guessed the inconvenience of it satisfied her mother's need for suffering; but Victoire woke most days feeling envy for her friends at court, all of whom could enjoy—at least most of the year—morning sunlight when they awoke. The Hôtel Berenguer didn't have bedroom windows; it had arrow-slits.

Under siege: that's how she felt this morning, anyway.

She dressed with little regard for what people would think—not her usual approach, she knew, but today promised to be unusual in all respects—and carefully made her way down the ancient stairs to breakfast. "Good morning, mademoiselle," said Fernet, the maître d'hôtel. "Will you eat now, or do you wish to wait?"

"My father is still asleep, I take it?" A safe guess: Papa seldom woke before midday.

"Yes, mademoiselle. And your mother—"

"Is in the chapel, annoying God."

His nod was barely perceptible. "She is concerned for her soul, yes. It is a concern that, if anything, seems to have grown since last year." If Fernet knew why this was, he didn't say. A very wise man, Fernet.

It serves me right for telling her what I was doing, and why I was doing it, she thought. "I have to talk with her, but it can wait until she is finished," she said. "I'm desperate for a good cup of chocolate, but I suppose I can settle for Madame Dutoit's." Papa had employed La Dutoit because she had previously served the Prince de Condé, not because she knew how to cook.

In the breakfast room Victoire ignored the riot of heavy cheeses and smoky, salty meats Father insisted on, wishing they could afford to bring in the light, flaky pastries that were the vogue now. Especially that Viennese thing—*croissant,* they called it, because of the Turks. She settled for a hunk of the heavy white bread that, if you didn't eat it straight out of the oven, cooled into the approximate texture of a cannonball. This loaf at least was still warm and hence still more or less edible.

Victoire was dipping a chunk of the bread into a cup of spiced wine, wondering how large a piece she would have to throw to break a window, when her mother entered the room.

"Good morning, Victoire," Maman said. "We missed you last night."

Once upon a time, Maman had dressed with a dazzling sense of style. Lately, though, she favoured dull, rough dresses of dark-brown cloth—brown only because black was too expensive—and caps of stunning hideousness. *You were beautiful once, Maman;* Victoire thought; *why do you do this to yourself?*

"I was out visiting," she said. No need to say where, or whom, she was visiting. Maman would only have been outraged anyway: Catherine had been nothing but a servant, and Maman had disposed of her when Catherine's fingers first became crippled, and after all what use was a seamstress who could no longer sew rapidly or well? It was definitely better Maman not know about Victoire's continuing friendship with Catherine. "How is Père Robillard?"

Maman's eyes narrowed. "He is well, as always. Why do you ask?"

"Did he return to Paris with you the other night?"

"Victoire, what is going on? You have never cared before for anything the good père said or did for me."

"That was before I was attacked and my goods stolen from me. Maman, how much of what I told you have you passed on to that priest?"

"Victoire! Show some respect, if not to you mother then to a man of God."

"I told you those things in confidence, Maman, and you have no right to pass them on to anyone else, not even a priest."

"How can you say that? When you know that I'll never go to Heaven if I am not utterly open to God, Victoire. And the way of openness to God is through his servant, Père Robillard. I can keep nothing from him." Maman looked so stricken that for a moment Victoire believed there might be truth behind the words, and that she was being wilful in standing between her mother and salvation. Then she thought about the nature of a priest who would drive a woman to condemn her daughter to the Bastille in the guise of a promise of salvation, and her standing animosity toward the Church in general, and Père Robillard in particular, returned.

"If that is truly the case, Maman, then I must from this moment forward consider your confessor to be no different from a paid informant of the customs inspectorate." Though it was hard to imagine a connection between the priest and Clopard, Victoire was confident she would find one.

Maman stepped back as if she'd been slapped. "No," she whispered.

"This is not the behaviour of a dutiful child," a deep male voice said.

Victoire looked to the door, and saw the object of her anger standing just inside the dining room. Père Robillard looked like the model on which Maman was remaking herself: thin, bony, pinch-faced and projecting sour rectitude through his every pose and gesture. It was a miracle, she thought, that a man as underfed and under-dressed as the père could cost so much to keep.

"Even one as lost to salvation as you should admit the sanctity of the confessional," Père Robillard told her. "I could no more inform on you than I could your mother, girl."

And no priest ever enriched himself at the expense of his flock, she told herself. "Think of this as my gift to you, then," she said with as false a sweetness as she could muster. "The less you know about me the less you will have to concern yourself with my soul." Turning to her mother she lied, "And you can stop worrying about me, Maman. Whether or not it was through your—your creature, there— that my enterprise was overturned, the fact remains that the business is done with. There will be no more money coming from that direction, now."

"Oh, praise be to God!" Maman said.

Hating herself, Victoire turned the knife. "And how," she asked, "do you propose to keep Père Robillard now that I can no longer contribute to his considerable expenses?"

"Oh." Maman looked stricken, but Victoire was disappointed to see no reaction at all from Père Robillard. The man merely nodded as though he approved.

"God will provide, of course," he said, placing a hand—a proprietary hand, Victoire thought—on Maman's shoulder.

"Then perhaps you should move yourself to our chateau," Victoire told him, "and work with our peasants to increase the yield of our estates. God helps those who help others, doesn't He?"

"Please, Victoire," Maman said, tears beginning to glisten at the corners of her eyes, "don't."

Victoire lowered her head. "I'm sorry, Maman. I should not have lost my temper. Please excuse me."

She turned around before she had fully lifted her head, so as not to have to look her mother in the eye. Maman had not, Victoire noted, answered her question about whether Père Robillard had accompanied her on the journey back to

Paris. Which was, she supposed, an answer in itself. *If he'd been with you, you'd have been eager to tell me.*

She set out to find Fernet again; the man would give her an honest answer about the priest's whereabouts the night her cloth was stolen. And after that—?

Suppose I find I have good reason to suspect Robillard. What do I do with it?

"You are looking well, Robert," the duchesse de Vimoutiers said, looking up at him as he walked into her salon that afternoon. He paused on his way to the wine; there had been an interrogative uplift at the end of her speech, and Maman was much more prone to the declarative.

"You are in doubt, Maman?"

"Not precisely," she said. Relieved, Robert poured himself a glass of wine, drank it quickly, and poured himself another. "It's just that by this time of the day I would normally have heard from at least two of my friends about whatever idiocy you'd got up to the previous night. But today? Nothing! And this is the second consecutive day I have had this odd experience. So naturally I am curious."

"Nothing to worry about, I assure you. I feel fine." And he did, he realized, and that despite the strange not-quite-a-threat he'd received this morning. If anything he felt better than he had in months if not years. "I just don't seem to find as much pleasure in gaming and drinking as I used to, that's all." *Perhaps I'm more grown up,* he nearly said before remembering, just in time, that Maman still felt shame over the scandal that, she often said, had forced him to grow up too quickly. To keep his mouth more safely occupied, he stuffed one of the new pastries—what did they call it? a *croissant?*—into it.

"So, you are partaking of more genteel entertainments in

the evenings now?" She smiled, a little thinly. "And how is dear Nicolette de Beaune?"

Once upon a time—say last week—such a question would have brought forth from Robert a choking, embarrassed cough and an explosion of flaky crumbs. This afternoon, though, it merely brought a smile. Robert finished chewing before he answered. "I'm afraid she's even more bored than usual. In fact, I've heard she's left Paris again." He sat beside Maman and took a more careful sip of wine, having decided against telling her of his interesting shopping trip with Nicolette's downtrodden cousin. "I've also heard—though not from her—that when she took her leave of the city she also took her leave of me."

"I cannot say I'm sorry to hear this. Even by your standards, Robert, the Beaune is a poor idea of a mistress. Such an odious woman! She's worse than her mother ever was."

"In which case I'm well to be done with her, I suppose." Finishing his wine, he paused to think again, this time for effect—that, and to build up some courage. He found none, and so poured himself a third glass and drank half of it before asking, "What do you know of the Berenguer family, Maman?"

"Oh, Robert, no! It's too much. She's at least fifteen years older than you are. Besides, she'd never have you. I heard she's become a God-botherer. And anyway, Berenguer's in debt to his follicles, they say."

"I wasn't proposing to offer myself to the comtesse as a lover, Maman. Really—whatever do you think of me?"

"It's probably best you never know," she said. The tone was prim, but her eyes sparkled, a little, the way they used to do, and Robert laughed.

"Only I met the daughter the other day," he said after a

moment, "and, well—you know." He felt his voice dry up in his throat; this conversation had suddenly become a lot more uncomfortable than he had expected. "Do you know her? Have you ever—?"

"Introduced you? As it happens, no. Not that I'd ever expect you to remember any of the eligible ladies I have paraded in front of you." She examined him carefully, and Robert felt seven years old again. "I haven't introduced you because I didn't think you'd suit."

"What's wrong with them?"

"On the surface, nothing at all. The title's old—six hundred years if it's a day, and maybe older than that. The comte is, in my experience, a genial enough man, though his snobbishness borders on eccentricity. He makes the duc de Saint-Simon seem reasonable." Robert struggled before finally suppressing a smile. To hear his mother accuse someone else of snobbishness was a new experience.

"The problem, dear Robert, is that they've got no money. The title may be old but it was an honour of war; there is no County Berenguer associated with it. And de Berenguer is snobbish enough to follow the old salic practise: what few small properties he does have will go, along with their mortgages, to some male heir, not his daughter. All she will inherit is his name and his personal debts. You're a younger son, Robert: you're not going to inherit enough to properly support a family."

"I'm not really thinking about a family—"

"Well, you should be. You're not going to be able to live here forever, you know." The duchesse shook her head. "Besides, there's something not right about that girl. Always disappearing from court without explanation— there's starting to be a scent of scandal about her, and the last thing this family needs is more scandal."

But, thought Robert, *the scandal is the most interesting thing about her.*

Aloud he said, "Perhaps I should pay another visit to Nicolette de Beaune's cousin Jeanette, then." He was greatly satisfied by the expression on his mother's face as he took his leave of her.

There were six names on her list. Victoire knew the villain who'd set the trap at Clopard's cellar could have been any one of a dozen or more women she had sold to over the past year, but only six of them had been in or close to Paris during the relevant period. And not all of those six had enough of a stake in the success of Victoire's enterprise to make it worth the risk to themselves. Antoinette, vicomtesse de Sauval was neither wealthy nor powerful—and the vicomtesse might not even know what Victoire looked like: she had always had a seamstress deal with Victoire, and Victoire couldn't remember if they'd ever met. She also dismissed Marguerite de Geoffroy, who besides being poor was also the closest to a friend she had among the six.

"I think we can concentrate our efforts on five people," she said to Marie-Louise, sitting beside her at the trestle table in the kitchen. "The duchesse de Beaune is the one I'm most interested in, so I'm going to ask about her first thing tomorrow, before it gets too hot." Marie-Louise nodded. She had met Nicolette.

"But we also have to consider the comtesse de Champcéry, the marquise de Lancie, the vicomtesse de Clermontagne, and the baronne de Sainte-Bertrille. None of them is especially friendly to me, and all of them still owe me greater or lesser amounts from the spring shipment. So, they all have a motive for betrayal."

"How can I help you with this?" Marie-Louise asked.

"I want you to find out the names and locations of the women who sew for these people," Victoire told her. "I can ask some questions"—very carefully—"about any unusual behaviour our clients might have engaged in recently. But I think I can learn if any of these women have suddenly got new cloth they haven't paid for. I just need to know which dressmakers I have to deal with."

Marie-Louise gave her a suspicious look. "Couldn't I talk to those women myself? After all, I'm of their class."

"I have no objections to you looking at their shops, if you think you can do so without drawing attention to yourself." Anything might help, after all. "But you can't approach them as a possible customer. I can."

"Won't these women know you?"

"Not the way I plan to appear to them, they won't."

Marie-Louise raised an eyebrow, then smiled. "It's a pity we only know about the blue elephants, mademoiselle. Any of the other pieces of cloth could be on one of our suspects right this moment and we wouldn't be able to tell."

"True," Victoire told her. "But you've given me another idea. You have a very good eye, and I trust it a great deal. So, while you are out and about today and tomorrow, see if you can catch a glimpse of any of our suspects for yourself. You might not know to a certainty that it's our cloth they might be wearing. But you will surely know if it's new. And that will give us something more to act on."

"I wish I could do more to help you. So does Catherine."

"I appreciate that, Marie-Louise. But we have to begin somewhere, and this is the best place." Marie-Louise got up; Victoire raised a hand to stop her. "There's one more thing," she said. "I also want you to set a watch on my parents' hôtel; you'll want Hachette to help you. If my mother's priest, Robillard, sets foot outside the house I want him followed. I need to know where he goes."

Marie-Louise raised an eyebrow. "Your own family, mademoiselle?"

"Père Robillard is not my family. And wasn't it you, Marie-Louise, who pointed out to me that the trap at Clopard's could just as easily have been set by a priest or monk as by a noble?"

Chapter Five

The Wrong Sort of Interest

THE IDIOT MEN who had banned cotton cloth ought to be forced to wear full court dress, of the heavy Italian silk, throughout the summer, Victoire thought. That way they might possibly understand why a woman might want clothing that didn't make her feel half-dead whenever she stood up. In this early September that felt much more like August even her cotton overskirt and petticoat were more weight than she was happy with. It didn't help that she'd had to walk so far.

The Hôtel de Beaune was a new mansion in the faubourg St-Honoré, and so within just a few minutes' walk of the gardens of the Tuilleries palace—but a long, sweating, exhausting distance from the Hôtel de Berenguer, which lay in the much less fashionable centre of the Right Bank. Victoire had only visited Nicolette here once, but she still was more than familiar with the location and the house, because her friend Jeanette Desmarais, Nicolette's cousin, also lived there—though not in the nicer wings of the hôtel.

The gatekeeper let her in without question, which made it a surprise when the maître d'hôtel told her that madame la duchesse was not only away from the house, she had left the city.

"Are you absolutely certain?" she asked the man, aware as she did so that of course he would be. "It's just that the emperor and empress will be back in Paris any day now, and it's not like madame la duchesse to avoid court like this."

"Terribly sorry, mademoiselle, but I only know what I have been told."

"Might I come in anyway? If the duchesse isn't at home I would like to speak to her cousin, mademoiselle Desmarais."

"Please come with me to the yellow salon," the man said, "and I will have the lady summoned." He stepped back into the entry hall, waiting until Victoire had stepped over the threshold before closing the door behind her, turning and walking away. She followed him, wondering if Nicolette had taken all of her personal servants with her. Unlike most of Victoire's clients, Nicolette had a dress-maker on her household staff; it would be very helpful to be able to interview that woman.

There was no point asking the maître d'hôtel about it, though. Jeanette would be more likely to know.

"If mademoiselle will be seated," the man said, gesturing her past him into the salon, "I will have mademoiselle Desmarais summoned." Victoire nodded in acceptance, then circumnavigated the salon looking for the least uncomfortable chair. She knew this salon well; it was not where the best visitors were received. *They won't offer refreshments either,* she thought, licking the dust from her lips.

In that assessment she was almost wrong: a few minutes after Victoire had settled onto a chair, one of the housemaids entered the salon, bearing a tray on which sat a stoneware jug and a somewhat battered pewter goblet. As she thanked the maid Victoire wondered just how sour the wine would prove to be.

It stopped just short of being vinegar. Still, it was liquid and very nearly cold, so she was grateful. She was on the verge of praising the stuff when the salon door opened behind the maid. Victoire caught a brief look of panic in the young woman's eyes, and then the maid shuffled silently to a corner as the duc de Beaune walked into the room.

"Mademoiselle de Berenguer," he said, bowing low. "I understand you were asking after my wife the duchesse." The duc was perhaps ten years older than Victoire—certainly no older than his late twenties—and good-looking in a dark sort of way. He wore a coat of deep burgundy, trimmed in silver and with enormous cuffs extending from his elbows to just above his wrists. His breeches matched; his long waistcoat was of lavender silk. The curls of his wig fell past his shoulders. He looked at her with appraisal verging on the arrogant. "I trust you were told of your mistaken assumption?"

Not at all how I'd put it, she thought, disliking him instantly. "I was told she had left the city, yes. I haven't been told where she has gone, though. I would like to visit her, if it's possible."

"Not possible, I'm afraid. My Nicolette has withdrawn from the world for a few days." Now his eyes were as cold as his voice. Victoire looked away from him—and saw the maid, shrinking back against the wall behind the open door, as though trying to make herself invisible. Her eyes were glazed with something Victoire guessed was fear. *How do I get this man out of here,* she asked herself, *when it's his own house?*

She was saved by the maître d'hôtel, who intruded into the doorway, not more than his head, saying, "Monsieur, a messenger from the baron de Geoffroy is at the gate and wishes to speak with you."

For a moment Victoire saw a look of utter hatred in the duc's eyes. It was gone almost before she'd fully registered the extent of that passion. "My regrets, mademoiselle," the duc said as he bowed a very formal farewell and gave her an utterly dead-eyed smile. "Until the next time we meet."

May it be never, Victoire thought as the duc disappeared. The maid fled the room almost immediately after the duc, giving Victoire no opportunity to say or ask anything. Victoire was not surprised the maid ran in the opposite of the direction taken by the duc.

She had only just realized the name she'd heard— *Geoffroy? I didn't know those two knew one another*—when Jeanette arrived. Victoire abandoned the thought, hugged her tightly and kissed both cheeks soundly. "Jeanette," she said, "I cannot thank you enough for whatever it is you have done when I've visited you to keep that man from crossing my path."

"Oh, dear," Jeanette said. "He was in this room?"

"He seemed to be—concerned—that I was inquiring after Nicolette." Victoire turned away from the door and asked, "What has happened to her? Where did she go, and why?"

"I know nothing more about it than you," Jeanette said. "I was a bit surprised myself that she left so suddenly, so I'm not sure how much help I can be. The chevalier de Vimoutiers thinks it is just because she has thrown him over and is making the acquaintance of a new lover, but I'm not sure I believe that."

"You are friends with the chevalier de Vimoutiers."

"Oh, not that sort of friend." Jeanette giggled, something completely unlike her. "He has been a help to me lately, that's all. And if you ask me he was more than grateful that Nicolette threw him over."

She did not want to get caught up in any discussion of Robert de Vimoutiers. "Well, has Nicolette suddenly come into some money? Or found another supply of painted cotton to replace the cloth I'd promised her but—but couldn't deliver?"

"I don't know of anything like that at all," Jeanette said. "If anything, I'd say she has even less money now than she's accustomed to. The gossip I've overheard among the servants is that the duc has finally lost patience with her profligacy—though not, apparently, with her adulteries. So perhaps she's been sent away as a punishment for spending too much." She took a large, defiant sip of wine, winced as the sourness hit and added, "I am not at all sorry she's gone, and I don't apologize for that either."

"I do not blame you," Victoire said. She took a small sip of the dreadful wine. The duchesse de Beaune could no longer occupy top place on the list of suspects, it appeared. She was a nasty enough person, though, that she couldn't be dismissed entirely. As long as she was out of Paris, though, Nicolette was less of a threat. For now.

"I'm not sure anyone else here is sorry she's gone. The servants are grumbling. Well, the male servants are, at any rate. The women are no more talkative with her gone than they are when she's here."

"They're not fond of Nicolette, that I have no trouble believing."

"They're not fond of her," Jeanette said, "but they're *terrified* of him. And I don't blame them a bit; I take great care never to be alone in a room with the duc."

"He did not strike me as wilfully cruel," Victoire said,

silently praying for the purity of the wine before she sipped again. "But there was something—"

"The word I use is *unhealthy*," Jeanette said. "He never speaks harshly to her, I've never seen him raise a hand to her. But something about him is very, very bad."

Bad enough to be the person who stole my cloth? "Jeanette, do you know if Nicolette took her dressmaker with her when she left?"

"I don't think she's here," Jeanette said, "so she must have gone with Nicolette's other personal maids. Why do you ask?"

"Please bear with me. Has Nicolette bragged to you about a fresh supply of painted cotton? Since the day I saw you at the Réalmont salon, that is."

"Oh, I see. Yes, if I were you I'd suspect Nicolette as well. Stealing your cloth and then blaming you for it is precisely the sort of thing she'd do.

"Unfortunately, I haven't seen any cotton in the house, and she didn't say anything to me either."

"*Peste*," Victoire said. "It would have been so easy had it been her."

"It could still be," Jeanette told her. "I didn't say the cloth wasn't here, only that I hadn't seen it. I'm not precisely a valued member of this household, remember." She pointed to the wine. "Even before I tasted it I knew how poor it is. My visitors are never given decent wine to drink—that's how well they treat me here."

"If I could afford to get you out of here, you know I would do it." Victoire gave her a pained smile. "You know that my situation isn't any better than yours. Instead of your cousin grieving you, it's my mother grieving me."

That gave her another idea. "I don't suppose you'd

know if Nicolette has any acquaintance with my mother's confessor, do you? His name is Robillard."

Jeanette laughed. "Nicolette, with a priest? Victoire, she's the sort of woman who sneaks out of the house to eat and drink at cabarets, not to go to church."

Lise and Rafael's lackeys were busily shifting trunks into the Hôtel de Bellevasse when Robert arrived. Leaning against an interior pillar of the port-cochère, Robert indulged himself in some pleasant voyeurism; watching others work, especially members of the Third Estate, was always entertaining. It was still hot and humid, but September was well under way now and it appeared Lise and her husband planned to make a prolonged stay in Paris; presumably the emperor and his family would be back in Paris within a day or two. It wouldn't be long—a month, two at most—before hunting season began, but Lise and Rafael wouldn't necessarily think of leaving Paris for the Chateau de Bellevasse because of that. Robert tried to remember if Rafael had ever shown an interest in hunting, and failed. *I really should pay more attention to non-female people,* he decided.

Spotting a gap in the flow of lackeys and trunks, Robert trotted across the courtyard and into the house. He was fortunate enough to find Lise in the entry hall, and even more fortunate to find her between lackeys. "Morning, cousin," he said. "You're looking busy today."

"That's only because I am, idiot." She smiled as she said it, though. Those people who said nobody respected him were clearly ill-informed.

"You surely aren't needed by these people more than you are by me." He nodded in the direction of a returning lackey. "They all seem to know what they should be doing. Which is all you can ask of a lackey, really."

"They seem to know," Lise said, "because I'm telling them. Is this really important, Robert? Or can it wait until lunch?"

"I suppose you'd have to tell me if it can wait." He smiled at her. "Is a threat from a well-known thief-master something that can wait?"

He'd expected a stronger reaction from her. Instead, Lise rolled her eyes. Then she put one—surprisingly strong— hand on his shoulder and pushed him to the side. "That one goes into the dressing room of monsieur le duc," she said to the man and boy carrying a new-looking trunk whose brass still shone. Only when the trunk had made its way to the grand staircase did she look again at Robert. "I'd have expected something a bit more creative from you, Robert."

"But it's true," he said, stung. It wouldn't have been so painful if he'd been lying about any of this. Not, of course, that he intended to come too close to the truth. "It was a man named Clopard. He accosted me in the street yesterday."

"I know of the man," she said, glaring. "So does most of the population of Paris. He's not someone I concern myself with, and you should follow my lead."

"Does he strike you as being the sort who'd be involved in an aristocratic smuggling ring?"

"No, he does not." Somehow, he seemed to have got in her way again; she pushed him to the side once more and directed a second pair of lackeys to shift their trunk to her own dressing room. "But the idea of an aristocratic smuggling ring doesn't strike me as being sensible in the first place. What is Clopard smuggling, salt? Sugar?"

"Indian painted cotton?" Robert was again disappointed by her failure to react. "That was the impression he gave me, anyway." It hadn't been Clopard, of course, but Robert had definitely got that impression from someone.

"Robert, the people who smuggle that cloth into France are rough, violent country people from the south-east. Their families have been smuggling for centuries, and they would eat Clopard and his gang for dinner. If you truly are thinking of getting involved in cloth-smuggling you're in the wrong part of the country. And I strongly advise you to stay here and stay out of it. You are not made for a life of crime."

"Nobody takes me seriously as a threat," he said with deliberate sadness. Lise punched him on the shoulder. "Please, not in front of the lackeys," he said. "I already find most of them disrespectful enough." He rubbed the shoulder. "So, what you are saying is I should just ignore this Clopard if he returns and asks me to cast my lot with him and his gang?"

"Are you saying that you *are* in fact smuggling cloth and are concerned he is trying to insert himself into your business?"

"Not as such," Robert said. "In fact," he added hastily, seeing her frown, "I am precisely as you suggest, and utterly innocent of any evil intent or action." *Though I wouldn't mind learning a bit more about them.* A pause to make it appear he was engaged in deep thought. "Are there lots of noblewomen selling or buying smuggled cloth in the city, then?"

"Everybody rest for a quarter-hour," Lise called out. Grabbing Robert by the arm she pulled him into a small room. "Sit," she said, pointing at one of the chairs.

He sat. It was an old chair, and uncomfortable. *Probably designed for interrogation purposes,* he thought. "I'm really sorry I interrupted your work," he began.

"Quiet," she said. "Robert, what is this about? Truly."

He looked up at her in mute reproach until she snarled and raised her hand to belt him again. "I didn't mean *quiet* in the sense of never speaking again, you idiot. I meant *quiet* in the sense of don't say stupid things until I understand what is going on here. Why are you suddenly so interested in crime and criminals? And why, in God's name, cloth-smuggling?" She was unable to keep the fierce expression on her face to the end of the speech, however, and Robert exhaled in relief. He had spent some time learning just how far he could push his cousin.

"I obviously can't give you any identifying details," he told her, "but it's true Clopard seems to think I am involved in cloth-smuggling. And if I am understanding him correctly he is himself involved, and wants to avoid competing with me. So, what this is really about, cousin, is: How serious a crime is this cloth-smuggling, and how dangerous is this Clopard to me? I may not be Maman's favourite child, but I'm the only one still living with her and I think that has to count for something."

"I sometimes think she puts up with you only because she sees it as a path to sainthood," Lise said. At least she sat in the other chair. "Lord," she said, "but this is a horrible chair. Reminds me of the ones in de La Reynie's office." Robert nodded but said nothing.

"Right," Lise said. "Cloth and smuggling. I have nothing to do with this, really. I know the emperor's financial advisors are upset because every piece of smuggled cloth is a piece of cloth that isn't being sold by French weaving mills. Nobody pays tax on smuggled cloth either. But in the grand scheme of things it is a small issue most of the time. So even though a lot of the people breaking the law are nobles, the police don't need me to track them down. Likewise, I am not involved with Clopard or people like him. The archers deal with that lot, and regular methods of policing are enough.

"So I'm not sure what you need me for. Do you want me to mention this to monsieur de La Reynie?"

"Good lord, no." *Should have thought of that; of course she'd want to report to her superior.* "I just wanted to know if I needed help," he said. "From what you're saying, it sounds as if I don't."

"And you won't need my help," Lise said, "right up to the point where suddenly you do."

The next day, Victoire stayed in bed late. After breakfast she reviewed her wardrobe until *Nones,* then hovered in the vicinity of the family's small chapel until her mother and Père Robillard were safely inside and chanting their way through the service. Then she climbed the stairs to the third floor of the house, where the servants' rooms were—and the cell in which Robillard ostentatiously confined himself at night.

She opened the unlocked door and was disappointed: instead of a hidden trove of self-indulgent luxuries she found only a primitive wood-and-rope bed, under the worn blanket of which was only a thin, straw-stuffed mattress that even a stable-boy would object to. *Wilful perversity,* she thought as she stepped back to close the door behind her.

There was nothing else in the room save for a very old and very small wooden chest whose lock—had it ever had one—was missing. The chest was far too small to contain even a single roll of the stolen cloth, but Victoire lifted the lid anyway: best to be certain. The chest was mostly empty; all it contained was a string of beads, an ancient crucifix whose edges were softened by age and handling, and a Bible whose covers were worn to the point the wood was visible beneath tears in the aged leather.

When she closed the chest's lid, a puff of air caused the tapestry curtain at the far end of the room to wave a little. *Hello,* she thought, *what's hiding behind you, then?* She lifted aside the *arras* and found a small alcove—and more disappointment. There wasn't enough space back here to hide anything incriminating either.

Not unless Père Robillard had managed to stuff a dozen donkey-loads of cloth into the aged *prie-dieu* sharing the space with nails, on which he had hung a robe (presumably the spare for the one he currently wore), a cloak, and some vestments he hardly ever used. Victoire looked on and inside the prayer desk, but found nothing save for a couple of very old pieces of paper on which someone had written in incomprehensible Latin. These were unlikely to be clues, because the edges of the papers were yellow enough to place them possibly two decades back in time.

Under the bed, she thought. She was on her knees, chin almost on the faded floorboards, trying to determine through the gloom if anything might be there, when she heard the unmistakable sound of approaching footsteps. *Dear God,* she thought, scrambling backwards to the *arras* and then behind it.

Of course it was Père Robillard. He grumbled something she couldn't quite make out as he closed his door behind him. Then, after a long sigh, he began to pray. The words weren't any devotional Victoire had ever heard; they didn't even seem to be Latin. Some odd dialect of French, perhaps—where was Robillard from? She realized she knew nothing about his background.

The smell of tallow assaulted her nostrils. No, not tallow—beef dripping. They were certainly the same substance, but their purposes were completely different. Victoire knew what tallow candles smelled like—they were all she could afford at the old house—but she also knew what roasting ox smelled like, and that was what she inhaled now. *He can't be cooking in here,* she thought. *So what is he doing?*

She heard him get to his feet and shuffle forward. *Oh God help me, he's coming back here.* A skinny, wrinkled finger appeared on her side of the *arras* and the cloth began to move. The *prie-dieu* wasn't big enough for her to hide behind, and at any rate he was probably coming back here to use it. She tried to invent a plausible reason for being in his cell—or at least a plausible reason that wasn't the truth.

Her mother saved her.

Père Robillard's hand stiffened, then withdrew as the sound of Maman's voice came through the closed door, calling for him. He grumbled something inaudible in that odd dialect, and Victoire heard the door open. Oddly enough he didn't seem to be upset at being called away. *God knows I would have been,* Victoire thought.

She didn't exhale and begin breathing again until she was sure her mother's and Père Robillard's voices were receding down the hall.

It was as she pulled back the *arras* to resume her interrupted search beneath the bed that Victoire realized where the smell had been coming from. Père Robillard's spare robe was smoking, and when she looked more closely at it she saw the remnants of a long, greasy stain evaporate into the hot air of the alcove.

What was this? Père Robillard was ostentatious in eating frugally—or at least he was when in the Hôtel de Berenguer. Papa loved meat, and the more of it he could get the better, but Père Robillard could be counted on to confine himself to bread and pottage, and maybe the odd piece of salt-cod from New France, even on non-fasting days. When he was in the Hôtel de Berenguer.

Most of us wouldn't be so anxious to hide the signs of eating well, she thought. She dropped to the floor again; there was nothing under the bed, not even shoes.

She was brushing the front of her dress when she remembered something Jeanette had said about her cousin, the duchesse de Beaune: *She's the sort of woman who sneaks out of the house to eat and drink at cabarets, not to go to church.*

"Your mother's priest?" Marie-Louise looked horrified. "A man of God?" The four of them were gathered in the kitchen of the old house; the kitchen door was open wide to encourage what breeze there was to come in and make itself at home.

Victoire nodded. "A priest, yes. Not necessarily a man of God. We hardly know anything about the man, you know." She thought back to the primitive cell: was it sincere piety and embrace of poverty? Or was it calculation, playing on an unhappy woman's susceptibility? "He might just be a horribly devoted man."

"So God might like him, but it still doesn't make him very nice for the rest of us," Hachette said.

"Not even remotely, so far as I'm concerned" said Victoire. "I know there's nothing that connects him to our missing cloth, not directly at least. But my feelings tell me I cannot trust his virtue. He's much too good to be true. And what sort of man feels obliged to hide an appetite for roasted meats? Whatever God feels, I cannot like him.

"But there's a difference, however subtle, between wanting to snub the man for a poseur and wanting to expose him for a villain." She gestured to Hachette. "Which is why I want you to help me, Rat-boy."

He stepped back and out the kitchen door, but he smiled as he did. "What do you want from me? Am I going to hate it?"

"Not at all. I just want you to follow our good Père Robillard the next time he leaves my father's house. See where he goes, who he meets."

"I don't know this man, mademoiselle. How can I follow him?"

"That might be a problem," Victoire said. She thought a moment. "And then again it won't be. Come over here, Hachette, and sit beside me. I am going to try to put an image into your head—no, no; I promise it won't hurt. You won't notice anything at all. But I want you to know what Père Robillard looks like, and this is the best way to do that. Now sit still, and don't fidget."

She conjured up a prayer from the recesses of her memory, then did the same with her memories of Père Robillard. "Are you seeing something?" she asked. She was surprised at how the effort had exhausted her: she felt as if she'd sprinted up the steps to the first floor of the old house.

"Yes," said Hachette, "but unless Père Robillard looks like a goose with red hair I think you should try again."

It was several minutes before Victoire was able to get her laughter under control and repeat the experiment. Only when Hachette was finally able to describe the père as "a scarecrow of a man, thin and hungry-looking—and old, even older than your father," did she consider the prayer a success. She had hoped Hachette would also be able to describe Robillard's narrow face and hooded eyes, or the way the skin on his hands looked like wrinkled paper.

But she was confident Hachette would know the man if he encountered him.

"Now," she said, "go out for a walk, Hachette, and see if you can't find this man."

"Paris is kind of big," he began.

"I know, and I realize this is a long shot. I just want you to get used to the idea of keeping your eyes alert for this man. I suggest you concentrate on the area around the Temple, and any other place where there are cabarets and taverns that offer a lot of food for not very much money. You wouldn't know it to look at him, but I suspect our humble man of God is a man of appetite."

Hachette nodded and started for the door. "One more thing," she added. "I know we haven't found any evidence yet that our cloth is on the market. But while you're looking for Père Robillard I'd like you to start looking for fences who might be in the business of selling stolen cloth. If such a person even exists."

"Oh, mademoiselle, there are fences who sell anything," Hachette said from the doorway. "And some are women, and I know of several in the *cour de miracle* near the *filles-dieux*. Not really close to the Temple, though, but I'll find a way to ask after I've found your priest—or given up on finding him."

"It would be perfect," Victoire said after Hachette had left them, "if he could find Père Robillard in the act of meeting with one of those fences."

"Sometimes prayers are answered, mademoiselle," said Catherine, and Victoire prayed that she was correct this time.

What an amazing place, Victoire thought. She had been

accustomed to buying her jewellery from the small shops inside the colonnades of the Palais Cardinal north of the Tuilleries. She was so accustomed to the shops and the neighbourhood, in fact, that she had used her experience of those streets in designing the escape route she'd had to follow the other night.

The shop of Fortune Vidal, in the east end of the Right Bank, was not a place she would have considered suitable. But now she was more than happy her search for Jeanette had led her here. Most of what she could see in the display cases at the front of this shop was garish and vulgar, but inside the shop she could see hints of what promised to be remarkable good taste; she was going to have fun shopping here. Once she had money again.

"I am looking for Jeanette Desmarais," she told the boy behind the counter. "Can you tell me if she's here today?"

"Jeanette Desmarais? You are looking for mademoiselle Desmarais?" An older man came into the shop from the room behind the counter.

Fortune Vidal did not look anything like a bourgeois jeweller. He didn't rub his hands unctuously, he didn't tug a forelock—in fact he didn't have a forelock to tug. And he certainly didn't look defensive or supplicatory. He looked, in fact, rather as her father did when he was poring over one of his genealogical treatises: a man of ordinary features but supremely confident in his abilities. "I believe I might know you, mademoiselle," he said to her, bowing. "You are the comte de Berenguer's daughter, are you not? I have seen you at the palace."

"You have the advantage of me, monsieur. I only know you by reputation."

"A good one, I hope," he said, smiling a little.

"I would not be here otherwise," she said, smiling

back in the same degree. "I was told I could find Jeanette Desmarais here."

"Now here you have the advantage of me, mademoiselle. Were you expecting to meet her here?"

"Not precisely," Victoire said. "I called for her at the Hôtel de Beaune and was told she was coming here." She looked back at the door. "Perhaps I was misled."

"Or she was making my shop one of a number of stops," monsieur Vidal said—just as the shop door opened.

"No, Anne," Jeanette Desmarais said, her back to Victoire as she spoke—somewhat harshly—to a person outside. "I do not wish you to come in with me. You will do as you are told, and wait out there."

"Jeanette," Victoire called out, smiling. "I am so happy to find you here." Jeanette's response was a furious blush, something that caught Victoire completely by surprise.

"Mademoiselle de Berenguer," she said, her voice tentative. "My apologies; I did not mean to intrude."

"What is this?" Victoire asked, just as monsieur Vidal told Jeanette to stop being silly and come into the shop. *That's an odd degree of familiarity*, she thought, *for a bourgeois to show to—*

"My profound apologies," the jeweller said. "I believe I am at fault here. I was unaware that you ladies were on a first-name basis."

"Because," Victoire said, guessing, "of our mutual connection with Nicolette de Beaune. Your confusion is justified, monsieur. Though it is in fact *because* of our knowledge of Nicolette that Jeanette and I are friends."

Jeanette laughed, finally, and Victoire was pleased— and mildly surprised, again—at the way her friend's face lightened, became so much younger, something she had to attribute to the presence of monsieur Vidal.

"If I am not being unforgivably forward," the jeweller said, "would you consider taking wine upstairs? That way you could have your conversation without having to worry about interruption. And I would be honoured."

Victoire wasn't certain about the desirability of this offer. Then she saw the look on Jeanette's face. *Just how long have you been coming here for your own reasons, my friend?* Victoire wondered. "Monsieur, I would be happy to accept your kind invitation," she said, smiling at Jeanette.

"His wine really is very good," Jeanette said in a small voice.

Monsieur Vidal cuffed his boy on the ear, telling him to stop gawking and return to watching the shop. Then he led Victoire and Jeanette up a steep flight of stairs to a first-floor apartment whose front salon was cozy and furnished in surprisingly good taste, for a bourgeois. Fortune Vidal's sofa was every bit as elegant as those Victoire had seen in the salons of the marquise de Réalmont. "I will leave you here," he said, eyes mostly on Jeanette, "and send up wine in a moment. I will be in the workshop if you need me; pull that cord to summon a servant."

Victoire wanted more than anything to demand of Jeanette, *What in the world is going on here, and what is Fortune Vidal to you?* But that would be both unfair and rude, so instead, once the wine had been delivered and poured, she made her expression one of seriousness and said, "Forgive me for asking this, Jeanette, but something you said yesterday has me wondering. Do you know of any particular taverns or cabarets Nicolette favours? I've just learned that somebody else I'm investigating also favours these places."

For a moment Jeanette looked confused; she had definitely been expecting a different question, Victoire thought with amusement. Then, speaking a bit slowly as if thinking her way through the answer, Jeanette said, "Is this to do with the last thing you asked me yesterday? About your mother's confessor?" Victoire nodded. "This really doesn't sound anything like her. A man of God?"

"He claims to be one, yes. And your cousin claims to be providing you with a home. I heard what you had to do to dismiss your maid when you got here, Jeanette."

Jeanette glowered. "They treat me as if I'm a thief in their house," she said. "I usually have to sneak out if I'm to"—she stopped herself, and smiled thinly. "I take your point. Very well, Victoire. I cannot give you any names at the moment—they're far from the top of my mind right now. But I will think about places I may have escorted her. Would that be helpful?"

"It certainly would," Victoire told her. "As will be your continuing discretion—for which I thank you."

"And likewise," Jeanette said, with a smile that crossed from knowing into pleading.

Chapter Six
A Question of Suitability

I DON'T SEE any chickens about, Robert said to himself, *so why is this street called Street of the Castrated Rooster?* Really, Paris had the most interesting places if you just took yourself a little bit outside your own neighbourhood.

Perhaps he should ask the man following him what his own neighbourhood was. Or whether he knew anything about how Capon Road got its name.

If that failed, he could ask the man following the man who was following him.

He'd become aware of his follower(s) shortly after he'd turned north onto rue St-Martin and had since been leading him on a zigzag route through the streets north of the hôtel de Ville and east of the markets. The man following his follower had joined them just a few moments ago, as they had turned north onto rue de Beaubourg.

At least he had taken care to steer this procession well clear of the street on which Victoire had her second house. *Her crime-house, I suppose.* So, if his shadow was one of Clopard's men at least he wouldn't be leading the man to her door. *Fart Street,* he thought, in vain trying to stifle the giggle. It was almost a certainty that young Hachette had found Victoire that house. Only a twelve-year-old could want to live in a house on the rue du Pet.

As for the second man, the best guess Robert could come up with was that the first man was known in some fashion to a Clopard equivalent on the north side of the river, and so the follower's follower was engaged in a sort of professional courtesy, an escort of sorts to ensure the intruder was able safely to return to his own side of the Seine.

Robert wasn't in any hurry, at any rate. His long-term goal was either to persuade Clopard's man to give up, or to take him and his own shadow past the old Temple and outside the crumbling north walls, which the emperor was busy converting into a broad, tree-lined path they were calling the *boulevard*, after the Dutch word for *fortress walls*. If need be they could walk all the way around the city.

Well, they could provided nobody decided to become confrontational about all this healthy exercise. *I should be getting in some practise,* he thought, *in the fighting prayers.* He brushed his hand across the hilt of his épée, and felt a little bit safer.

A burst of shouting from behind him informed Robert that his follower had discovered that he himself was being trailed, and had taken objection to this fact. Nobody paid any attention to Robert when he turned about and began walking back along the way he'd come; this was because everyone on the street was now clustered around the two fighting men. Additional spectators were flooding in from adjacent streets, suggesting to Robert that this sort of excitement wasn't too common around here.

The men were using cudgels on each other. Well, they were trying to, at any rate. Neither of them was all that proficient with the weapon, and neither cudgel was much more than a slightly large stick. Still, each man had been bloodied, and one had an eye swelling shut when Robert, taking advantage of his class and the fact he carried a sword, got close enough to them to see.

They were shouting at each other as much as they were trying to hit one another. *I really don't understand the criminal mind,* Robert thought as one called out, "He's on our side of the river! So he's ours!"

"Sucks to you, we saw him first!" Thump; a cheer from the crowd.

"Isn't anybody betting on this?" Robert asked the elderly woman next to him.

"No point," the woman said, spitting a plug of tobacco onto the street just in front of Robert's shoes. "No skill involved. Where's the pride in the job? That's what I want to know." Spit. "Time was, a street-tough was a man to reckon with. Today? Ha. Nothing but cheap-talking kids."

The men circled around some more, and at first Robert thought they were looking for advantage. Then he decided they were simply circling because that was what street-fighting was about. "Do you know either of them?"

"The one with the closing eye, that's Croque. He's one of Batteur's gang, from up by rue du Renard. The one with the bloody nose I don't know."

"From the left bank, I gather," said Robert. "I wonder what they're fighting about."

"Probably," the old woman said, "about which gang gets to rob you and break your head."

"I did wonder about that," Robert said, smiling.

"Going to head back to your domestic fortress, then?" she asked, beginning to sidle away from him.

"And miss the ending? Wouldn't dream of it." He rested one hand on the hilt of his épée, and with the other smacked away from his purse the approaching paw of an urchin. "Besides," he told her, "I want to have a word or two with whichever one of them is still standing when the fight ends or the archers arrive. Whichever comes first."

In the end it was Robert who had to leave first. An entire squad of archers broke up the fight and arrested both men, thwarting his desire to learn from the victor the real reason he was being followed. So many of the spectators had left by then—more than one of them throwing clods of horse-dung at the fighters for being such poor entertainment—that Robert found himself too obvious a part of the remaining audience.

He was preparing to make his way south-west and back to his domestic fortress when a familiar ratlike visage flickered through his line of sight. *So I wasn't the only one curious about this event,* he thought. *Did Victoire send you out to follow me? If so, just how much trouble are you— and I, I suppose—in, after the other night?* Had the boy been following Robert as well as the two inept shadows, it was possible he or Victoire knew more about Clopard and company than they had told him.

He caught up with Hachette on the rue de La Corderie, along the south wall of the Temple. At first the boy started, preparing for flight, when Robert called him. Then, on seeing Robert's face, the boy settled back, smiling. "You're far from home, monsieur le chevalier."

"Too true," Robert said. "I have been trying to shake off those two pugilists."

"Those what?"

"Fist-fighters," Robert said. "Though not very good ones."

"I thought you were calling them men who have sex with

sheep or something," Hachette said, giggling. "They sure aren't very good. They won't last long in a gang, that's for certain."

"I wanted to ask you about that," Robert told him. "Someone in the crowd said something about a gang run by a fellow named Batteur."

"I might know about him," Hachette said, suddenly wary again.

"You don't have to know much about him as far as I'm concerned. I just want to know why he might be interested in someone like me. Batteur's man was following another man, who in turn had been following me for about an hour before they started fighting. But why?"

"Isn't it obvious?" Hachette sucked his teeth. "I mean, you're an aristo and you dress good and you've probably got a whole fistful of *livres* in your purse right now."

"Yes to the first two, more or less no to the third," Robert told him. "But I've always been an aristo, and I'd like to think I've always dressed pretty well. So why are the street gangs of Paris so interested in me *now,* when they haven't paid me the slightest notice before?" *Before I met your mistress Victoire, that is.*

"How much time have you spent in this neighbourhood before?"

"A touch," Robert admitted. Seeing the confusion on Hachette's face he added, "That means you've made a good point. In fact, I haven't been out and about in these parts of the city at all, really." *Until my visit to friend Clopard's cellar, that is.* He put a hand on Hachette's shoulder and turned the boy, looking him in the eye. "How much do these gangs control, really? Does somebody like you have to be in Batteur or Clopard's good graces in order to survive on the streets?"

Hachette stiffened with outrage. Or pride; Robert couldn't be certain. "They think they run things," he said with a snort. "They don't really control the likes of me any more than the archers do."

"Could be dangerous, though, if you have everyone against you." *Come on, you can trust me.*

"Only if you call attention to yourself," Hachette said. "I make sure I don't."

"Until now?"

"Hey," he said, sucking his teeth more aggressively. "I didn't have nothing to do with—with that thing you got caught up in. But you should listen to me and stop making the gangs notice you. Then they'll leave you alone."

"I'm sure you're right," Robert told him, not believing a word of it.

"Do you want me to tell mademoiselle Victoire about you and me meeting this way?" He grinned in a suggestive fashion that appalled Robert.

"Do you really think knowing about this will make her feel warmer towards me?"

Hachette's grin faltered, collapsed. "A touch," he said, disappointed.

"The sorts of people we're interested in don't come out much in the daytime," Hachette said. "So, I don't know how much luck we're going to have here."

Victoire, wearing her glamour as Hachette's older brother, turned to him. "I don't feel safe in this sort of neighbourhood at night, so I want to be doubly certain a trip into one of these miracle courts will justify the risk before I actually take that risk."

"Oh, that's being smart, mademoiselle." Hachette

grinned his approval. "And it gives the bad men less chance to make us suffer." His expedition of the previous night had established little of any use: Père Robillard had stayed within the walls of the Hôtel de Berenguer, and while Hachette had made contact with a couple of women who sold stolen goods, neither of them had any cotton cloth, nor had they seen any, they claimed, in months. He could have all the brocades he wanted, mind, save that even the newest of them were in last year's styles.

So Victoire had, reluctantly, decided to expand the scope of her investigations to include male fences, uncomfortable though this made her. After her unwilling visit to Clopard's cellar she found she had a strong dislike of the criminal underclass of Paris.

An old woman passed them and Hachette nudged Victoire. "Take a look," he said and turned around. Victoire turned slowly, hoping not to draw too much attention to herself. She was just in time to see the old woman lean against the side of a filthy building, lift one leg up and suddenly sprout a wooden leg where a whole limb had been just a moment before. "Behold," Hachette said. "A miracle. And without magic." The old woman produced a crutch from somewhere within her greasy dress and hobbled around the corner onto the rue du Temple.

"I have heard about this, but I believe that's the first one I've ever seen," she said. "Hachette, you're a good-luck charm."

"Tell me that again after I've found you our cloth," he said with a grin.

Victoire saw a second non-magical miracle a moment later, when a blind man came around the same corner from rue du Temple and then suddenly could see. As the first thing he saw was Hachette and the disguised Victoire he scowled for a moment. Then, having taken in their dress and Hachette's bare feet, he shared a big smile with them, rattled his begging-cup to show off the morning's haul, and skipped past them into the court of miracles in rue Portofrère, the one they were headed to themselves.

While the beggars who made up most of the population of the area paid little to no attention to them, Victoire could tell from the way the back of her neck burned and twitched that somebody, or somebodies, watched them very carefully. "Even though we look as if we should belong, we don't belong," she murmured to Hachette.

"People in these neighbourhoods have to trust one another," he told her. "And they have to know you for a long time before they trust you even a little bit."

"Am I making this harder for you, then?" She didn't know precisely which neighbourhoods Hachette was known in, but that he was fairly well known in certain neighbourhoods he had been eager to tell her when they'd met and she had taken him into her second household. It made sense, now that she was forced to think about it, that she'd fit into his world no better than he would into hers. Even if she could glamour him to look like the chevalier de Vimoutiers or one of his cronies.

"People here probably wouldn't care for me anyway," he said. Victoire detected a suggestion of sour grapes about his tone, but ignored it. "Maybe we'll have more luck in the court around the *Petit Lion*. They know me a lot better there. More important," he said, thrusting out his chest, "they know I can stand up for myself."

Alas, though many people in the miracle court of the small lion knew and greeted Hachette, none of them knew anything about stolen cloth. Or, if they did know, they considered the knowledge worth a price Victoire couldn't have paid even had they told her what it was.

They were just about to turn back onto rue St-Denis, having given up for the day, when Victoire realized something behind them was bothering her. Uncertain as to what it could be—she knew no more about the court of the small lion than she had about the first court they'd been in—she turned, slowly, to look behind her.

The thing that had bothered her was the blind beggar— the same blind beggar they had seen in rue Portofrère. When her gaze lighted on his face the man rattled his begging-cup again... and then gave her a big smile that now didn't seem as friendly as it had an hour before.

"Good morning, mademoiselle! To what do I owe this undeserved honour?" Mademoiselle Le Point's smile was predatory, and Victoire couldn't help contrasting it unfavourably with Catherine's smile, which was practically a plea for favour. Still, to be a successful artisan probably did require a certain amount of predation.

"I am interviewing dressmakers," Victoire told her, stepping forward to allow a worn-faced servant to close the shop door behind her. "You have a good reputation, courtesy of the marquise de Lancie. So, I have decided to come see for myself if your reputation is justified." *I, too, can be predatory,* she thought as the dressmaker's smile curdled for a breath, before returning to its fixed cheeriness.

"I'm certain I will be able to provide satisfactory service, mademoiselle. The marquise is not my only noble client"

Victoire did not reply immediately, instead walking around the shop with a calm deliberation she did not quite feel. She had not, after all, used a glamour to disguise herself, and she could not help but feel exposed. But Marie-

Louise had warned her that the better dressmakers of Paris made a study of the aristocratic women who were their best potential customers, and Victoire had decided she ran a greater risk if she tried to present herself as someone else—or, worse, as someone who did not exist—than she would appearing as herself. She was wearing one of her best dresses as compensation, making the point that whoever she was, she knew how to dress.

"I intend to be at the height of fashion," she said when she finally returned to facing the woman. "Tell me about your materials. Can you provide them, or will I have to see to it myself?"

"Mademoiselle might wish to keep control over the choice of cloth," Le Point said. "But if she is prepared to trust me, I am not being over-proud when I say that I can myself obtain the best cloth, thread, and lace there is to be had."

"And painted cotton?"

"Is forbidden, mademoiselle."

"And you make up dresses of it anyway. I have seen them, mademoiselle. The ones I have seen are admirable, but I do not want to follow fashion, I want to lead it. Do you have cotton nobody has seen yet this year?"

Mademoiselle Le Point's eyes shifted away from Victoire. "Not as such," she said, apparently finding something fascinating on the street outside her window. "There have been some disruptions in the trade this summer." She returned her gaze to Victoire, her face a portrait of honesty. "I am sure these problems will be resolved when the weather cools." As if the problem was simply a matter of too much heat.

"Perhaps I could speak with your supplier. My request

might carry more weight than yours, admirable though your reputation is."

The woman's expression shut down, hard. "We never discuss our sources, mademoiselle. You understand, it is not that I wish to insult, but it is a forbidden matter you have spoken of. So, we are all safer if none knows the identities of more than one or two links in the chain."

Victoire sighed with an exasperation that was very real. "I will not press, then," she said. "Nor will I be making a decision anytime soon." She turned to the door. "I will let you know," she said. "Eventually." She tapped one foot until the servant arrived to open the door.

She waited until she had reached the end of the street and turned south before pausing to let out the breath she had been holding. *Is there any point in continuing?* This interview had produced the same result as her first. Either her stolen cloth had not yet been introduced into the market, or the dressmakers of Paris were too afraid of the thief or thieves to talk. *Either way I appear to be wasting my time,* she thought. *I hope Marie-Louise and Hachette have had better luck following Père Robillard.*

I'm impressed, Robert thought. *I've only had to stand here for a few minutes.*

"What are you doing here, monsieur?" Clopard looked nervous, possibly even agitated. *I wish Lise could see this. At least* somebody *thinks I'm worth worrying about.*

"Why wouldn't I be here? This is a public street in Paris. I grant you it's much more of an alleyway—or even a gutter—than it is a street. But a man's allowed to stand in a street, last I knew."

"Not in front of my door, he isn't," Clopard said. Robert smiled; the man was finally beginning to recover a sense of equilibrium. Now he looked like the dangerous underworld figure he was supposed to be."

"Afraid I'll draw undue attention to you?" Robert asked, in the sweet and mild voice he would use with his aunts should they ever visit. "I agree, that would be a real shame."

"It's not safe for you to be just loitering out here," Clopard said. Somewhere up the end of the street of the fishing cat Robert could hear muttering and the occasional thump of a sabot on the rock-hard dirt of a cross-street.

"I'm not sure it's any less safe for me to be here than it is for me to go walking on my own side of the river," he said. I'm happy for your boys to take sticks to the thieves on the Right Bank—or even to each other—but I resent it when I can't go for a walk without having to worry about what sort of creature is dogging my footsteps."

"You weren't supposed to notice that boy," Clopard muttered.

"You sound like a baby yourself," Robert said. "It's not my fault your people are clumsy and stupid." Clopard growled, but Robert detected an impotence in it. The man wasn't accustomed to dealing with people who could fight back, he decided. "At any rate, I thought I might just drop by your cellar and ask you, face-to-face, why you suddenly think I'm so important to your peace of mind."

"Isn't that obvious? We talked about this not even a week ago, you know." Clopard began to edge his way along the street in the direction of the river. Robert stayed where he was, and eventually Clopard sidled back, scowling.

"I really don't understand what you expect me to do, monsieur Clopard. What precisely do you mean when you ask me to join in with you and your chief? And how could I justify to my mother my going into business with someone I've never met?"

"Your mother?" Clopard's face seemed to grow pale under its coating of dirt, grime and hair. "You've talked to your *mother* about this?"

"Not in so many words, no. But she does take a sort of fond maternal interest in my doings—well, not in the ones that involve undressing ladies, as I'm sure you'll agree— and I can't help but wonder how she'd respond if I was to behave in as simple-minded a fashion as you seem to expect."

"Look," Clopard said, raising a fist, "it's not simple-minded. It's in your best interests to join up with us."

"How can it possibly be in my best interests to agree to something you haven't told me anything about?"

"But you *know* what I'm talking about."

"No, I do not. I haven't a clue. Which is why I can't agree to anything until you give me enough information for me to make a good decision."

Clopard seemed to give up. His fist lost its threatening nature, his hand dropped back down to his side, and he turned and walked away from his door, up to the corner where his henchmen waited. "The only clue you need," he called over his shoulder, "is that it is going to go very badly for you, and very quickly, if you don't stop screwing about and come around to my chief's side of things."

Robert's attempt at a reply was drowned out by Clopard's shout of "Stop hanging around my damned door!"

He found himself singing one of Lise's off-colour country songs as he crossed the river. He wasn't any more enlightened today than he had been yesterday, but at least he might have succeeded in making Clopard's mysterious chief a bit more unsettled.

He was still singing when, as he was about to turn

onto the rue des Lombards, he realized that he was being followed again.

"This is a happy coincidence, mademoiselle," Robert said to Jeanette Desmarais as she closed up beside him, her maid trailing behind. "People are going to begin to suspect, you know."

Jeanette dimpled with pleasure, and curtsied. "Monsieur de Vimoutiers," she said. "It is a great pleasure." As though it had been an accident.

He read the question in her eyes, and smiled. "Mademoiselle, it appears we happen to be walking in the same direction. If so, may I do you the honour of escorting you there?" He offered her his arm. "I see you have managed to, ah, lose your maid already."

"They have stopped making me take a woman with me when I go out. I suppose this constitutes a victory of sorts—though my cousin's servants view it otherwise. And that, too, is a victory of sorts. Nobody in that horrible hôtel cares about me anymore," Jeanette said, smiling up at him as they walked. "Or at least they don't so long as my cousin is out of town."

"Long may she remain away, then," Robert told her. He found himself pleased with the change in Mademoiselle Desmarais lately: she looked considerably more lively, and less grey, than she used to be. Mere weeks ago, for instance, she would not have laughed so at his remarks about her cousin; now she seemed so amused that it was only polite that he joined her in laughter. "I assume," he said, "that we are going to the same place as always?"

"Is it so horribly wicked of me, monsieur? Monsieur Vidal is such a charming man, for all that his birth was so humble. And he behaves so much more beautifully toward me than any of my cousin's fine friends—present company excepted, of course." She giggled for a moment at the look on his face; then her own face took on a more serious cast. "He insists on giving me fine things, and I have to keep them all hidden because if the servants discover them they'll tell Nicolette, and she will steal and sell them."

"It does surprise me, a little, that dear Nicolette can be so wealthy and yet always so pinched for free coin."

"Oh," she said, tugging on his arm to bring him to a halt. "May we stop here? I should like to bring a bottle of wine to—to Monsieur Vidal. He is forever giving me wine to drink, and it is always so good, that I thought—"

"What, buy wine? What a concept." *Still,* he thought, *this might be a better way of delivering a gift of wine to— well, to someone deserving of a gift of wine—than trying to persuade Maman to part with something from the family cellar.* "You know this place?"

"No, but isn't one wine-shop pretty much the same as another?"

"Remind me to never allow you to buy my wine, mademoiselle." He opened the door for her. "Still, we've nothing to lose by investigating."

He was more than a little surprised when one of the men inside the shop showed every sign of recognizing him. The man was a complete stranger, a short skinny man dressed in lawyer's black and an enormous grey wig, but from the expression on his face he clearly saw something familiar in Robert—or thought he did. For a moment it appeared the man was going to approach him, which would have been deeply embarrassing—for both of them.

Then the lawyer muttered something inaudible to the proprietor of the shop and hurried out the door and into the street.

"Are you able to tell me who that man was?" Robert asked. "He was being extremely forward, in my opinion."

"Mine as well," Jeanette said. "In fact, I'd say he was being quite ill-mannered."

The proprietor shrugged. "My apologies, monsieur. I can tell you the man's name and occupation, because he is sometimes a customer of mine. But more than that I do not know. The monsieur is not a friend of mine."

"Who was he, then?" Robert asked. "And what did he say to you as he was leaving?"

"His name is Antoine Chenal, and he is a lawyer who, he tells me, has the right to plead before the Parlement de Paris."

"And?"

"And, and he asked me if I knew you, monsieur." The proprietor swallowed. "He thought you were the chevalier de Vimoutiers. I told him I could not say, because I had never seen you before."

Robert shook his head. "I've never seen you either, so it must be true." Could Chenal be Clopard's chief? It might make sense, because lawyers were fairly powerful as bourgeois went; some were even given titles by the emperor for their services to the state. *If this one's the chief of a smuggling gang, he's probably not on the short list for a barony,* he said to himself. "The lady is hoping to buy some wine, monsieur. Have you anything suitable?"

"I'm sure I have," the man said, sounding very grateful to be talking business at last.

They were nearly at Vidal's shop when Robert was forced to stop, because Jeanette had begun to fuss with the lace at her bosom. Then, to his surprise, she pulled it all away, exposing a pleasing décolleté. Before he could compliment her, she had stuffed the lace into her muff and pulled, from the same place, a thing of sparkles and pleasant tinkling noises. "Is this not beautiful, monsieur?" she asked as she hung it around her neck.

It was. The stones were emeralds, or some equally green cousin, and he was sure there were diamonds set amongst them. Now he complimented her, on both her appearance and the loveliness of the necklace. *Vidal really does do nice work,* he thought. It was no wonder he was the court's favourite jeweller. "This is one of the nicer pieces of his I've ever seen," he told Jeanette.

"He agrees with you, monsieur." She dimpled again, looking up at him. "You may not be aware of it, but he has been paying very careful attention to what you say to him whenever you—when you take me to visit him. He told me, after our last visit, that he considers you to have exquisite taste, monsieur."

"Good lord," Robert said. "Is he quite right in the head?"

"You may joke, monsieur, but I assure you he is quite serious. And I, it seems, am to be the prime beneficiary of your tutelage, however inadvertent you may think it is."

Her smile drooped again. "I can only wear the things he gives me when I am able to visit him," she said. "That's so unfair—but it's still worth it, to see the way his face lights up when he sees me wearing one of his gifts."

"He sounds quite the fellow," Robert said. "Perhaps you two ought to just elope."

"You needn't dissemble or joke with me," Jeanette replied. Now Vidal's shop and home were just a few doors away. "I know that what I'm doing is very wrong, and that he is not at all suitable. I just want to be able to enjoy a little bit of happiness, while Nicolette is away, before I have to return to the life that God insists I lead."

"Do you know, I'm beginning to wonder about that," Robert said, thinking.

"About happiness?"

"And about suitability," he said. "I'm beginning to wonder if in fact it's all that important.

"And I'm not joking."

"Is there really a law prohibiting the import of cloth?" Robert asked his mother after dinner that afternoon. He already knew the answer, but he was curious about how much she knew of the matter.

"What a peculiar subject in which to show interest," she said by way of reply. She set her wine glass on the table beside her chair. "What brings you to this new concern with the law? Or is it—please tell me you aren't thinking about business."

"Really, Maman. A de Vimoutiers going into business? The earth would cease its motion."

"I should hope so. It is not to be contemplated."

"I happened to admire a lady's petticoat the other day," Robert told her, "and she laughed at me when I didn't understand her statement that she was breaking the law by wearing it."

"She was breaking the law," Maman admitted. "This is not, however, something about which you ought to concern yourself. If you really want to give dresses to your mistresses, you make a financial arrangement with the woman who makes up her dresses; you don't worry about buying the cloth yourself."

"Even if it's something rare and, well, illegal?"

"Especially if it's illegal. Good heavens, Robert, what is getting into you? A woman who wears illegal cloth can have her dress confiscated and burnt. But a man who causes that cloth to be imported can end up in prison. And don't think it wouldn't happen to you because of your birth. You know full well about the cells in the Bastille reserved for people such as you."

"I wasn't proposing to become a smuggler, Maman," said Robert—who had in fact begun contemplating that very thing. "I suppose I was trying to understand why anyone would take such a risk."

"They take risks because they want to stand out. For women, or at least for women at court, fashion is a competition, of the same sort as tournaments used to be for men. If you are wearing something nobody else can find, you win the competition—at least for the day. You should know this. It's not as if you men don't compete in the same way."

"I would have thought, Maman, that it was how one wore clothes that determined fashion, more than the clothes themselves. We mock the bourgeois because they wear rich clothes badly, don't we? They use very much the same cloth we use." Robert paused, noting the darkling expression on his mother's face. "Of course, I could be confused about this."

"Everything about the world confuses you, Robert. You dress in a way that makes me proud, most of the time—and then I hear from friends that you have worn magenta and brown at the same time."

"I'll have you know that ensemble has garnered me plenty of compliments. Well, comments."

"I rest my case," said Maman. "You'll take my advice, Robert, and avoid anything to do with business entirely."

"I can get into all the trouble I can handle at Respire's", Robert said in reply. Though the truth was that he was becoming disenchanted with the sorts of trouble he'd been able to get into at Respire's lately.

Time for a change? he asked himself.

Chapter Seven

Hurluberlu

ON THE FOLLOWING Saturday the heat broke in spectacular fashion, the lightning and thunder at first coming from a sunlit sky before a heavy rain washed Paris clean—while leaving the crops in the fields more or less untouched.

On the Sunday the imperial family arrived back at the Tuilleries Palace to take up residence again in the emperor's capital. On Sunday evening there was a mass at Notre Dame to celebrate the emperor's safe return, with echoing celebrations in most of Paris' churches.

And on Monday evening there was a grand reception at the Tuilleries, to which the entire court was invited as well as the more exalted members of the Parlement. Victoire had her hair done up in the riot of curls that was the *hurluberlu*—hurly-burly—style and wore a costume she had been saving since the middle of spring: a daring low bodice, and overskirt the colour of ripe limes, and a petticoat of a pale rose. The edgings of the overskirt included knots of ribbon whose colour matched the petticoat, and ruffles of white lace covered her upper arms, ending just below the elbows in more rose-coloured knots. The dress was heavy, but at least it was legal—though she owned numerous cotton petticoats, Victoire wanted to impress tonight but not stand out.

She had been circulating for about a quarter of an hour when she saw Jeanette Desmarais in a corner of the grand salon, almost as far away from the emperor and empress as it was possible to be. Jeanette's dress was probably something handed down by her nasty cousin, because while perfectly suited to the court—as it had been two years ago—it nonetheless managed, by virtue of being white with gold embroidery around the hem and an overskirt that resembled an apron, to make her look pale and dull. "My dear Jeanette," Victoire said, marching up to her friend. "Are you unwell?"

"I am in perfect health," Jeanette said, looking miserable. "I'm just out of sorts—and to be honest, *bored*. I have never much cared for court life, and I cannot make myself be outgoing and—and *conversational*. I would have stayed at home, except—"

"Oh, no," Victoire said. "Is Nicolette back already? Is she here tonight?"

"No, but it seems she is coming back, and soon. And so the house is in an uproar as everyone tries to ensure she can find no fault with them.

"Everyone but the duc, that is, who is in a foul mood and wants everyone else to be equally unhappy."

"I would not care at all about what is happening between those two," Victoire said, "if it were not for the way it affects you." *And I'm still not convinced Nicolette had nothing to do with what has been happening to me, either.* "Would you be willing to come to my father's place? You'd be welcome, you know that."

Jeanette flushed, looking even less happy than before. "You are too kind, Victoire, but I cannot bring myself to impose. Besides, I cannot see myself staying here much longer, and not for my life would I make you leave a reception at court so early in the evening." She smiled, or at least tried to.

"I would do so for you," said Victoire, who really did not want to leave. When Jeanette shook her head No, Victoire, embarrassed at how grateful she was, kissed Jeanette and went back to her circuit of the salon.

After a further quarter-hour of shouted greetings and catching up, she saw Marguerite de Geoffroy emerging from a circle of laughing young women. Several of those women, Victoire noted, were wearing cotton gowns, but Marguerite was not one of them. "How are you, my dear baronne?" Victoire said, kissing her and then offering her cheek in return.

"As well as one can be in last spring's fashions," Marguerite said, smiling in a sour manner. "As you can see"—she circled slowly, the heavy blue skirt billowing— "I still cannot find anyone to sell new cotton to my woman. Is Inspector Grenier making life miserable for everyone in this city?"

"Poor, poor Marguerite." Victoire laughed. "I do wish I could help you."

"You've still no idea where the cloth is?"

"None whatever." She found herself frowning. "And it's not for lack of trying, I assure you. This is an unusual experience for me, Marguerite, and I am at a bit of a loss as to how to proceed." She forced a laugh. "But tomorrow is a new day, and I will start a new search. Don't lose hope, dear friend, and we will all be well at the end."

The jewel-purple of twilight still decorated the southern sky as Victoire and her escorts emerged from the eastern gate of the palace grounds. "Call you a chair, mademoiselle?" asked the lackey.

"It's a lovely night," Victoire told him. "I'd like to walk." A chair would cost money, and she was on a strict budget now. Besides, it wasn't much more than a quarter-hour's walk from the Place de Tuilleries to rue des Petits Champs and home.

"Are you certain, mademoiselle?" asked Genevre, her maid. "It's nearly dark and the streets aren't safe."

"Genevre, we're right outside the imperial palace. There isn't a safer place to be in all of Europe."

There were archers patrolling the streets closest to the palace, the better to encourage the criminals of Paris to prey on the lower orders someplace else, and so Victoire was paying no attention to her surroundings when she heard Genevre giggle. "Mademoiselle, look," the maid called. "The threads are dancing!"

Victoire turned to see her maid hopping up and down in apparent delight. Around her was a flimsy cloud which, on closer inspection, was indeed made up threads swirling around the bottom of Genevre's skirt. As Victoire looked on, the cloud began to work its way up towards the maid's knees while the girl continued to coo with pleasure. Victoire wasn't so certain this was something to be enjoyed.

Taking care not to touch the cloud, she crouched to take a closer look.

Cotton. It was cotton thread wrapping around her. *I really don't like this*, she thought, *no matter how pretty Genevre thinks it looks*. Victoire closed her eyes and summoned a prayer to unravel the stuff—but it fought back against her. Something did, at any rate—she could feel a heavy, liquid sort of pressure resisting the essence of her prayer. She stepped back, not wanting to alarm her maid and definitely not wanting to touch those threads. "God, help me," she muttered, and summoned up the strongest force she could find within herself.

A soft *thump* pressed against her ears. When she opened her eyes again Genevre was clapping as tiny demons of fire leaping into the night air marked the destruction of the magicked thread. "Is it not marvellous, mademoiselle?" Genevre asked. Then she finally seemed to become aware of the look on Victoire's face. "Did you do this, mademoiselle? I thought it was some sort of going-away gift from the emperor."

"I don't know who did it," Victoire said—though she certainly wanted to know this, and to know why the prayer had targeted Genevre and not herself. *Perhaps it was intended for me but Genevre got in the way.* That made more sense. But though Victoire was certain the attack had been made by the same persons who had stolen her cloth and lured her into Clopard's trap, she still had no idea who those people might have been.

"I'm glad you enjoyed it, though," she added with a smile she did not feel.

Perhaps I really should do as Maman suggests, Robert thought, *and get myself established at court.* He had been forced to run an embarrassing gamut of flunkies and officials in order to gain entrance to even the public salons of the palace; it defied the imagination to speculate about what might have been required of him had he wanted to watch the emperor dine or go to bed.

As a rule, younger sons did not get established at court, which was crowded enough already. But Victoire de Berenguer was a regular at court, and court was, Robert had decided, the best place to look for her—or at least the best place to look to find her wearing skirts rather than trousers.

So here he was, at the first evening entertainment following the emperor's return from the north—and here, apparently, Victoire wasn't. *You should have come to last night's party,* he told himself. *Guaranteed she was here last night.* He tried to stay in the doorway of the salon while searching for her, but the press of new arrivals forced him further into the room and the crowd. Everyone else here seemed to know everyone, putting Robert in an unusual and uncomfortable position; he wasn't used to being a stranger.

Being ignored by everyone else did make it easier for him to search the room for Victoire, and so make it easier for him to conclude with certainty that she hadn't come tonight. Well, it was still early enough in the evening that he could get to Respire's before the play and partying got fully under way. Robert turned and began to fight his way back upstream in the direction of the door.

"Robert! Good God, what are you doing here?" *Oh, no,* he thought. *Why in the world is* she *here? Maybe I can pretend I didn't hear her.* He pressed onward, but a brace of women in especially broad skirts blocked his way, and before he could will himself to barge between them a strong hand was on his shoulder. "Didn't you hear me?" her voice demanded in his ear.

"Hello, Lise," Robert said, abandoning all hope. "What brings you here?"

"Idiot," she said. "We're almost always here in the evenings. It's your presence that's remarkable. Come on." She gripped his shoulder firmly and spun him around. As she propelled him further into the salon, he saw with horror the group toward which she drew him stood in the centre of a broad and respectful space.

At the centre of which was His Majesty, Charles XIII.

The emperor did not look well. His face was pale and drawn, and while this could be the result of nothing more than the heat of the room and the crowd surrounding him, the lines on the emperor's face did not appear to have arrived this evening. *He's been ill again*, Robert thought.

No, he realized as Lise pulled him toward the emperor's group, it wasn't the heat of the room. His majesty was enveloped in a cocoon of cool air, possibly prayed into existence by himself but more likely the gift of his companions, two people he absolutely did not want to see: his cousin's husband, Rafael, duc de Bellevasse; and Nicolas de La Reynie, lieutenant-general of the Paris police. That Lise was also part of this group argued strongly that they were not talking about parties.

"Your majesty," Lise said, "you remember my cousin Robert?"

"Of course," the emperor said. "Though we have not much had the pleasure of your company lately." He nodded in acceptance of Robert's deep bow. "I trust your good mother is well?"

Robert nodded. For some reason his tongue seemed to have dried up and stuck to the roof of his mouth.

"As well-spoken as ever, I see," Rafael murmured. "Lise, was this necessary?"

"Robert keeps company with a different set than you, my heart." Lise smiled at Robert, and he felt a deep chill. Lise in a smiling mood was not safe for him. "I thought that since fortune has presented him to us here we might ask if he's seen or heard anything." She narrowed her gaze at him. "And have you?"

Enlightenment washed over him. "Oh, this is that spying thing you were going on about at the beginning of the month, is it?"

"Could you speak a little more loudly, Vimoutiers?" Rafael asked, his voice all vinegar. "There are some near the door who may not have heard you."

"If it was all that deep a secret," Robert found the nerve to say, "then you shouldn't have asked me about it in the first place."

"It isn't a serious matter," lieutenant-general de La Reynie said, wheezing a bit. *Shouldn't you be retired and living on a fat pension?* Robert asked him inwardly. "But it is still an open issue and so one is curious nevertheless."

"Well, I'm sorry to disappoint," Robert told them, "but none of my friends has suddenly come into money. If they had perhaps they wouldn't feel the need to borrow quite so much from me all the time. Likewise, none of them has suddenly started speaking—what was it, again? Italian? Spanish? No, it was German, yes? By which I mean No, none of my friends has suddenly declared allegiance to the Holy Roman Empire."

"I think," said Rafael, "that your majesty's empire is safe from this one, and from all who know him. Your friends, my dear Robert, couldn't conspire their way into a brothel if the women led them on by the—"

"That's quite enough, my heart," said Lise. "We all get the idea." She shook her head, violently. "Too well, in fact."

You don't know all of my friends, Robert thought. And was suddenly glad Victoire de Berenguer had not, after all, graced him with her presence here tonight. "I'm sorry to disappoint," he said to the emperor and his trio, "but if there's nothing else, might I be permitted to withdraw?"

The emperor nodded, and by the time Robert had retreated, his majesty appeared already to have forgotten him.

"You never did tell me what you were doing here tonight," Lise said as she caught up with him.

"You're right. I never did." Robert smiled. Then he adopted a more serious expression. "Is his majesty well? He doesn't look it, you know."

"This is not to be spoken of," Lise said, serious now herself, "but he was ill for much of August. The priests and physicians don't know what it was. He is better now, thank God, but still tired from the illness. He suffers from this heat, too. I am from the south and so find these conditions quite pleasant. His majesty would wish it otherwise."

"Well, is not the palace full of nobles and priests?" Robert asked. "Couldn't the lot of you get together and chill the air all around here, rather than just surrounding him? At least until his majesty is feeling better."

"And they say you don't have a brain worthy of the name," Lise told him. "That's a marvellous idea, cousin. It won't be easy to manage—chaining prayer together is damnably difficult—but it is certainly worth the attempt."

"Feel free to take all the credit for yourself," Robert told her. "I have no desire to come to his majesty's attention." He turned from her; the door, at last, was within reach.

"Nor to that of monsieur de La Reynie."

"You look unhappy, mademoiselle. What is it concerns you?" Marie-Louise poured Victoire a second cup of well-watered wine. Catherine and Hachette were still out, the one hovering in the vicinity of the Hôtel de Beaune and the other trailing Père Robillard—the priest having left the

Hôtel de Berenguer this morning even before Victoire had been able to slip away to the old house on the rue du Pet.

"I'm still worried about that affair the other night," Victoire told her. "It was not an accident."

"Didn't you tell your maid it was just a joke someone was playing?"

"Yes, Marie-Louise, and I trust she still believes me. I might wish she could have kept her mouth shut, but she would go and laugh about it amongst the servants, and somehow it got to my mother. Making light of it is the only way I can think of to keep Maman—and other people—from asking too many questions about it."

She swallowed an unladylike volume of wine. "It was not a joke, though. In fact, I think it was an attack."

"An attack? But nothing happened, mademoiselle."

"No, because for whatever reason the attack went awry. The threads were trying to wrap themselves around Genevre's legs, and God only knows what might have happened if the force moving them had been stronger. I don't mind admitting, Marie-Louise, that it is bothering me a lot."

"Is there any way of telling who did it?"

"None that I'm aware. There are rumours the duchesse de Bellevasse can work that sort of magic, but I don't believe them. My father is obsessed with history and he doesn't believe the rumours, and says there's no evidence such a person as could do this has ever existed.

"And anyway, even if she could do it, I wouldn't want her involved. She is the Law, and I want to stay clear of that."

"Somebody wants to harm you, mademoiselle. There must be something we can do to stop him—or her."

"Until we have a better idea of who that person is,"

120

Victoire said, frowning, "what we are doing now is the only thing we can do."

"I'm sorry I haven't been able to learn anything useful." Marie-Louise had finished investigating Victoire's customers as Victoire had finished interviewing their dressmakers, and the results had been—nothing.

"It was certainly useful," Victoire said, "to learn that none of those women has been wearing new cotton this season. Just as I am happy to know that their dressmakers are suffering from the same lack of cloth as we are. We eliminate the people who can't have our cloth and eventually only one person will be left, and that will be the person we—" she stopped, realizing she didn't know what she wanted to do with that person. *Kill them? Ostentatiously snub them at court?*

All she really wanted, she decided, was to have her cloth back and to restore her business to its usual state.

"What do you want me to do this afternoon?" Marie-Louise asked.

"I don't have anything for you to do except to wait here for Catherine and Hachette to return. If either of them has anything interesting to say, send me a message and I'll come back here immediately."

"Where will you be?"

"I am going back to my parents' home," Victoire told her. "I am tired of asking questions that have no answers, and I want to get some rest."

Chapter Eight
A Damsel in Distress

VICTOIRE CAUGHT HERSELF trying to surreptitiously sniff for the smells of a fat-laden big dinner when Père Robillard passed through the breakfast salon. She felt her face flush and turned away before—she hoped—the père noticed what she was doing. She and her gang had been following, or trying to follow, the confessor for over a week, and so far they had seen nothing to indicate he was the enemy they sought. *Are we wasting our time?* she asked herself as she got up to leave the table.

The problem, she decided, was that she wasn't thinking well on the empty stomach that was the consequence of the family cook. There was a good bakery not far from the Hôtel de Berenguer, and she still had a few sous left in her purse; a better breakfast, and more comfort, likely awaited her there.

She was in the garden, and making her way towards the gate, when she saw and heard a confrontation between an urchin—not Hachette, but definitely of his ilk—and one of the gardeners, who had arrested the child on its way to the door of the house. "What do we have here, Dufort?" she asked, approaching the contentious pair.

Before the gardener could respond the child burst out,

"Pardon, mademoiselle, but is you the lady de Ber—de—um, the lady of this house?"

Victoire examined the child. Male, female? It was impossible to tell. "I am not the lady of the house, no. But I believe I am, however, the lady you are looking for. I am Victoire de Berenguer. Are you looking for me?"

"I think so. A beautiful lady give me this to take you." A grimy hand thrust a somewhat crumpled piece of paper toward her. "She give me four sous to give it you, and said she'd give me another six if I bring you back to her with me. So you'll come, hein?"

"I have to read this first," she said. The first thing she saw when she unfolded the paper was that it had been sealed—and that the impression on the seal belonged to the duchesse de Beaune. *This is not good,* she told herself.

The note was not from Nicolette de Beaune.

Nor did it make much sense. The handwriting was Jeanette's, and it read *My dear Victoire, I have urgent need of your assistance. My cousin has discovered my secret and all may be lost if you cannot help me. Please follow this child as quickly as you can. I dare not write any more than this, but will tell you everything if only we can meet.* It ended, *your most affectionate Jeanette Desmarais.*

"Her secret?" she asked.

"Hein?" asked the child.

"I was speaking to myself, child," she replied. Then she realized the secret Jeanette had referred to. *They know about her jeweller now.* "You wait here." To the gardener she said, "Please keep this child here, Dufort. I will be right back." She set off, at a brisk walk, back to the house.

This wasn't exactly how she had expected to spend the day. It was better than another fruitless exploration of a *court de miracle,* however. And if she was able to do some small service for poor Jeanette Desmarais, then perhaps God would smile on her and return her stolen cloth to her.

As quickly as she could do so—to Genevre's considerable annoyance—Victoire got herself into a dress more suitable to a visit to a duchesse's hôtel. Then, strapping her dagger onto her right calf—she didn't intend to let the duc de Beaune anywhere near her if the man happened to be at home—she rushed out of the house again, to find the urchin and gardener at an impasse, glaring at each other in barely arrested hostility.

"Thank you, Dufort," she said, grabbing the urchin's smock and hoping her glove wouldn't be too badly stained. "No need to say anything about this to my parents, please."

Robert, puzzled, read through the note again. *How in the world am I supposed to help Fortune Vidal?* Still, that's what the note was: a request for his assistance. No other information, just a plea for a rapid reply.

Then he felt a smile settling onto his face. *What does it matter how I'm supposed to help him? He wants my help, and I want something to do.* Buckling his shoes, he got to his feet and made his careful way to the back of the house, allowing him to vacate the Hôtel de Vimoutiers without risking his mother becoming aware of his escape.

This wasn't exactly how he had expected to spend the day. It was better than drinking alone, however. And if he was able to do some small service for the lowly but wealthy monsieur Vidal, then perhaps God would smile on him and alleviate his own miseries, at least a little bit.

It was apparent from the moment Robert greeted Fortune Vidal in the jeweller's private office, something truly had the tradesman on edge. The happy predatory ebullience Robert had become accustomed to was missing, leaving a grey-faced man who looked two decades older than he had just a week ago. Though Robert had given him several opportunities to explain the abrupt summons, the jeweller had done nothing more than turn a brooch over and over in his hands, lips moving ceaselessly, but what he might be saying inaudible. *How difficult can this be?* Robert asked him silently. *You're the one who called out to me, monsieur.*

After waiting in vain for him to do or say something practical Robert reached out a hand and gently stopped him worrying at the brooch. "Monsieur, don't you think it time you explained why you sent for me?"

"I am thinking I made a mistake in writing you," he said in a quiet, hesitant voice. "I am unable to think of how you could help me." The look he gave Robert then suggested tragedy. Or treachery. Possibly both. Who knew bourgeois were so prone to melodrama?

"I believe I might be the best judge of whether I am able to help," he said, "but only if I know what has happened."

"It is Jeanette," Vidal said after a painful pause. "I have not had a word from her in nearly two weeks."

"That hardly seems like the end of the world, monsieur," Robert told him. "Things are always a bit unsettled when the court is newly returned, you know. I wouldn't be surprised to find the Hôtel de Beaune is still disordered, especially if our dear duchesse de Beaune is also newly returned to Paris. Nicolette requires a lot of attention, you know. You shouldn't be surprised if Jeanette hasn't been able to visit."

"It's not that she hasn't seen me," Vidal said. "There has been no word at all. When her cousin returned from the north I had a note from Jeanette saying that the woman was refusing to allow her out of the hôtel without an escort. After that there have been no notes either. Nothing at all."

"I don't think it's the done thing to lock up spinster relatives that way," Robert said. He patted Vidal on the shoulder. "But at least you've suggested to me a way in which I can help you." He got to his feet. "Why don't I pay Jeanette a visit, monsieur Vidal? She may not be allowed to see you, but surely she could see me. I could always threaten to reattach myself to Nicolette if they don't let poor Jeanette out from time to time."

For the first time since Robert's arrival Monsieur Vidal's eyes seemed to come alive. "If you would be willing to do such a thing for me—for us—I would be grateful, monsieur le chevalier. Very grateful."

"I would be honoured to be able to do this for you. In fact, I will take myself to the Hôtel de Beaune as soon I finish this admirable wine you have given me."

"There is one thing I should tell you about Jeanette before you go to see her," Vidal said. He took the stopper from a fine glass decanter and refilled both glasses.

Handing his glass back to Robert Vidal said, "Two weeks ago I asked mademoiselle Desmarais if she would be my wife. She consented."

"This is without doubt the most unusual conversation I have ever had with you," Victoire said to the hole in the wall. She laughed. "I suppose I should congratulate you, Jeanette, on your ingenuity."

"I didn't know what else to do, Victoire," Jeanette said from the other side of the masonry. "I am so miserable now. I haven't seen my Fortune in nearly a fortnight, and now Cousin Nicolette will not even let me write to him: she opens every piece of paper I try to send out of the house.

I had to throw my note to you over the wall, Victoire, and trust to the discretion of that child—"

"And the greed," Victoire pointed out.

"—and the greed, yes," she said, laughing without pleasure, "for which I am most grateful." The laughter faltered. "Victoire, she is threatening to send me to an abbèe if I make any effort to contact him."

"That horrible, *horrible* woman," Victoire said through gritted teeth. "If I could, I would take back every single *denier's* worth of cloth I ever sold her." For a moment or two she fantasized about the various tortures she could inflict on Nicolette de Beaune. Then, pulling herself back to the real world, she asked, "What are we going to do, Jeanette?"

"I had hoped that you could suggest something," Jeanette said. "You're always so clever, Victoire."

It's not what I'd prefer to be doing, she thought. *But if I can stick a knife into Nicolette de Beaune, even if it's only metaphorically, then I'll enjoy it.* "Give me a few minutes to think," she said, "and we'll see what I can come up with."

"I am sorry, monsieur," said the maître d'hôtel, "but mademoiselle Desmarais has asked me to tell any visitors that she is unwell and unable to receive at this time." The expression on the man's face was bland as a nearly-set *blanc mangier,* but Robert was certain he saw something smug and even superior hiding beneath the still features. Even as he tamped down on a condescending reply, he realized at least one of the meanings behind that expression: poor Jeanette had no friends at all in this hôtel, not even amongst the servants.

"I wonder," he said, in a voice as thorough a parody of a

sanctimonious priest as he could achieve, "if poor Jeanette will ever again be well enough to receive visitors."

The servant's response was to close the door in his face, leaving Robert in no doubt about his current reputation in the duchesse de Beaune's household. *Well, I had already decided I was better off without her anyway.*

He had just turned onto the rue de la Madeleine when he saw a familiar form leaning into the back wall of the Hôtel de Beaune, across the narrow lane that ran between the hôtel and the monastery of the Benedictines. *Hello,* he said to himself. *What a remarkable coincidence this is.*

"I take it," he said, sidling up beside her, "that you didn't get to see Jeanette either."

Victoire started, but aside from a strangled gasp she said nothing. *Admirable sang-froid,* Robert thought. Which was more than the person on the other side of the wall displayed. A horrified squeak came through a small hole in the wall: "My God, who is it? Is it disaster?"

"It's not disaster," Victoire said into the hole. "It's the chevalier de Vimoutiers." After a pause she added, "Although I suppose that could fit some definitions of *disaster.*"

"Unfair," Robert said, feeling the smile tug at the corners of his mouth. "Only m'mother is allowed to think that way about me." Before Victoire could reply, he added, "I take it Jeanette is on the other side of this wall? What is going on, mademoiselle? At the door they say you are too unwell to receive visitors."

"Cowards! Scoundrels! Liars!" The voice on the other side of the wall, while it still squeaked, was doing so in outrage now.

"Nicolette has found out about Fortune Vidal," Victoire

told him. "She is threatening to commit Jeanette to an abbèe if Jeanette tries to communicate with him in any way."

Monsieur Vidal's not going to be happy to learn this, he thought. To the hole in the wall he said, "I can't think that you would make a very happy nun, mademoiselle Desmarais." He resisted peering through the hole, and asked instead, "What should we do about this, mademoiselle? You can be certain that your monsieur Vidal knows something is wrong. He sent me here to find out what that might be."

"Oh, would you please take word to my Fortune, monsieur, and ask him to apply his whole mind to the question of getting me out of my prison? I know he'll be able to rescue me once he knows all."

"I'm not sure Monsieur Vidal would wish to act so firmly against Nicolette," Victoire said. "She and her husband are valuable customers."

"Fortune has asked me to marry him," Jeanette said with quiet dignity. "I have accepted his offer. We are both prepared to deal with the consequences."

"What?" Victoire actually took a step back away from the wall. "Does Nicolette know of this, Jeanette?" Robert, recalling with a small flush of discomfort that elopement with monsieur Vidal had actually been his own suggestion, held his tongue.

"You do not have to say a word to me about my duties to my class, Victoire," Jeanette said. "I fully realize I will be casting myself out of the circle into which I was born. And some will surely say I will be bringing disgrace onto my name. But," she added in a much more stubborn tone, "I do not think any name I might ever have shared with Nicolette to be capable of disgrace.

"And anyway, it was your friend the chevalier there who suggested this idea in the first place." She giggled, and

Robert was unable to turn away quickly enough to avoid the look of exasperation that spoiled Victoire's face.

"Just trying to be helpful," he said. "I really can't see much of a happy future for the lady in this household, y'know."

"I should have guessed you'd be involved," Victoire said. "Any time you seek to be helpful something is certain to explode, so it stands to reason that if something explodes it's because you've decided to be helpful."

"I don't think that's right," he said, "but I can't precisely say why. You're being a bit confusing."

"It *isn't* right," Jeanette said. "It is not enough for Nicolette to keep everything in this house for herself, and expect me to be satisfied with scraps. No, she must also set out to destroy even the small happiness I might be able to build for myself. And as for my class, what has this class ever done for me? I have no money, no property, no dowry—no future. So far as I'm concerned, then, since I have nothing to my name, I also have no obligations to my class."

"I wasn't criticizing or even questioning, Jeanette," Victoire said. "In fact, I think it's a wonderful idea, and I hope you will be very happy. I sometimes think I feel no more obligation to our class than you say. And certainly, I have no love for your cousin." She glared at Robert. "I just can't see how I can help you if you can't get out of that place and I can't get in."

"I suppose you are still being watched by the servants?" Robert asked.

"I cannot get to a door or even a window onto the street without one of the thrice-damned maids or footmen lurking nearby."

"And at night?" The initial gleamings of a plan were beginning to sparkle at him, teasingly.

"I would never be allowed to leave the house after dark, monsieur. It isn't safe."

"I think perhaps you might be missing the point, mademoiselle. It can't be much less safe for you on the streets of Paris at night than it is for you to stay here, if Nicolette is determined to make a nun of you."

"What are you getting at?" Victoire whispered at him, glaring.

"Oh. Yes, yes, I see what you mean, monsieur." Jeanette's voice trembled. "But my dresser sleeps in the chamber beyond my boudoir," she said, "and I would most certainly wake her if I tried to get past her."

"Let me—let *us* think on this for a while," he said, grinning at Victoire. Leaning over so that his mouth was nearly touching the wall, he told her, "Mademoiselle Victoire and I are going to go visit Monsieur Vidal now, mademoiselle, and between us we will come up with a plan that will get you away from this place—and with any luck, before too many nights pass."

He paused a moment to think of logistics; when Victoire showed signs of wanting to dispute with him again, he said, "While we are away, I suggest you return to the house for a while and allow yourself to be observed, dragging listlessly about and in general giving no suggestion whatever of a woman on the verge of flight, or of someone engaged in clandestine meetings through a garden wall." She giggled, though why she would do that he did not know. "About an hour from now, come back out here with a book, so that you may pretend to be occupied with something unimportant while you await our return. If we don't come back later today, then come into this part of the garden every day at this time until we do come back."

"Is there anything else I can do, monsieur?"

"Yes: pray it doesn't rain before we return."

"What in the world are you trying to get me into?" Victoire turned on Robert as soon as they'd reached rue de la Madeleine. "The de Beaune are a powerful family and he especially strikes me as being very dangerous. Don't you ever think?"

"I didn't think you'd object," he said, grinning at her in his infuriating fashion and not addressing the question. "You seem to like adventure, after all. And adventure seems to like you." He stopped abruptly, flushing. "All I meant to say," he told her, obviously embarrassed, "was that if there was any way we could help poor Jeanette we ought to try."

His obvious embarrassment seemed to be contagious, because she felt herself flush in turn. "I didn't mean to sound so harsh," she said. "It's just that the duc de Beaune really does seem to me to be a most frightening man. But I should have given you credit for a generous impulse, however misguided. And dangerous, in case I hadn't made that clear."

"Well, I confess I mostly did it because I was annoyed with Nicolette. But I really do think that I, at least, have to follow through on this now, having sort of pledged myself to mademoiselle Jeanette." He grinned at her again. "I suspect my cousin Lise would heartily approve of the situation in which you and I seem to have got ourselves caught, mademoiselle. Lise," he added as if it signified anything, "is a friend of lady novelists like the Marquise de Lafayette. She pretends to be practical but in fact Lise is in love with romance and high adventure." Looking back at her and apparently realizing he was moving at a faster pace than she could easily match, he slowed his stride.

"And anyway, I have rather come to like Jeanette. How she can share even a drop of the same blood as Nicolette is a mystery to me. And one I don't propose to spend any time investigating, I should add."

"Monsieur Vidal is not going to like the way Nicolette appears to have made a prisoner of Jeanette," Victoire said.

"I'm afraid you are right, mademoiselle, about how dangerous the Beaune family could be. Vidal *is* a mere bourgeois, however much money he has." He paused a moment and then said, "Come to think of it, with as much money as he does have, perhaps he won't stop at just not liking this."

"I am developing the impression that you and this bourgeois are much better acquainted than anyone suspects."

"Not my fault, I assure you. It certainly wasn't my idea. Oddly enough, my involvement in all this began almost immediately after I first met you, mademoiselle de Berenguer. It was that day I saw you at the Réalmont salon: Nicolette asked—all right, ordered—me to accompany her cousin to Vidal's on an errand." Victoire remembered that day very well, but felt uncomfortable about admitting that. "No matter. Odd as it must seem, I've rather come to like Vidal. I think he and Jeanette make a charming couple. Perplexing, but still charming."

"I only wonder it took them both this long to notice that," Victoire said. She felt an unaccountable need to change the subject. "Do you have a plan to help her?"

"Was rather hoping you would," he said. "You're the one with the organizational skills. You could probably lead an army, whereas my family are convinced I couldn't find my dinner if you started me out at the dining-room door."

"It probably doesn't make any difference," she said,

wondering why this conversation was so upsetting. "That is, and always has been, a doomed relationship."

"Is and has been, perhaps," he said, and there was that annoying grin and tilt of one eyebrow. "But always will be? I'm beginning to wonder about that.

"At any rate," he said, beginning to pick up his pace again, "We do have to have a conversation with monsieur Vidal, whether or not doom enters into it."

It was, Robert decided, a sign of how much in love was Fortune Vidal with Jeanette Desmarais that the jeweller ejected all customers from his shop the instant he perceived Robert's entrance with Victoire at his side. "It doesn't matter about them," Vidal said after escorting Robert and Victoire to the private office behind the shop. "They'll be back, if they were ever serious in the first place. Nobody does gold-work as well as I do. Nobody!"

"I'll let others be the judge of that," Robert told him, smiling. "My reason for being here with mademoiselle de Berenguer is probably easy for you to guess. But I'm afraid our news is not good."

"That doesn't surprise me in the slightest," Vidal told him. "That bitch cousin of hers has forbidden her to see me, hasn't she?"

"Somewhat worse than that," Robert said. "Jeanette tells me that her cousin means to put her into a convent if Jeanette persists in trying to communicate with you."

"If it were within my power," the jeweller told him through clenched jaws, "I would call in every livre of debt that woman de Beaune owes me. As it is not within my power, I will have to settle for doing what I can: I shall inform the jewellers of Paris that their membership in the guild is dependent on their no longer doing any business

134

with the de Beaune family. I will happily give up that
woman's business, and we will see if the aristocracy can
amuse itself without the assistance of the guilds."

"You could also attack her rather more directly," Robert
pointed out. "By stealing her cousin from under her nose, I
mean." He heard a heavy sigh from beside him; turning, he
saw Victoire gazing at him sadly.

"I had really hoped you were joking about that," she said.
He favoured her with his most engaging grin.

"That sort of theft is easier said than done, monsieur,"
said Vidal.

"Oh, I shouldn't think it all that difficult," Robert told
him. "You could take her to Navarre, or Lorraine—or even
England, if that was your idea of a good time."

"I could, if I had to. I don't believe I would have to,
though. The duc de Beaune may be powerful, but I have a
good many friends—and a good many nobles dependent on
my good will. If we had to live outside Paris for a period, it
wouldn't be for long. Getting out of Paris, though—"

"Not a problem at all," Robert said. "The Hôtel de Beaune
is already outside the city. What will be a bit of a challenge
is getting her outside the hôtel itself."

"A bit?" Victoire snorted. "That suggests it might be as
difficult as deciding what hat to wear. If you are serious
about this, then you face two problems. First you have to
get monsieur Vidal through any of the city gates—he's a
bourgeois and that won't be as easy as you seem to think.
And while that house is outside the city, are you just going
to leave Jeanette out there once you've rescued her? I
think monsieur Vidal will insist on her being brought to
him—which means you will have to get both of them out
of the city. And yes, getting Jeanette out of that prison of
a hôtel is going to tax all of our intellects. And I'm being

generous when I call your mind an intellect, monsieur de Vimoutiers."

"I think she likes me," Robert said, favouring Victoire with another smile, if only because he enjoyed the expression his smiles always seemed to inspire.

He moved to the door. "I suggest we sleep on this for now. I'm trusting Jeanette will not be too upset if we aren't able to free her from her prison today—though I am definitely developing some ideas as to how we can do this—and is prepared to act once we do present our plan to her."

"I have every confidence in her," Vidal said.

"Of course you do," Robert told him. "It's only right that you should. In the meantime, let us all think about the best way of safely removing you two from the city, and meet again here immediately after dinner tomorrow."

"And that is when you propose to rescue Jeanette," Victoire said. Her voice was flat, disbelieving.

"That is when I propose that *we* rescue Jeanette," he said, smiling. "You're in this as completely as we, mademoiselle."

Chapter Nine

Dressing the Part

"TELL ME YOU weren't waiting here for me," Victoire said as he approached her on the rue des Francs Bourgeois the next afternoon.

"I would gladly tell you this," Robert said, "if I thought it would make you happy. Wouldn't be true, I'm afraid, but I'll still say it if you want." He had, in fact, been waiting for nearly a full half-hour; he'd tried to convince himself it was only because he hadn't wanted to arrive at Fortune Vidal's shop alone.

"Idiot," she said. She seemed to be struggling with her frown, though, which pleased him very much.

"That's what my cousin Lise is always calling me," he said happily. "My cousin Lise quite likes me, y'know."

"And here I thought she was an intelligent woman."

"Oh, of the first intelligence. And I'm her favourite male relative, after her husband of course."

"I'd wager, then, you're her only male relative. After her husband, of course."

"You and she are going to get along wonderfully."

She grimaced, and the pleasure left her face. "Stop being foolish," she said, "and let's go tell monsieur Vidal about the brilliant plan you've come up with."

"Do you mean to say you haven't thought of anything?" They had reached the shop; he paused in the act of opening the door.

"I didn't say that," she said as the door opened. "But this is your adventure, monsieur le chevalier, so you get to speak first."

"Good afternoon, monsieur, mademoiselle," Vidal said before Robert could respond to Victoire. "Welcome, and let me give you wine." He waved them into the shop, which again was empty.

"It can't be good for your business to empty out your shop on first a Monday and then a Tuesday," Robert told him. "Surely we could have our discussion upstairs while your apprentices keep the business going."

"I want to be thinking of nothing but escape, monsieur," Vidal said. "Though it is true that we will be more comfortable upstairs, and that is where we will go."

When he had them seated in his comfortable chairs and drinking excellent wine from crystal-clear goblets, Vidal turned to Robert and said, "And so, monsieur le chevalier?"

Robert reached inside his waistcoat and retrieved the sealed paper he'd written this morning. "I have here a letter of introduction for you, monsieur, that I believe will provide you with sanctuary once you've made your flight from Paris." That piece of the plan he'd been formulating since yesterday had clicked into place as he and Victoire had parted after leaving here yesterday.

Lise and Rafael are likely to kill me over this, he thought, hardly able to suppress a laugh, *but as I already owe the dowager duchesse my life, what's a bit more debt added on top?*

"Do you have access to a carriage, monsieur?" he asked.

"I have an excellent carriage, monsieur le chevalier, and four very strong horses to pull it."

"It's in Paris?"

"No, at my house near St-Germain-en-Laye. Are you telling me to bring it into the city?"

He looked at Victoire, who shook her head decisively. "No, I think not. You should send word to your house to have it made ready for departure tonight or, at the very latest, at first light tomorrow. You'll be going north; this letter is addressed to my good friend the dowager duchesse de Bellevasse, who lives in northern Picardy. That will be more than far enough from Paris, should you decide your house isn't far enough to go.

"And you should obtain a conveyance of some sort to take you and your lady from here to your home and that carriage, tonight."

"Rent or borrow a cart, monsieur," Victoire said. "You don't want to draw undue attention to yourself."

"I can certainly do this." Vidal took a fresh sheet of paper from a stack on his desk, sharpened a pen and dipped it into the inkwell. "What precisely are you proposing, my friends?"

"I wasn't aware that *we* were proposing anything," Victoire said, her face set into an expression that suggested she had been a very obnoxious child. "This would appear to be the work of the chevalier de Vimoutiers all on his own."

Ignoring this ill-natured comment, Robert glanced around the office. "That looks like a rather nice Cognac on that shelf, monsieur. While I do not normally drink brandywine before sunset, I believe in this instance I will make an exception, much as I admire the quality of your wine. Pour us a glass apiece, my good man, and whatever mademoiselle wishes to drink, and I will explain to you my thinking. I am sure between the two of you, you and mademoiselle de Berenguer will easily point out any flaws in my reasoning, and that between the three of us we will easily come up with a plan that is simple, safe and yet elegant. And, better yet, something that can be effected within the next few hours."

"*We* will come up with a plan? Do you mean to say you don't actually have one?" The expression on Victoire's face could have frosted a window.

"Of course I have one," he said. "I just happen to believe that you can make it better than it already is."

The weather had cooperated and it had not rained on Jeanette, who had perfectly followed instructions and was waiting in the garden when Victoire and Robert arrived to inform her of the part she was to play in Robert's plan.

"I am most happy to hear your voice," Jeanette told her. "My Fortune has sent you to me, hasn't he?"

I was under the impression it was Robert de Vimoutiers's doing, she thought. Aloud she said, "All is set now, Jeanette. I have the chevalier de Vimoutiers with me and he will tell you what to do."

She was suddenly aware of the pressure of Robert's body against her as he approached the hole in the wall; she hurriedly stepped away as he said, "You have only to follow my instructions and you will be safe with Monsieur Vidal before next sunrise."

"I knew that my Fortune would not fail me," Jeanette said, sounding almost breathless. "What will he have me do?"

Wait—whose plan is this? She decided, shaking her head,

that there was no accounting for the wits of women in love, and Jeanette must surely be in love—and with a bourgeois no less. *I give you leave to hold on to your illusion, Jeanette.*

Ignoring the slight, Robert said, "Your part is simple, mademoiselle." Withdrawing from his coat pocket the small, heavily wrapped package Vidal had given him, he said, "I am about to throw something over the wall. Please pick it up and put it someplace hidden about you." He tossed the package, which obligingly arced over the wall; Victoire heard a rustle of leaves as it fell back to earth. Robert waited a moment, then asked, "You have it?"

"I have!" she whispered, clearly thrilled at the surreptitiousness of it all. A pause. "What do I have?"

"It is a vial of syrup of poppies, mademoiselle. Tonight, you are to order a cup of chocolate at bedtime. Drink some of it, then mix in the syrup. Pass the cup to your dresser and invite her to finish it, as you have had your fill."

"Ah," Jeanette said. "And then the horrid woman will sleep, and not notice my departure."

"Precisely." Robert paused, looking at Victoire as if seeking—what? Inspiration? "Mademoiselle," he said, "there are several lesser exits from the house into the garden in addition to the grand doors, are there not?" Victoire tried to build for herself a mental map of the Hôtel de Beaune, but could not quite complete it; she had only visited the duchesse a handful of times, and when visiting Jeanette, she had never been given the freedom of the house. "I seem to recall seeing some, but I have only ever used the main exit."

"There are," Jeanette said. "Including one at the far west end of the house, which would allow me to walk almost directly under the wall to this place."

"I see you anticipate the next step in the plan," he said.

Victoire nodded; this situation—and the promise of rescue from it—would sharpen to a fine point the wits of someone only half as bright as her friend. "At one o'clock tomorrow morning you will dress yourself for travel and make your way here. If you insist on bringing anything, it must be only what you can fit into a small bag—and you'll have to pack it in the dark, because you cannot risk anyone discovering you if you try to pack before you have—dealt with—your dresser."

"But how can I travel with nothing but what I wear?"

Robert stepped aside and waved Victoire back to the hole in the wall. "Monsieur Vidal has charged me to inform you," Victoire said, feeling a trifle awkward at being a go-between in such matters, "that he has provided for all you will need. You are to put yourself entirely in his hands, Jeanette."

"Ooh," she said, and Victoire felt the flush leaping up the back of her neck: Jeanette liked this idea rather too much for her taste. "I will do as my Fortune commands," she said. Victoire could not suppress a sigh. "Don't worry, Victoire," she said, completely misunderstanding. "Some day you will find yourself as happy as I am today."

"No doubt," Victoire said, keeping her voice level. "Once you are here you will speak softly through this hole, to let monsieur de Vimoutiers and myself know you are ready. At that point we will throw a rope over the wall. You will catch up the end of the rope and begin, carefully, to pull it toward you. Attached to the rope will be a rope-ladder, which we will make fast on this side of the wall. You will use the ladder to climb over the wall, and then back down this side."

"And into my Fortune's arms," she breathed. "It is a splendid plan, Victoire. I knew he would not fail me."

"No doubt," Victoire said again. She found herself beginning to feel sorry for Robert, who seemed to have actually engaged in careful thought in preparing this plan. "Once you are over the wall you and Vidal will depart in a conveyance he is arranging, and then you will both be away to a place Nicolette won't dare follow."

"Italy?" Jeanette breathed, nervously. "Lorraine? Germany? Pray God, not England."

"According to the chevalier de Vimoutiers, he has someplace rather closer to home in mind," Victoire told her.

"What in the world are you wearing?" Victoire glared at Robert, then pointedly shifted her gaze up to the astonishing hat that crowned his head. "And where in the world did you get it?"

"Demands the woman disguised as an ill-bred weaver's brat," he said as if they'd been discussing the latest horse races. "I'll have you know this outfit cost me five sous and took me several hours to locate. Never again will I trust my valet to shop for lower-class clothing."

"That hat makes your head look like the full moon," she said. "At least your breeches and coat are dark brown—and I can only trust that they were dyed that way—but the straw in your hat is going to look bright white to anyone watching us."

"And anyone watching us," he replied, "is going to remember someone in a ridiculous floppy straw hat. And that's pretty much the only thing they'll remember."

He rubbed his hands together. "I hope this cold doesn't make things awkward. The empress could have chosen a better night to have a skating party in the Tuilleries."

"Another month and it would nearly have been cold

enough without the need for all that prayer from all those priests," she said, nodding. "But I think we will be well." The chill tonight might have been magically induced but that didn't make it any less real; she was glad she had decided to wear woollen mittens in addition to the heavy stockings Catherine had insisted she wear.

Robert made a show of looking her up and down. "Any watchers likely won't even notice you're using a glamour, despite the fact we are most likely to be spied upon by monks if we're seen by anybody." A gesture over his shoulder took in the monastery of the Benedictines de la Ville-l'Évêque, with the buildings themselves only a few dozens of paces to the north of the Hôtel de Beaune, along the rue de Surène. "It's a good face," he added, "even if it does uncomfortably remind one of your criminal associate Hachette."

"He will be pleased to hear that, monsieur," she said. "Where have you put Vidal's cart?"

"Back around the corner on rue d'Anjou," he said. "Thought I should wander over here myself first to be sure you'd arrived."

"I know how to dodge the archers," she said, "rather more than you do."

"We could have a very pleasant discussion about that sometime, because I'm not sure you've been out drinking and gambling after curfew quite as frequently as I have. But this isn't really the time or the place for that." He stepped back from the lane into the street and waved his hat; a moment later Victoire heard the clop of hooves and the creak of wheels. *Why didn't you just shout?* she thought at him. *Anybody awake right now couldn't have missed that even wearing a blindfold.*

She had to admit, though, the chances of someone being

awake at this hour were pretty small. Even she had been reluctant to be out so late during her cloth-moving sorties, and those had taken place during the warm nights of spring or summer.

"When the cart gets here, you bring it to me," she told Robert. "I'm going to go ahead and make certain Jeanette is waiting." He nodded—the floppy brim of his hat moving like a flag—and she couldn't resist a small smile as she turned away from him.

Jeanette was indeed waiting by the hole in the wall, and if anything she sounded more excited now than she had earlier in the day. "Is my Fortune with you?" she asked. Her voice squeaked in her excitement and her determination to be quiet.

"Alas, it is just myself and the chevalier de Vimoutiers," Victoire told her. "Monsieur Vidal awaits you at his shop. He is, I believe, preparing your trousseau." Jeanette giggled.

After a moment's pause she said, "I do hope you can get me out of here quickly. It's cold and I couldn't find any gloves, I'm afraid."

"You'll be warm soon enough," Victoire told her. "Be patient, Jeanette. Ah, here comes de Vimoutiers now."

The cart was humble, but Vidal did not stint on its upkeep, so though the wooden wheels creaked a bit as the cart approached her at least it did not squeak. "Do you mind if I do the honours, mademoiselle?" he asked Victoire.

"By all means proceed, monsieur. Do let me know if you need any assistance."

Robert pulled two coils of rope and a suspicious-looking rope-ladder from the back of the cart. "Tell her the rope is on its way," he whispered. As Victoire repeated his message into the hole in the wall, Robert took one end of one coil in his left hand, and with his right threw the remainder of the rope over the wall. It skittered down the other side of the wall like a squirrel dancing.

"I have it," Jeanette said, and Victoire nodded at Robert. As he began to tie his end of the rope to one end of the ladder, Jeanette added, "now what do I do?"

"When I give the word," Victoire told her, "pull the rope until the ladder attached to it reaches the ground on your side of the wall. Then, when I signal you, climb to freedom."

Robert watched with approval as the rope he'd tied to the upper end of the ladder straightened, tautened and then began, just, to pull against the cart-wheel to which he had secured the whole assemblage. Then the rope slackened. Then it tautened again—and slackened.

He walked to where Victoire crouched, shivering, beside the wall. "Um, she did understand you meant her to start climbing, didn't she?"

"I don't know that the problem is," Victoire told him. "She told me several minutes ago that she was going to climb the ladder. She should have appeared on top of the wall by now."

"Try to get her attention, please." He was beginning to feel a bit nervous, though he would not have wanted to suggest this to Victoire. It really was a good plan, he told himself. And up until now it had gone along quite well. That the cold weather had been his own suggestion was...unfortunate. He was glad for the darkness and the outrageous hat he wore: it was less likely Victoire would be able to see the blush on his face.

"I believe," Victoire said, "that she is crying. She isn't answering me when I call her."

"Oh, dear." He looked at the rope, which would be much more difficult to climb than the rope-ladder. "I suppose I should climb in there and see if I can help."

"I'll do it." Victoire got to her feet, grimacing and cursing softly as she straightened up out of the crouch. "It's better for you to stay here and defend the cart, I think." She tucked her hands into her armpits for a few moments, then grabbed the rope with both hands and began to walk her way up the wall. Robert sucked in a long, slow breath in appreciation of her dexterity. "Listen for me at the hole in the wall," she told him. "As soon as I find out what's bothering her I'll let you know."

As Victoire disappeared over the top of the wall Robert crouched down and put his ear to the hole in the wall. He tried not to think about his soft, warm bed and about the hot spiced wine he could order up with just a word to Janvier. *Time enough for indulgence,* he told himself, *when the night's work is done.*

"She can't climb the ladder." Victoire's voice was tight with frustration. "Her hands are too cold to grip it and she's not strong enough to climb using her legs alone."

"Damn," Robert said. "That is …unfortunate. Do you think you can help her somehow?"

"What I think," Victoire said crisply, "is that we should tie the rope around her waist and haul her up like a sack of turnips." Robert smiled, absurdly pleased at the thought that Victoire would never have to be hauled like turnips or potatoes or any lumpy vegetable.

"Have you suggested this to mademoiselle yet?" he asked.

She laughed. "I think she'll take the suggestion rather more kindly if it comes from you."

"She's your friend, you know." He was about to chastise

Victoire for a coward when her sudden gasp stopped the words in his throat. "What's happened?"

She cursed in a most un-ladylike fashion. "Men are coming," she said. "Not the duc, I don't think. Thank God for that, at least."

"Lackeys or guards are bad enough," he said, as much to himself as to her. "I'm coming over."

She didn't say anything to that; there wasn't anything she could say, really. *I should have taken account of the fact Jeanette was being guarded,* he told himself. *But then again, why would Nicolette go so far as to put a watch on her? They're only cousins, for God's sake.*

He was at the top of the wall and ready to climb down to face the attackers when Robert realized that his sword was where he'd left it, tucked into the back of the cart. Immediately after that he realized that the cold night air had created frost on the top of the wall. Slippery frost.

"I knew she was up to something," a man's voice said.

"You did not," a second replied. "You had to be dragged away from the kitchen fire even though we'd been told to watch her. Ow." The last sound followed a soft thump that suggested these two knew each other pretty well.

Can I use that against them? Victoire asked herself. Then a second, much louder thump from behind her, followed by an exasperated groan, announced Robert's arrival. Victoire darted toward a piece of topiary large enough to hide behind, waving at Jeanette to follow. Her friend was on the verge of panic but clearly hadn't crossed over, because she obeyed.

Victoire fumbled together a mental image of a de Beaune lackey, or at least as good a one she could build from a

148

memory that hadn't ever been given that much to work with. *Good enough,* she decided, and began to pray. "Find me a rock," she told Jeanette when the prayer was complete and God worked His transformation on her appearance. Victoire could more easily have found what she needed herself, but she wanted Jeanette to have something to think about that wasn't the amount of danger they were all in.

"That's a man," the second voice said, his exclamation ending on an upward note of alarm.

"Don't be thick," the first said. "The Desmarais isn't much of a woman but she's still not a man."

"In which case this isn't the Desmarais. Ow." This time the last sound followed a smack that resounded with considerable force around the garden. "Get him," the second said, in a voice half-strangled with pain.

Victoire took the stone Jeanette had offered. It was, naturally, too small. But it had a projection that promised a certain useful sharpness. "I'll get him," she said, stepping out from behind the bush.

"Where did you come from?" the first voice asked her. The voice belonged to a thick-bodied middle-aged man whose squashed nose suggested he had been on the losing end of more than a few fights. *Here's another to add to your score,* Victoire told him silently, before smacking the stone into the side of his head. The man went to the ground without a sound.

As did Victoire, thrown off-balance by her strike to the man's head and unable to recover because the grass was slick with frost.

Victoire realized the lackeys had clubs—finding the one her victim had dropped—just as the second lackey scored a hit against a particularly bony part of Robert's person. She heard Robert's "Damn," and grabbed for the club on the grass beside her. She had struggled to her feet again when Robert and his opponent came into view, circling one another as the lackey tried to force his way past the ridiculous floppy hat, which Robert was now using as a shield, the way a swordsman might use a cloak.

He glanced at her, and his eyes widened. On impulse she tossed the club at him. Her aim was good, but Robert's feet slipped out from under him and he sat down on the grass with painful haste. "Sorry," she hissed.

"I've fought in much worse conditions than this," he said. Then, shooting her a quick grin, he swiped the club against his assailant's ankles just as the lackey was raising his own club overhead for a *coup de main.* The man squawked in pain and surprise, joining Robert on the ground. Victoire kicked her own man in the head to ensure he'd stay down, then picked up the stone she'd used to fell him.

"My God, my God," Jeanette muttered from behind the bush. "I am lost. Oh, God, save me."

God's busy, Victoire said to herself. "En garde," she snarled, skidding across the grass toward the second lackey. He turned his head toward her just as she reached him—allowing Robert to deliver a well-aimed blow to the back of the man's head.

She dug her boot-heels into the turf, trying to stop, but was still moving forward when she hit the unconscious lackey's body. She flung the rock away as she thrust out her arms to brace herself. And then she was somehow on top of Robert, knocking him backward from his crouch and landing on him as he sprawled onto his back.

He was bleeding from a broad scratch beside one eye. In the moon- and starlight his blood looked like the finest black cloth, napped to a shine. Holding her breath, she reached a finger toward the wound.

"Please, please, won't you get me out of here? I can hear more people coming, and I'm cold." Jeanette's voice trembled. "I want to leave this place and never come back." Victoire pulled back her hand, feeling unaccountably frustrated.

"I hope," Robert said as he closed his eyes and shifted Victoire's body away from him, "that Fortune Vidal is as generous as he is rich. Because that man now owes me a lot."

"I'd rather not go through another fight like that," Victoire said, slipping as she tried to get to her feet.

"I don't understand why you had to use stones and clubs when prayer would have been so much faster," Jeanette said. She was still weeping, and her voice shook. It might even have been petulant.

"I didn't want those people to know they were dealing with nobles," Robert told her. "If I'd used any magic to fight them, Nicolette would have guessed who was behind your escape." He tilted his head in the direction of the hôtel. "Yes, I hear more voices. Somebody is definitely about to join us." He held out a hand to Jeanette. "You are right, mademoiselle: it's time we left. Are you certain you can't climb that ladder?"

"I'm sorry, monsieur Robert, but my hands are so cold." She held them out, as if she and Robert might somehow be able to see frost growing on them. Looking up at him she added, "I'm sure I could manage if you helped me."

Robert drew in a deep breath, letting it out in a long sigh. "I'm beginning to think that perhaps it's time to pray."

"You didn't want them to know we're noble," Victoire pointed out.

"While we were fighting them," he replied. "I think

there's a prayer that would help us here, and we could start it up while our friends there are still asleep."

"Help *us?*" Victoire glared at him. "I'm already uncomfortable with my degree of involvement in this *plan.*"

"I could use your help, is all. This is a prayer I use at Respire's and some of the other gaming houses I visit. We make a sport of levitation, you see." He closed his eyes for a moment and she watched his lips move. "Yes, that's it," he said. "It's a simple prayer, really." He recited it to her, slowly but with enough urgency that she could hear it.

It was certainly simple; it was also French. "You had it translated from the Latin?"

"Oh, it wasn't I who did it," he said, smiling in an embarrassed way. "Clever idea, though, wasn't it? It was to prevent undue advantage going to those with classical educations, you know. A sort of handicap to our races."

"Very clever," she muttered. "I am surrounded by brilliance." She took a deep breath. "After you, then, monsieur."

Robert began to pray, his voice smooth and practised. After listening through one round, and watching with some small surprise as Jeanette began to float upward, Victoire added her voice to his. At once she felt a warm flush move outward from her breast, until her whole person was suffused with a remarkable sense of pleasant well-being. She couldn't resist looking up at him, and saw his eyes staring, wide, back at her. After a breath, a smile appeared around the corners of his mouth. "This is working very well," he told her. He shifted a bit, so as better to watch Jeanette's progress up to the top of the wall.

Jeanette's face had settled from fear or petulance into a slightly startled pleasure, and it appeared that however cold her hands were, they were not incapable of grasping the rope-ladder once she had reached the wall's summit.

"Time for us to go, now," Robert said. He reached for her hand.

Victoire, inspiration striking, pulled back.

"I'm not sure we should all be trying to get away," Victoire said to him

Robert could only stare. "What in the world are you talking about? We have to leave, and you can't stay behind."

"Oh, it wasn't me I was referring to," she said, pointing back at the house. "I've thought about it, and I believe we'd be better served if you stayed behind to distract de Beaune or his people, while I take Jeanette to monsieur Vidal."

"What? That's insane. I'm more useful helping you get her down on the other side of the wall." *You aren't going to get rid of me that easily,* he decided. "Once I'm up there I can just as easily come down on the right side of this wall as on the wrong side."

"Yes, yes," Victoire said, pushing the words at him as if she were spitting seeds. "And then what? They hear the cart going away and come after us. I suspect they could catch up to that horse of Vidal's on foot—and some of them at least won't be on foot."

"How does leaving me behind prevent them from chasing the cart?"

"Because, you great idiot, if you're here when they arrive there won't be any reason to chase. They'll have an explanation for the fight, and the explanation is you."

"No doubt you've got a good reason why I would have been fighting de Beaune lackeys."

"Of course," she said, and the crazed look of triumph

in her eyes made him wonder if perhaps he had erred in thinking it would be exciting to get involved with Victoire de Berenguer. "You came here because you were absolutely desperate to see Nicolette again. She threw you over at the beginning of the month, didn't she? Well, you thought you were over her, but you aren't. So, you've been out drinking—you can act drunk, I presume—and you got it into your head that if you could just speak to her you could persuade her to take you back again."

"*What?*"

"Well, you asked me if I had a reason for you being here, and I do. And it's a pretty good reason too, I think."

"I most certainly don't." He wondered why his voice was shaking, then decided he didn't care. "This is the most ridiculous thing anyone has ever asked me to do." *No, it isn't,* a treacherous voice inside his head reminded him. "I'm not the sort of person who would ever do something as demented as this." *A surprising number of people seem to think you are.* "Besides, it's clearly implausible. Nobody would be so stupid as to believe I'd suddenly decide to go chasing after Nicolette again after nearly three months of happy solitude. *Nobody* is that—"

"Nicolette would believe that," Jeanette said from atop the wall.

Victoire nodded. "And yes, she *is* that stupid." Jeanette giggled, but Robert was unable to detect any reason for laughing.

He stared at Victoire. "Let me understand this," he said, speaking very carefully because the cold had clearly got to her brains. "Having risked my—well, not my neck, I suppose—getting her up to the top of the wall, I am to help her down the other side, and then I am to climb *back down* the rope-ladder to here and meekly wait to be beaten up by more of de Beaune's lackeys. Is that it, or have I missed something?"

"You likely don't have to climb up," Victoire said. "That prayer should work just as well with you here, no? And they won't beat you up," she added. "I'm pretty certain they won't. What would be the point? You just want to see their mistress, after all."

"Something I will only be too happy to say if the duc is a member of the approaching party."

"Which is *approaching,* monsieur!" Jeanette threw a bit of ice at him. "Stop arguing and get me down from here!"

I am certain to regret this, Robert thought, as Victoire began the prayer and that astonishing sense of—utterly inappropriate to the current circumstances—wellness filled him again. *And yet here I am.*

A sense of release told him the prayer was no longer needed because Jeanette was on the ground now. "You won't object if I leave it to you to get up and over the wall and remove the ladder," he told Victoire. "And you won't mind if I hope, just a little, that you fall on your head getting down."

Then he sat down to await capture, interrogation, lies and only God knew what else.

Fortune Vidal was waiting in the doorway of his shop, a vibrating silhouette surrounded by the glow of numerous candles and, Victoire hoped, a really big fire. "My darling!" he whispered as Victoire presented Jeanette to him. "Are you hurt? You are so brave, my little one. Praise God I have you with me at last."

Robert and I may have had a little to do with this, Victoire thought. *No doubt God could have done it all on His own, but in fact He did not.* "I believe that mademoiselle Desmarais did not suffer too much from tonight's cold," Victoire told him. "Which ought to end soon anyway, if it's true this was created for the empress' amusement. Still, I would hope you have something hot for us to drink, because we did suffer somewhat."

"She is a strong and brave woman," Vidal said, and though the jeweller spoke of her as if she wasn't there, Jeanette still preened at the praise. "I knew she would do her part, if only we did but do ours." This was all rather too melodramatic for Victoire's taste, but even so she had to admit planning an elopement and *mésalliance* might over-set even the most phlegmatic of temperaments. No doubt the happy couple would have to spend the first several weeks of married life recovering from the excitement of the marriage itself.

"And, of course I have hot wine for you," he added. "And a good fire. Come in and warm yourselves, both of you, while I see to having hot bricks put into the cart." He stopped abruptly, and Victoire could actually see him counting them, even though it should have been readily apparent that the count stopped at two. "Where is the chevalier de Vimoutiers?" he asked. A brief pause and he added, "Surely he's not hurt, or…or—"

"No, nothing serious," Victoire said, pushing past Vidal to enter the private office and its promise of warmth. "He had to stay behind, I'm afraid." She found four filled cups on a sideboard, and took one. It was still, blessedly, hot. Her fingers tingled as the cold drew out of them.

"They have both been so clever," Jeanette told Vidal, "nearly as clever as you, my love. Monsieur le chevalier has stayed behind to pretend that, rather than breaking me out of that horrible house, *he* was trying to break *in*."

"Which will give you the extra time you need," Victoire said as Vidal stared, uncomprehending, "to get outside of Paris before anyone thinks to search for mademoiselle.

"Speaking of which," she added, "You two will want to keep this with you at least until you have reached Monsieur Vidal's house." Victoire unfolded the paper she had been keeping in her muff. "I wrote this a few hours ago, while waiting for our rendezvous, and have attached my seal to it. It's a pass to get you two through the Porte du Temple. Jeanette could, of course, have written something like this herself—but that would provide evidence of the direction by which you left the city. This doesn't name you—the assumption is that as you're non-noble your names don't matter—but confirms you in my service. I doubt there will be any questions, even if you do reach the gate before it officially opens for the day."

"Mademoiselle, I thank you." Vidal bowed low. "I confess I had not thought of that."

"You thought of everything else, though," Victoire said, giving credit where it was due. "I trust, by the way, that you have everything you'll need—and more importantly, everything Jeanette will need—packed and ready to go. Robert—Monsieur de Vimoutiers—and I more or less promised Jeanette that you would provide everything she could possibly need." She glanced at the astonishingly ornate clock on the mantelpiece of Vidal's office. "It's rather late—perhaps I should say early—in the day to head to the shops, after all"

"Mademoiselle, I have had everything ready for this event for more than two weeks now." He smiled, proudly. "We but awaited the arrival of a brave chevalier to assist us—and somehow we were given two of you."

"Ah. Glad to be of service, I suppose." She felt a sudden

flush of understanding of Robert's response to praise. He wasn't used to it, she realized, and neither was she. She thought about repercussions, shivered, and added, "Don't feel any great need to praise either me or the chevalier to anyone else, though. As far as we're concerned—and I feel safe in speaking for the chevalier—we're happy for you to claim full credit for this, monsieur."

"You are too kind, mademoiselle." Vidal broke into a broad smile. "I will pray, though, that someday you obtain the credit you deserve."

"I'm prepared to wait for that," Victoire told him.

Chapter Ten
The Best of Interests

"I HAD THOUGHT you a wiser man than this," the duc de Beaune told Robert. He glared at Robert, tied to a chair in the hôtel's winter kitchen. "I can't for the life of me imagine why I thought that."

"In my defence, I had been drinking. It seemed a good idea at that time." Robert made a tentative tug against his bonds. His head ached, as did his left shoulder; the lackeys who had subdued him had not even understood the word *gentle*. He didn't think he had slept more than an hour after being shut in here, and the morning sun had brought no cheer. "Is it really necessary I be tied up? Do you honestly want to keep me here?"

"Honestly? I'd rather throw you into one of the canals with stones tied to your feet. You are not precisely a splendid advertisement for the attractions of my wife." The emphasis the duc put on the words *my wife* suggested he spoke of an ulcerated leg. *Not much love in this home,* Robert said to himself. *Why didn't I think to notice that before?*

"Disposing of me won't help you much," he said aloud. "Our entire society seems to be built on us not noticing our various peccadilloes. Can't think you want to come across as being jealous of your wife." The suggestion didn't seem to be welcomed. "Just trying to be helpful," he offered.

"You should stop trying," the duc growled.

"Happy to help," Robert said. He thought about that. "Or, as it were, not help."

"Do shut up, Vimoutiers."

Robert shut up.

After several very long minutes in which the duc did nothing save to stare, frowning, at him, Robert was driven to risk speech again. "You seem rather more upset than I would have expected, de Beaune. I promise you I didn't tell anyone at Respire's I was coming here. I would not embarrass you."

"The betrayal I'm wondering about goes a bit beyond simple embarrassment. You are not helping me to make a decision about that, nor doing yourself any favours."

"Sorry about that," Robert told him. "I'm just not used to so much silence."

The duc laughed abruptly. "Thank you," he said with sour humour. "I have just entertained a most enjoyable vision of you as a monk." He crouched slightly, bringing his eyes level with Robert's. "Very well, let's to it: What, precisely, has been your relationship with Nicolette since—oh, let's call it the end of August?"

"Mostly that of discarded swain, I should think." De Beaune's expression was most odd. *Not the look of a jealous husband at all. But what is it that's eating at him? This makes no sense.*

"You've had contact with her? Or with her other— acquaintances?"

"Not to speak of. I think I've only spoken to her once in the past three weeks, and that wasn't so much speaking as me listening to her tell me that she wasn't pleased

with me anymore and would I please stop pestering her."
He ventured a smile at the duc. "I didn't think I'd been
pestering. I thought I'd been very polite in my attentions.
Tasteful, even."

The duc straightened. "Who is her new lover?"

"Y'know, I haven't the slightest idea. As a rule, I take
care never to know this sort of thing. If it's somebody I'm
on a first-name basis with, I'll find out soon enough from
the party in question. And if it isn't, I'm just as happy not
knowing."

"You're not really much of a man, are you?"

"That question only ever bothers me if it comes from
a woman," Robert said, smiling brightly. "No offence
intended, I assure you." *There's that look again,* he thought.
Then he realized, *He knows who it is. He wanted to know if
I knew as well.* That was very interesting.

Robert was about to ask about that when the maître d'
hôtel oozed into the kitchen, bowing ostentatiously. "My
lord duc," the man intoned, "I regret to inform you that the
cousin of the duchesse has disappeared."

"Disappeared? What in the name of all that's sacred does
that mean? Has God plucked her from her room? Did you
see this disappearance?"

"Monsieur, she is not anywhere in the house. And her
dresser is claiming she was drugged last night."

"How is this possible?" The duc turned on the man.
"The house is guarded, is it not? Are you trying to tell me
somebody was able to get in here and steal her away?"

"Not at all, monsieur, not at all!" A glow on the man's
forehead suggested nervous sweating. "If the dresser is
to be taken at her word, mademoiselle Desmarais herself
administered the sleeping-potion."

Slowly the duc turned to Robert. Then he spun around

and, with a curt wave, dismissed the maître d' hôtel. Only when the functionary was gone did he—slowly—turn back to Robert. "You'd been drinking," he said. "You had a sudden whim to break into my house and try to seduce my wife."

"I did say it seemed a good idea at the time," Robert said, not liking the look on the duc's face. "I didn't say I still think it a good idea."

"I could justifiably challenge you and run you through, you dissembling bastard." The duc's face now bore a look of icy, almost inhuman anger. "Stealing from me, even if it's only the Desmarais, is an insult of the grossest proportion."

"She wasn't stolen from you, de Beaune. She was stolen from your wife."

The duc stepped back. He stared at Robert for a long moment. Then he smiled—though it was the sort of smile that dropped the temperature in the room still further. "I had not considered it in that light," he said, his voice soft but with menace still very much present. "I suppose it's just possible that you might actually have done me a small favour, de Vimoutiers." Robert smiled back at him, but before he could say anything the duc added, "Don't presume to take advantage, boy. I would still be fully within my rights to challenge you for what you've done." A pause. "What, exactly, *have* you done?"

"Ah, you probably don't want to know the precise details," Robert said.

"What you mean is, you don't want to *tell* me the precise details."

"As you will. At any rate, all I did was help. Aiding the course of true love, as it were."

"True what?"

Of course, you'd have to have that explained to you,

Robert thought. Aloud, he said, "Jeanette's fallen in love with a very wealthy man. She and he needed some help from me in order to put the him and the her of it together. So, once she'd got out into your garden last night I helped her to climb over the wall. I just wasn't able to escape with her because of your lackeys interrupting me so enthusiastically."

"Desmarais? A very wealthy—do you mean a wealthy *bourgeois?*"

"Does it really matter? You no longer have to support her, and Nicolette—well, I suppose Nicolette can no longer use her as a go-between." *If Jeanette was being used this way, why didn't she say something to us?* "Was Nicolette using her that way?"

"I don't know, Vimoutiers, and you *really* don't want to." He stepped around and behind Robert, who felt a brief tug and then freedom as the rope came away from his wrists. "I think it's time we ended our acquaintance. You can leave through the back gate—the fewer people who see you the better. And do yourself a favour, Vimoutiers: don't talk about this.

"To anyone."

"So, of course the first thing I thought of was to tell you about it," Robert said to Victoire.

"Well, strictly speaking it was the second or third thing. My first thought was to get myself back into m'mother's house without anyone seeing me, so that I could wash up and get into some proper clothing.

"And my second thought was to ask Jeanette what in the world her cousin has been getting up to." He looked around the kitchen of Victoire's old house; it was nowhere near as nice as the kitchen from which he'd just escaped, but it felt so much better to be here than there. Only one of the inhabitants—was her name Marie-Louise?—was there with Victoire, and that hardened female looked completely uninterested in him. "But, of course you probably already know that she and her Fortune have left Paris."

"As I was the one who wrote the pass to get them through the gate," Victoire said in a dry, amused voice, "yes, I did know that."

"Normally I'd be thrilled to learn they'd got safely away," Robert said. "But I'm really beginning to wonder just how *normal* my life has become, lately. I am thinking I really ought to talk to Jeanette, to find out everything she knows about what Nicolette has been up to this month. The duc was enormously upset, Victoire—it *is* all right if I call you Victoire, isn't it?—and that's not the sort of reaction I should expect of him. I'm not really sure how to explain this—"

"Try," Victoire said. "I just might be able to understand it."

"I don't mind you mocking me," he said, very nearly meaning it, "but the fact is there's something really off about this. It wasn't *that* Nicolette was having an affair that bothered him, I think—it was with *whom* she was having it. He seemed to think he was at some sort of risk because of it."

"Perhaps he believes the man was so déclassé that it was an insult to his honour."

"It's always possible. He wouldn't be the first noble to be that self-absorbed. But I don't think that's the case here. He seemed—perhaps *nervous* isn't the word for somebody like de Beaune—let's say *concerned* about this new lover of hers. What's more, he was very concerned about whether I knew who the new lover was."

"Do you?"

"Happy to say I do not." He sighed. "Though I suppose I am going to have to find out, now. Something tells me it's going to matter a lot."

"Will it help me to find my missing cloth?"

"Who knows? It might." *I hadn't really been thinking about that. I'd been thinking about the danger to you—and to me, I suppose—if Nicolette is involved in something very bad.*

"I'll take that as a No, then," Victoire said. "I'm really sorry, monsieur de Vimoutiers, but now that Jeanette is safely in the arms of her monsieur Vidal, I have to return my attentions to my own problems. You may be able to depend on your family for support, but that's not a luxury I have. I'm not going to be able to help you."

"Not really sure I was asking for help," Robert told her. *Though I thought we worked quite well together last night; don't you?* "Just wanted you to be aware, that's all. And to see if you'd noticed anything about Nicolette that I hadn't, I suppose."

An idea occurred to him. "So how can I help you find your missing cloth?"

"I already declined your offer, monsieur. There isn't any way you can help me."

He smiled at her. "Don't be so quick to judge," he said.

I really ought to get some sleep, he thought as he walked away from the house. A lot of people seemed to be looking at him. *I suppose I should also start dressing in a less-flamboyant fashion.*

Victoire watched from the door until de Vimoutiers disappeared around the corner onto rue St-Martin. Then she grabbed a shawl and wrapped it around her—the weather was more than seasonably warm again, but for some reason memories of the magical cold were making her shiver today—and slipped out the door, walking the opposite way along rue du Pet and taking a dog-leg that put her on rue St-Denis. Hachette had gone this way an hour earlier, and Victoire hoped that by following the boy she might somehow locate Père Robillard in the act of committing some foul deed related to her missing cloth.

It was better than sitting with Marie-Louise trying to work out whether de Vimoutiers might have had a point about the duc de Beaune's behaviour, which truly was more worrisome than she had let de Vimoutiers see.

There was a cabaret on St-Denis at the corner of the rue des Deux Portes, only a moment's walk from the Porte St-Denis. *If I were a wicked priest with a habit of gluttony,* she thought, *I might seek my pleasures as far away from the centre of the city as possible.* And this place was as far away from her parents' hôtel as one could go without crossing to the left bank of the Seine. She had had Hachette investigate all of the cabarets and taverns on St-Denis and St-Martin, leaving only the Hungry Fox to be investigated on this side of the river. They weren't any closer to finding the cloth than they had been two weeks ago, but Victoire knew a lot more now about the less-salubrious parts of Paris than she ever had.

"Mademoiselle."

She stopped. The voice came from the shadows, a narrow gap between the wall of an hôtel and a shop-front whose sign suggested either an oculist or a publisher. *Will I draw too much attention to myself,* she wondered, *if I bend and lift my skirts to reach the knife strapped to my leg?*

"Mademoiselle, I have some advice for you." Now she

could see the man. He was on the short side, thin but not skinny, perhaps in his late thirties—though his silver wig made his age difficult to guess. His occupation was easier to guess, though no less confusing for that: he wore a lawyer's black. *What's this about then?* Her first thought was that one of Papa's creditors had somehow obtained a *lettre de cachet.*

"What advice do I need from a lawyer, monsieur?" she asked.

She thought she heard a frustrated growl before he said, "Advice that will keep you out of the Bastille, mademoiselle, and possibly even keep you alive."

She felt herself stiffen, alert to a danger this fussy-looking man should not have possessed. "I am in no danger of the Bastille, monsieur." She looked around her; plenty of people in the street, but none near enough to give immediate aid save perhaps for the shabby old man sweeping the street just beyond arm's length away. "Perhaps you are accosting the wrong person?"

"No, mademoiselle de Berenguer, I am not accosting the wrong person."

This is bad. Where is Hachette when you need him? She said, "Monsieur, you are being rude, and I wish you to go away." As she spoke she carefully stepped back and over until she could rest against the hôtel wall and lift her foot from the ground. Hating her skirts, she fumbled for the knife in its sheath.

"For the moment, mademoiselle, you indeed are in no danger of going into the Bastille. But this is only because you no longer have cloth to sell. I am here to strongly advise you against trying to obtain any more. Your supplier has agreed to use, shall we say, a different distribution service—a different individual for the sale and delivery of his cloth. Your services are no longer required, and you will be safer if you simply accept this fact."

"My—my supplier?"

"Don't pretend you don't know what this conversation is about, mademoiselle. We both know I'm referring to the chevalier de Vimoutiers."

"The chevalier."

"That's what I said, mademoiselle."

"Robert de Vimoutiers." She felt a burning growing in her, but kept her voice as steady as the demands of her anger allowed. "You think that my cloth is coming from that bumbling—you utter *imbecile!*" The burning overwhelmed her attempts to suppress it.

She charged at the lawyer, who squeaked in alarm and backed further into the shadows. When he saw the knife in Victoire's right hand he screamed and tried to spin around.

The gap was too narrow to allow an easy turn—nor did it allow Victoire the room to brandish the knife with the degree of threat she wanted. The absence of flourish didn't seem to make a difference to the lawyer, though: once he'd picked himself up off the filthy ground he ran with an impressive turn of speed until he disappeared into the gloom.

Victoire wasn't interested in following him. Which was, she decided, a good thing because the narrow gap between buildings threatened to crush her skirts and petticoats completely if she did anything but back out carefully along the route she had taken in.

She emerged onto rue St-Denis just in time to see Père Robillard emerge from the doorway of a shop whose sign proclaimed a seamstress resided there.

"Robert de Vimoutiers! He thought I *worked for* Robert de Vimoutiers! Aahh!" Victoire flung her shawl onto the old chest in one corner of the kitchen. "*Men.* If I'd stuck my knife into his throat he would have assumed de Vimoutiers had told me where to aim it!"

Hachette laughed and mimed the lawyer taking a blade to the neck. Catherine shushed the boy. Marie-Louise quietly asked, "And who was this lawyer, and how did he know you?"

Victoire paused at the point of shouting a response. *Think, don't shout.* "A very good point, Marie-Louise," she said, "and thank you for raising it—and reminding me to calm myself."

She took a deep breath. "I have no idea who he is, nor do I know how he knew me. Though it's easy enough to guess. I haven't made it too much of a secret, amongst our customers, about the fact that it's an aristo selling them their cloth."

"Possibly this lawyer works for one of our customers?" Catherine suggested.

"Possibly. Though we haven't found any evidence that the cloth was stolen by one of our customers. And anyway, what really interests me is what that man said about other means of distributing smuggled cloth."

"Surely we're not the only ones who sell smuggled cloth, mademoiselle."

"Of course we aren't. But we don't try to force our competitors out of business, either. This man—or the people he seems to represent—is trying to do precisely that."

"Do you think the chevalier works for them now?" Hachette asked. He seemed upset by the prospect.

"How could he?" Victoire demanded. "Robert de

Vimoutiers doesn't know how to work at anything. He's another of those useless younger sons who give our class such a great name with the bourgeois and the peasants." She took a deep breath. *You're going to start shouting again.* "I don't know how they got the idea that monsieur de Vimoutiers is a genius smuggler, but that they did get the idea is their problem to deal with, not ours."

She smiled, feeling the tension seep out of her. "What we must deal with, I'm happy to say, is my good friend Père Robillard. I found him this afternoon coming out of a seamstress's shop near the St-Denis gate."

"You did?" Hachette jumped up. "Not fair! That was my job."

"I wasn't looking for him," Victoire lied, wanting to salve the boy's feelings. "I was trying to figure out how to get my knife into that thrice-damned lawyer. It was the purest chance I saw the good father."

"So now we know who took the cloth and where he's hiding it?"

"Well," Victoire said, her smile faltering a bit, "not exactly."

"'Not exactly'?" Marie-Louise said.

"I talked to the seamstress and while she might have been lying, she told me that she had never seen Père Robillard before. She claimed he was *looking for* cloth, not trying to sell any."

"Looking for cloth? That doesn't make any sense," Hachette said. "Why would a priest want to buy painted cotton?"

"A very good question," Victoire said. "But at least now we know for certain there is a connection between Père Robillard and our cloth.

"Now we just have to find out what that connection is."

"Vimoutiers! Where in heaven and hell have you been?" The sound of popping corks accompanied the greeting, and there was a brief burst of fireworks over the gaming table, the most that prayer could accomplish in these heavily warded rooms. To Robert it all seemed forced, and sadly so; he wondered why he'd never noticed this before. Still, he prayed up his own fireworks in return, because it was expected.

"Seriously, though," du Rochefort said, pulling back a chair for him, "what have you been up to lately? I can't remember the last time I saw you."

"It was yesterday," Robert said. "I passed you on the street. I waved; I was fairly certain, at the time, that you had waved back. Perhaps I was mistaken."

"Idiot," du Rochefort said. "You know what I mean. I don't believe I've seen you here for nearly a week. Don't tell me you're in mourning for Nicolette de Beaune; I won't believe you. Is it some actress taking up your time and your...energies? I promise, you won't be able to keep her hidden from me." Catching a waiter's attention, he obtained a cup and filled it for Robert.

"This is a decent Burgundy. You must be winning tonight." Robert raised the cup to du Rochefort. "Your continued good luck."

"If you're not going to wish the same for me," said the chevalier de Senez—whose winnings were a hillock against du Rochefort's mountain—"I wish you would keep your sentiments to yourself."

"I am, in fact, having a terrific night," du Rochefort said. "And you, Vimoutiers, dissimulate. Let's have the truth now, and before the next game begins."

"The truth is," he lied, "I'm broke. And m'mother won't advance me any more." There was no point even trying to explain the truth of his circumstances to these men, he realized—any more than he could explain why it was he was suddenly finding his presence here so disappointing.

"I could front you the money," du Rochefort said—but slowly, as though he was preparing to accuse his own self of prevarication. "God knows you've done it for me." *And have you ever paid me back?* Robert wondered. It was a little embarrassing to realize that he himself didn't know.

"I'd rather you didn't," he said. He sipped, stared into his cup, sipped some more, and wondered once again why he had thought it a good idea—well, an idea—to come here tonight. "Do you ever get bored?" he asked. They stared at him, uncomprehendingly.

"Bored?" Du Rochefort's expression suggested Robert had addressed him in Persian or Turkish.

"Bored. Bored with this life." Robert struggled to put unfamiliar thoughts into words. "We stay in bed until noon; we visit the same people during the afternoon; we dine with the same friends; we gamble at the same three or four places in the evenings—and we do this day after day after day. Don't tell me you don't sometimes wonder about this."

"I only wonder when we're going to return to the game," said de Senez—rather sulkily, Robert thought.

"My dear Robert," said du Rochefort, "I try my hardest to wonder about little and think about even less."

"Thanks for your help," Robert said. "You're a great comfort to me, my friend."

"What would you have me say, Robert? What other life is available to me? I don't have enough money to join the church, even if I seriously wanted to give up women.

Which, now that I come to think about it, I don't. And the army? It is to laugh: horses make me break out in a rash, as do gunpowder and sharp, pointy things. I have no estates to manage, and no bookseller cares about my philosophy—such as it is, and I happen to believe it's a good one." He smiled at Robert. "Now tell me you're any different, my lovesick friend. Come on, Robert: who is she?"

"It's nobody," he said. But it occurred to him this might no more be true than anything else he'd said so far tonight. "I'm just out of sorts, I suppose." *You're out of sorts,* he said to himself, *because you haven't seen her for eight hours—and the last time you did see her she rejected every offer you made to help her.*

"Maybe you should spare us your ennui," said de Senez, "until you're back in sorts. In the meantime, I prescribe you to let us return to our game while you run off home."

"Much as it pains me to admit it," Robert said to de Senez, "you are in the right of it. My regrets, messieurs, and I will join you some other time." He did not let du Rochefort's protests—and they seemed quite real, he was pleased to note—keep him at the table, nor did he let Respire's splendid supper keep him in the house at all. *Maman will be astonished to see me home so early,* he thought sourly.

He hadn't gone more than twenty paces away from Respire's place when a deep voice called out from the night-shrouded shadows of a building set a little back from the street. "Monsieur le chevalier de Vimoutiers?"

"Who asks?"

"My name will not be known to you. I have the honour to represent—certain parties, whose interests are similar to yours, if only adjacently." The man stepped into the street, and in the pale moonlight Robert thought he recognized the lawyer from the wine-shop the other day. What was his name? Chenan? No, Chenal, that was it.

The lawyer bowed, formally, almost to the point of dislodging the wig from atop his head. "I am most fortunate indeed in encountering you here."

"A funny thing," Robert told him, guessing that fortune had had nothing to do with the man's presence, "I don't know that I feel fortunate at all in this meeting."

"Believe me, monsieur, I have nothing but your best interests in mind."

"I keep hearing those words," Robert told him, sliding his hand across his body to the hilt of his épée. "Hearing them with remarkable frequency lately, in fact. And perhaps I simply lack the brains, but I am unable to see any of my interests at all in you, much less the best of them."

The smooth, self-possessed smile faded from the lawyer's face; in the moonlight his eyes took on a dangerous, obsidian glitter. "I'm surprised, monsieur, that you don't consider staying out of prison to be in your best interests."

"I consider it so important, on the contrary, that I do nothing at all to put myself on the wrong side of the law." *Nothing so far, at any rate.* "If you've heard otherwise, you've been misinformed. My friends, you should know, are notorious practical jokers."

"I know more about you and your friends, monsieur le chevalier, than you may be comfortable with. You should know that I, Antoine Chenal, plead before the Parlement de Paris, and so am much better able than you to adjudge any threats to your personal liberty."

"I know who you are," Robert said, slowly, "And speaking of threats, did I just hear one from you?"

"I have no need to make threats. Not when I have these—ah, gentlemen—standing behind me." Chenal stepped to one side, and two unpleasant-looking individuals moved into the moonlight. "I promise they won't hurt you too dreadfully. Did you hear that, you two?" He turned to look at his companions. "I've given my word, so no broken bones or serious blood-letting."

Robert summoned a sphere of God-light and sent it to hover over the two men. He laughed at what he saw. "The next time you do this," he said, "I suggest you instruct Clopard to give you bravos I haven't actually seen before." He made an elaborate bow. "Good evening. Please be gentle with me: I bruise easily."

If Chenal blushed at this the colouring wasn't visible in the greenish cast the moonlight now had. "You're talking nonsense," he said. "I don't know any Clopard."

"We'll see how long that claim lasts once you're put to the torture," Robert said. He regretted his response almost immediately.

"I take it back, you two," Chenal growled. "Feel free to kill him. Send me word when it's done." He turned and walked away, in the direction of the river. Robert toyed briefly with the idea of tangling the lawyer's feet, to keep him around until he'd dealt with the bravos. But he was forced to alter his tactics when he felt a kind of claustrophobic warmth hovering just beyond his spiritual form.

Somebody, somehow, had warded the wooden cudgels the two men carried.

He tried to ward himself, then attempted a prayer to lift the weapon from one of them; both times, the warm bath, a sickly parody of the warmth one always felt in the emperor's presence, spilled over from the man's right arm and onto Robert's spiritual self. *That's disgusting*, he thought; it suggested bathing in semi-congealed ox-fat.

And possibly painful, came to him as the man brought the cudgel down towards his head with arrogant precision.

He almost completely dodged the blow.

"I'd love to know," he gasped, rubbing his left shoulder as he dodged backward into the middle of the street, "who it was who did that work for you."

He had a bit more luck dodging the other man's blow. "Want to give him my personal regards."

He drew his épée just in time; the first man swung out at him again, and Robert's block was clumsy. He deflected the attack but obviously didn't hurt the man at all; this worthy gave Robert a gap-tooth grin and prepared to come at him once more, at the same time as his companion came in low, from the side, aiming at Robert's knee.

Robert slashed out from left to right, knee up to shoulder, not caring whether he hit so long as he wasn't hit himself. A profane outburst told him he'd done something even as the slight shock up his right arm told him the contact hadn't been much. Still, his knee and head hadn't been broken. And this time he'd drawn blood.

He skipped back, hoping he wasn't about to crash into a wall. "This is hardly playing fair," he said, gasping just a little. He reached back to his sword belt and pulled out the long dagger. He got it into position just as the first man came at him for a fourth time.

Training took over; he set his feet and shoulders and blocked the blow with his dagger hand, forcing cudgel and arm upward and across the man's face as his sword-hand thrust the épée into the man. The shock into his right arm was more substantial this time, and his target did not curse, hardly said a word as he sat down, blank-eyed, in the middle of the street.

At which point his companion smashed a blow into Robert's left knee.

"By God that hurts," he said. He pulled his épée out of the first man and made another wild cut at the second, even as he was falling himself.

Sprawled in the street, without thinking, he threw a spiritual punch at the man—and felt it connect. "Right," he said, gasping as the pain began to flow outward from his knee. "Shall we begin in earnest now?"

In response the second man scrambled to his feet and staggered away, taking the same path the lawyer had a few minutes earlier. *No sense of fair play whatever,* Robert thought. He cast a levitation prayer at the abandoned cudgel, watched it begin to rise, and dropped both prayer and weapon. Something had happened to the ward on the thing, but he wasn't the one to find out what that was.

And he didn't really want to talk about this with the one person who could help him.

With some difficulty Robert made his way to the bravo he had stabbed, and tried to pray the wound closed. The man died a moment before the sounds of shouts and boots on stone announced the arrival of a company from Respire's.

Chapter Eleven
Trusted With a Name

"You did *what*? And to *whom*?" The duchesse de Vimoutiers stood, mouth open and arms limp at her side—a pose Robert did not think he had ever seen her adopt before. The sight, he decided, was a trifle unnerving.

"A lawyer?" he said. "At least, it was a lawyer who was behind it. The men who attacked me were just common criminals." He felt queasiness coming over him. "If I could, Maman, I'd like to sit down. My knee hurts. A lot."

"Sit, then." She pulled a fragile-looking chair towards him; big soft comfortable armchairs were evidently not something the duchesse required in her boudoir. Robert thought he'd been in pews more comfortable than this chair. "And how," she asked softly, "did you know that the men were common criminals?"

"Um," he said. *Why can't I be as clever as she is?* he wondered. *If I were, it would make fooling her so much easier.* Aloud, all he could think of to say was, "I may have encountered one of them before." She said nothing, but the temperature in her room seemed to drop. "I suppose that if you insisted on looking at this only in—in a certain way, it might look, well, somewhat suspicious. Or at least coincidental. Yes, that's the word: coincidence. But we all know that coincidence isn't causation. Or something like that. Don't we?" *Really, it's just astonishing how women can set you to babbling. You're never like this around your friends.*

"Let me be certain I understand you," Maman said. "You were accosted by—by a lawyer? Who had two armed men with him? And you don't know why? Or, rather, you *say* you don't know why."

"Absolutely true, Maman," he said. He was sweating now; it had to be the pain. "I'd never met the man before, but he claimed to know me. And when I suggested the law might be interested in his accosting me that way, he told his men to kill me. So, I had to fight back. I was just defending myself, and they were street-scum."

"And you explained all this to the archers?"

"Um. Not as such, no. My friends from Respire's thought it wasn't necessary I should wait around for the archers to arrive, so I didn't. But I'm—well, I'm still a bit concerned about this. So, I thought you should know."

"You *thought*. Robert, what am I going to do with you?"

"Sending for a priest or physician might be a start," he offered. "And then perhaps some advice? I'm feeling a bit lost here."

Her expression softened. A bit. She rang for her maid and instructed the sleepy woman to go wake the family priest. After the maid had left she turned back to Robert.

"Perhaps we should remove you from Paris for a while," she said. She rubbed her eyes for a moment, stopping abruptly as if suddenly aware of what she'd been doing. "At least until we can be certain monsieur de La Reynie has not developed an interest in you."

"Not that I want to deny the wisdom of your suggestion,"

said Robert, "but the last time I left Paris I got shot, you'll recall."

"Well, that's not likely to happen again, is it? It's not as if there are unknown members of the d'Audemar family lurking in the bushes waiting for you to pass by. Whereas, by your admission to me tonight, there appear to be a number of people in the city who wish to do you ill."

"And even if I've finally understood what happened to you tonight, Robert, I still have no idea *why* it happened."

"You and I are both alike in that," Robert told her, hoping he was lying convincingly for a change. "But I can't help but think it might not look good if I suddenly fled the city. Don't want to give the authorities the wrong impression."

"You may be right," Maman said, though in a tone of voice suggesting she'd really believe this on the morning she found pigs nesting in the trees. "In which case I think the best thing to do—and I regret this as much as you likely do—is to talk to your cousin about this."

"I'm not sure how *Tell Lise About This* equates to not giving the authorities the wrong impression."

"She is family, Robert. She is not a policeman, and only occasionally is she a servant of his majesty."

Robert tried to think how Lise would react should he tell her everything, or even just more than he'd told his mother. All he could think of, though, was how badly his knee hurt.

Even the pain was obliterated, however, when the maître d' hôtel appeared at the bedroom door. "Madame," he said, glaring at Robert with disapproval, "there is an officer at the gate. He wishes to speak with monsieur le chevalier."

"Tell me his name again," Lise said. She looked unhappy;

at this hour of the day she had every right to be. "I want to be certain we looked for the right man."

"Antoine Chenal," Robert said. "He said he had the right—"

"To plead before the parlement," she said. "So, we were looking for the right man."

"Were? You—they—haven't arrested him?"

"He's disappeared."

"He can't have. It hasn't even been ten hours since—well, since last night. I saw him walk away from me toward the river." Robert leaned forward in the chair, rubbing his knee. Père Roffroi had worked his usual miracle of healing, but the leg still felt stiff, almost unreal.

"He did not come home last night, according to his maître d'hôtel. Which means," she added, sadly, "that you are apparently the last person to have seen him."

"That can't be true," he said. To himself he said, *That can't be good.* "There's at least one street-bravo who saw him leave at the same time I did."

"Robert, do you have any idea how many men in this city match the description you gave me?"

"I'm pretty sure he worked for a man named Clopard," he told her. "I can take you to his—well, his cellar, I suppose."

"I've been there. It's empty. Abandoned," she said. When he gaped at her she added, "How much of what you are involved in do you feel like sharing with me? I can't think it's a simple thing to drive a man like Clopard away. Lieutenant general de La Reynie has been trying to do that for years."

"Could I have something to drink?" He licked his lips. "Cognac would be nice. This feels like a Cognac sort of morning." He looked around the room—they were in a

small, sunlit salon at the back of the Hôtel de Bellevasse—
but failed to spot a decanter or bottle of any sort.

"I'll have one of the servants go out for coffee," she
said. "The last thing you need right now is alcohol." She
frowned. "Coffee is something we ought to be able to brew
ourselves. Remind me to talk to Rafael about that."

"I'm going to be drinking Cognac at some point today,
but for now I will be grateful for a cup of coffee. No, make
it a whole pot of coffee." Lise summoned a servant, issued
the order, then turned back to Robert. "What is going on,
Robert? I promise you can trust me."

Trust you to what? he asked, silently. To Lise he said, "It's
all a gigantic mistake. Somebody thinks I am something—
or some*one*—that I am not."

"All right. Let's start with the something. What would
that be?"

Robert knew he wasn't a good enough liar, so he didn't
even try. "A cloth smuggler," he said.

He hadn't tried to guess what her reaction would be, but
laughter definitely wasn't on the shortlist.

"Oh, Robert," she said, trying in vain to swallow a fit
of giggles. "How on earth could you have given them that
impression?"

"I'm not at all certain," he said. Which was the truth,
but only in the sense that he'd made a very educated guess
and hadn't had the chance to ask Clopard to confirm the
accuracy of that guess. "I think I was in the wrong place at
the wrong time."

"And I think that you're dissembling. You don't do that
very well, you know. Never did." She pierced him with a
look, then closed her eyes, humming tunelessly. "Clopard,
hmm? And you said you knew where his place was. Very
interesting. Now, I'm pretty certain none of your friends—

and forgive me, but I'm using that word very loosely—is possessed of the sort of mind a smuggler would need. So, it has to be somebody new in your life. I've heard stories about you and Jeanette Desmarais, but she isn't your type. So, who could it—oh, I'll wager I know." She opened her eyes and smiled at him in a leonine sort of way.

"It's Victoire de Berenguer, isn't it? There certainly are rumours about where she gets her money, and she dresses with a sense of style most of your mistresses only pretend to." She pointed a long, strong finger at him. "Tell me I'm right."

Robert exhaled, defeated. "I didn't mean to get mixed up in it," he said. "I was only trying to help. But she was in disguise—as a young man, something I'm sure you'll appreciate, cousin—and so I was the only noble in the room when the magic started flying. In retrospect it was only natural Clopard would think I was their master."

"*Their* master? Just how many people are involved in this?"

After he had given her as much information as he possessed, along with the few bits of guesswork he was prepared to share, she leaned back in her chair. "This is awkward."

"Not nearly as awkward as you being accused of murder," he told her. Which she certainly had been, and Robert had got himself shot trying to absolve her, so she owed him.

"Tactless of you to bring that up, cousin." She smiled as she said it, though. "It's my position that's awkward, not yours. You might even be able to avoid mentioning mademoiselle de Berenguer's name in the process of clearing your own. But I have just been told about a criminal conspiracy. And while it's definitely a small thing as far as the safety of the empire goes, it's still something I should report."

The seed of an idea sprouted in Robert's mind. "I'm not asking you to say nothing," he told her. "I'm just asking you to help me out a little bit and to maybe be in a bit less of a hurry to say anything to de La Reynie."

He could help himself, he realized, by helping Victoire. And he could help her by getting them both of them out of the city for a while.

The court was in a partying mood again. It had happened, Victoire learned, that the emperor had been ill for much of August, and it was only just before his return to Paris that his health had been restored. She thought she likely would have heard of this much earlier than today had she not been so caught up in the process of importing—and then losing—the year's second shipment of cloth.

The good weather drew people out-of-doors, and this afternoon both the imperial family and its courtiers were in the enormous gardens of the Tuilleries Palace. A cooling breeze made the stiff brocade of Victoire's dress almost comfortable to wear, and the young women with whom she spoke as she circulated were clearly enjoying the day. Victoire noted—with some disapproval—the ridiculous heights the new head-dresses were reaching; it was a pleasure to be unmarried and so not required to wear anything atop her curls.

A flash of brilliant colour caught her eye and she turned to see a bright painted-cotton overskirt disappear behind a hedge. "Sorry," she said to the girl she had been speaking to. "I have to run; just saw somebody I've been wanting to speak to." In truth she had only caught a glimpse of the cloth, and had no idea who wore it. But the cloth was patterned in a way she hadn't seen before, which meant there was a good chance it was a new arrival—and possibly hers.

The woman wearing the painted skirt was Marguerite de Geoffroy.

"Marguerite, you lucky woman," Victoire said when she finally came alongside her friend. "You've found some new cotton."

"Isn't it pretty?" Marguerite said, beaming with pleasure and pride. "And aren't those reds brilliant? I don't know what these curly designs are called, but they almost seem to move, don't they?"

I could have made *them move,* Victoire thought. To Marguerite she said, "They are beautiful. There's nothing like this in Paris just now, I'll wager." She took a careful look at her friend; she was still smiling. "If it's not too forward of me, where did you find this? I've been having no luck for the past week."

The smile didn't vanish, but it did seem to Victoire to have become more brittle. "I was only able to get enough to make this one skirt," she said. "Sorry."

"Not at all, Marguerite. I wasn't asking for you to give me any, or even sell me some. I just hoped I could ask your supplier if she—or he—could provide any cloth to me. My dressmaker is too idle lately." She punctuated the last with a small laugh, but Marguerite did not join in.

"I am not sure I'm at liberty to say," she said. "Much as I'd like to. You of all people should appreciate the danger of speaking hastily."

"And I do, believe me." *I would not have been so reluctant with you, Marguerite.*

As if she had heard the words, Marguerite smiled again. "Let me ask the person," she said. "After all, if anyone could be trusted with a name, it must be you."

"That would be very good of you."

"I'll try to get word to you by tomorrow. But please don't be too upset if it takes me a day or two longer. The person may not even be in the city right now."

"Of course," Victoire said. "And thank you, Marguerite. I am most grateful."

She continued to look at Marguerite as her friend skipped down the path and then turned around a flowered corner. Marguerite was not a wealthy woman, and had seemed upset when Victoire had first told her of the theft of her cloth. *So how did you come across that cloth, really? And why did you look so uncomfortable when I asked you about the source? Surely, I'm not the first person who's asked you about that.*

Perhaps she had been too quick to assume that Marguerite, as a friend, would never have been involved in the theft of her cloth.

Well, she now had a description of the cloth she could give to Marie-Louise. If Marie-Louise remembered buying that particular cloth in Milan, Victoire would know a bit more about how she had been betrayed.

And, of course Marguerite had visited the Hôtel de Berenguer many times. So, she knew Père Robillard.

"The curly things are called *paisley*, mademoiselle," Marie-Louise told her. "I believe it's a Persian thing, even though the cloth comes from India."

Victoire stopped her pacing. "And you bought this particular cloth for us?"

"I bought paisley cloth, yes. And it had really brilliant reds. I cannot swear that the cloth you saw this afternoon is the cloth I bought, mademoiselle, but it seems like it is, doesn't it?" Marie-Louise frowned. "Is there any chance of my seeing this skirt?"

"I wish there was. But if Marguerite is somehow involved with the theft of the cloth it doesn't seem to me she will want me to see it again." Victoire walked to the front door of the old house, turned and walked back to Marie-Louise. "I still have a hard time believing that a friend would betray me." She had returned to the house after dinner, to discover that neither Catherine nor Hachette had returned yet. It was still bright as mid-afternoon out in the streets, though; it might be hours yet before Hachette, in particular, made his way home again.

"It's possible the baronne didn't," Marie-Louise told her. "Perhaps it's as she suggested, and someone sold her the cloth without telling her who brought it in."

"I'd like to believe that," Victoire said. "But I don't know that I have that luxury at the moment." She was back at the front door again. Pacing wasn't doing her much good, and if she continued it she'd likely develop a headache. "Do we have any wine left?" she asked.

"I wouldn't feed what's left to Hachette," Marie-Louise began.

"I will happily provide some wine for us," said the chevalier de Vimoutiers from the open doorway. *Don't you ever knock? Victoire wondered.* "It turns out I've discovered a decent wine shop with affordable prices, and it's not that far from here. Well, it's on this side of the river at any rate." He waggled a finger at them. "Don't you go away, now. I'll be back in a few minutes. Well, before dark."

"That's wonderful," Victoire said to the now-closed door. "All I needed to make this a perfect day."

She'd been wrong in that, she realized once Robert de

187

Vimoutiers had returned and explained his reason for intruding on her privacy. No matter how badly things might go, they could always be worse.

"It's out of the question," she said—and held up a hand to stop Marie-Louise before the latter could object.

"I don't see why," he said. "You're short of cloth"—*and money,* she thought, and found it rather pointed his not mentioning this—"and it so happens I've got some spare money I'd be happy to invest in another trip over the mountains for you."

"You really are very kind," she said, not wanting that to be true, "but you've overlooked something important."

"I can always borrow more money if that's necessary," he said. Victoire guessed his smile was supposed to be supportive.

"What you've overlooked isn't money. It's the date. It's getting on to the end of September now."

"I hadn't overlooked that. I tend to make a note of the date, well, pretty much on a daily basis. Not that my present life really requires this, of course."

"If it's late-September now," she said, speaking to him as she would to a child, or at least any child who wasn't Hachette, "then it will be the end of the month at the earliest before my people can set out for the Italian lands. That means it will be at the very earliest the first week of November before they can reach Milan. With the best possible organization and luck they might—might—be ready to begin the trip home by the end of November."

"Still in time for Christmas," he said.

"Next Christmas, that is. Clearly you've never crossed the mountains before," she said.

"One of the reasons I was rather looking forward to it," he told her.

"I hope you have sufficient funds to support yourself, Marie-Louise and your servants until next spring," she replied, "because by the time you could be ready for the return trip the passes would be closed by snow. You would freeze to death if you were foolish enough to try the trip before spring."

"Oh." He looked more than upset at this news, which didn't make sense to Victoire, who had assessed his offer of financing as having been prompted by little more than boredom. "That is going to make things awkward," he added.

"Why? How could this possibly affect you?" she asked. The look he gave her made her cheeks burn, a little, and the back of her neck twitched, for reasons she didn't understand.

"I had been hoping to be out of town for the next few weeks," he said. "I understand now that I haven't really thought this through. But," he added, "if I don't find something to get me out of the city, m'cousin says, I might be in a bit of trouble. Um, because of you." He shrugged, and gave her a distinctly wobbly smile.

"Because. Of. Me." Victoire advanced on him—hating that the closer she got the more she had to look up at him. "You will please explain that," she said through clenched teeth.

"You won't like it, I think." When he saw the look on her face he rapidly retreated a couple of steps. She trusted the look made it clear how much she already disliked whatever *it* was. "It was when I helped you escape from Clopard's dungeon," he said.

"You mean, when you interfered in my private business with Clopard."

"I don't believe he thought of it that way. Two nights

189

ago, a couple of his men attacked me, under the orders of a lawyer who was—and is—a complete mystery to me."

She felt cold. "A lawyer?"

"A man named Chenal."

"Short, very thin, gigantic wig?"

"That's the fellow." He paused. "I suppose this means you know him."

"I do not," she said, with extra emphasis on the *not*. "I encountered him in much the same way as you did."

He grinned. "You see? We *are* working together. You just don't realize it yet."

"I do not see us as working together. Nor do I understand why in the name of heaven anyone, much less a lawyer, would think that I was taking orders from you." She suppressed the urge to hit him with the heaviest object available to hand: the broad. iron lid of the cook-pot.

De Vimoutiers turned his face away, closing his eyes. "I rather think he believes I'm the person running your, um, operation. Enterprise. That thing you do with the cloth. Because of Clopard. It seems to me Clopard was expecting you to have a noble with you—remember, mademoiselle, that you were disguised as a street-urchin that night—and then I arrived. Clopard has been following me around ever since, making crude threats about what might happen to me if I didn't throw in my lot with him and his chief. I kept telling him it wasn't me. For some reason he doesn't believe it."

"Clearly he doesn't know you very well," she spat.

"I really don't feel any better about this than you do," he said. "At least the police don't have you under suspicion."

"Oh, this is too much," she said. As if it wasn't bad enough that she now had to treat her friends as suspects, this aristocratic idiot was bringing the police into her orbit.

"Why are the police suspecting you, monsieur?" Marie-Louise asked.

"That lawyer I mentioned earlier? The one who seemed to be working with Clopard in trying to get me to hand over your business? Well, he's vanished. And as I killed one of his men who attacked me—"

"The more you say," Victoire said, "the more I agree with your cousin who thinks you should get out of town. Might I suggest you start now?" Her image of him, she realized, did not really support the concept of de Vimoutiers as killer of criminal lackeys.

"But where should we go?"

"We? There is no *we*, monsieur." *And I am not going anywhere, and especially not with you.*

"I thought we might accomplish more working together, mademoiselle. Or have you in fact recovered your cloth already?" He didn't come any closer, but the expression in his eyes seemed to. "We have already been yoked together by your enemies—my enemies too, now—and so it only seems reasonable to me that we should pool our strengths to defeat them."

"Strengths? All you seem to have done, monsieur, is to lead the police directly to me through this vanished lawyer. Please don't feel obliged to give me any more of that sort of help." *Don't forget,* a voice in her head spoke up, *that it was you who had Hachette bring him to the watch's attention that night.*

Chapter Twelve

Wounding and Healing

MARIE-LOUISE WAS OUT of breath when she burst through the front door of the old house two days later. "Hachette," she said, gasping. "Says. Père. Robillard. Is on. The move again."

"At last." Victoire leapt to her feet. Grabbing her shawl and gloves she met Marie-Louise in the doorway. "You can tell me about it while we walk."

"Fine, mademoiselle," she said, gulping enormous breaths. "Just not too fast, please. At least until I feel better."

That process took longer than Victoire had wanted, but she held her frustration in check; Marie-Louise was older and certainly wasn't used to running—if she ever had been. They were on the rue des Gravillers and still going east when Marie-Louise finally said, "Hachette says he came out of your parents' hôtel well after breakfast and walked north on St-Denis." *Of course he'd want to eat well first,* Victoire thought. "But he turned east almost immediately, so Hachette has decided he's going someplace new today. He went up St-Martin for a bit, then turned east again."

"Where does Hachette think he's going? Where are we to meet Hachette?"

"There is a cluster of cloth-merchants between rue

d'Orleans and the old rue du Temple," Marie-Louise said. "We think the priest is going there."

"Haven't we already visited those merchants?"

"Yes, but they were among the first we looked at, mademoiselle. It has been weeks since we last checked them. Something may well have happened since then."

I still find Robillard's behaviour peculiar, she thought. *But this gives me something to do and keeps me away from Robert de Vimoutiers.* "An excellent idea," she told Marie-Louise, and was pleased to see the older woman flush with pride.

The area into which they walked featured some of the grandest noble houses Paris could offer—hôtels owned by the de Guise, de Sourdy, and d'Estre families just to begin with—but as with most of Paris these magnificent homes existed mere paces away from the meanest sort of slum. They found Hachette in one such neighbourhood, a cramped block of crumbling houses whose upper floors didn't just project over the street, they seemed to be reaching toward their opposites across the road in order to provide mutual support. Victoire was reminded of the drunks she too often saw on the rue du Pet, staggering as they tried to hold each other up.

"Mademoiselle!" Hachette's grin was visible from the far end of the block, and he started to run towards Victoire and Marie-Louise, his bare feet kicking up dust from the dry street. *I ought to be in disguise,* she realized. It was too late now, though, and Hachette's enthusiasm had caused at least some of the neighbourhood's inhabitants to pay her more attention than she was comfortable with.

"He's been in that shop since the last quarter-hour rang," Hachette said once he was close enough that shouting wasn't required. "Maybe we've got him, hein?"

"Not so loudly," Victoire began. She froze, the rest of her admonition evaporating.

Across the street, a man had emerged from a doorway. He wore smoked glasses and carried a cane, and Victoire knew him: he was the blind-man-who-wasn't from the miracle courts. She was still calling up a prayer when the man drew a horse-pistol from beneath his mud-spattered cloak. The prayer wavered, then disintegrated when it encountered the steel of the pistol. She had only begun to shout a warning when the lock spurted flame and the shot erupted with an ear-crushing bang and a cloud of smoke.

It took a moment for Victoire to realize that she had not been shot. And another to realize that Hachette was on the street before her, not moving.

She heard herself scream, but it was anger and not fear that drove her voice. The false blind man looked directly at her, and she could see startled surprise in every visible aspect of his face even though his eyes were hidden from her.

Then he reached under his cloak again. *He's got a second pistol,* she thought.

"Marie-Louise! Your shoes!"

God bless her, Marie-Louise did not question the order, simply pulled off a sabot and tossed it to Victoire. Marie-Louise was still removing the second shoe when Victoire's new prayer sent the wooden shoe at high speed into the blind man's face.

She didn't need the second shoe.

The impact of the sabot on his nose caused the man to drop both pistols. And though they were still close enough to him to make Victoire's next prayer difficult to cast, they weren't close enough to prevent the spiritual blow from lifting him off his feet and slamming him into the wall behind him.

When she was certain the man wasn't going to get up anytime soon, Victoire rushed to Hachette and dropped to her knees, joining Marie-Louise in examining the boy's body. "I don't think he's badly hurt," Marie-Louise said. "I don't even see a hole in him, just a sort of tear across his arm. Good thing that was a blind man, I suppose." She laughed, in a brittle fashion that came close to tears.

"The man wasn't really blind," Victoire said, "and he wasn't aiming at Hachette."

"Good God," said Marie-Louise. "What does it mean?"

"At the very least it means we should pick up Hachette and get out of here as quickly as we can."

They had left the slum and were on rue des Quatre Fils when Hachette came to his senses again. "Put me down!" he shouted. "I'm not a baby and you don't need to carry me."

"Shut your mouth, boy," Marie-Louise snarled. "The mademoiselle has saved your worthless skin. The least you can do is thank her before you start shouting at her."

"Never mind," Victoire said, stopping and setting Hachette back onto his feet. "At least we're far enough away that we can do a proper job of treating that wound." She looked into Hachette's eyes. "Does it hurt very badly?"

"I've hurt worse when Marie-Louise boxes my ears," Hachette said. The fact that he winced as he was speaking somewhat spoiled the effectiveness of the bravado, but Victoire felt herself smiling nevertheless.

"Still," she said, "I'm going to try to stop the bleeding before we go any further. And then I want to have a priest

look at you. There's far too much blood here for my liking."
She gripped Hachette's good arm to keep him still, closed
her eyes, and began whispering the best healing prayer she
knew.

A rush of sensation so intense it was almost physical
pleasure flowed through her. For a moment she lost her
place in the prayer; then she realized she had felt something
like this before. She opened her eyes, and saw Robert de
Vimoutiers mouthing the same prayer, his eyes on her.
He looked unhappy, much too unhappy. She found the wit
to wonder, *Why is he so upset at a simple bullet-wound?*
And then: *Is it this way every time two people chain their
Blessings together?* Then the connection broke, and de
Vimoutiers was saying, "I believe this should hold him
together until you can get him to a priest." His expression
became more settled. No: more *guarded.*

"I tell you it's just a scratch," Hachette said. "The bastard
didn't even have the guts to look me in the eye when he
shot me." Hachette looked around. "Where is he?"

"It doesn't matter now," Victoire said. But her next words
were drowned out by a shriek from Marie-Louise.

"Mademoiselle, watch out! The threads!"

Victoire, startled by the fear in Marie-Louise's voice,
pulled back from Hachette—and felt herself stumble. She
tried to widen her stance, but her feet would not move;
as she tried, in fact, the force drawing her feet together
increased. "Damn it," she snarled, and hiked up the hem
of her skirt. Sure enough, the prayer-cursed cotton threads
had reappeared, and this time it was Victoire's feet and
ankles they were wrapping around. By the time she had
fully understood what was happening to her the threads had
swirled outward and were beginning to spin themselves
around her skirts. Cursing again as the threads began to

crush her skirts against her legs, Victoire crouched down to claw at the swirling cotton.

And cried out in pain as the magicked cotton sliced through her gloves as though they had been made of tissue paper. Losing her balance, she toppled to one side, cracking her elbow on the cobble-stones.

"No!" she shouted as de Vimoutiers grabbed at the threads. "Don't touch them!"

It was too late; he recoiled, grunting in pain and with his hands bloodied. Ignoring the evidence of his own eyes Hachette made to pull the threads away; he ended up screaming.

The threads wrapped themselves around the hem of her skirts and petticoat, drawing tight as they worked their way up to her knees. *I'm turning into a cocoon*, she thought. Then, absurdly, *I wonder what sort of butterfly I'll make?*

Marie-Louise ran down the street towards the gates of the Hôtel de Guise, screaming for help. But however many people had been on the rue des Quatre Fils when Victoire had reached it, nobody stood there now.

Victoire threw up her arms so that her hands were over her head, ignoring the pain in her bruised elbow. Whatever happened, she intended to keep her hands free as long as she could. She tried to slow her breathing, searching her mind for prayers that might be of some use. A prayer to assist in undressing ought to have had some impact on the growing cocoon, but it did not. Nor did any other prayer that could conceivably had anything to do with unwinding or unwrapping.

"All of you," she said, keeping her voice level. "Stand back, please."

"What are you going to do?" Hachette asked, his voice a sob.

"The only thing that's left to me. Get well back, and then—well, I suppose you should be ready to help me out if this prayer works."

She closed her eyes and, breathing deeply, summoned up the most powerful prayer she knew.

The pressure against her was surprisingly gentle. So was the soft *whump* she heard as the prayer countered and then destroyed the prayer that had made the cotton thread attack her. She flexed and then threw her feet apart; it happened easily. *You have to move quickly,* she told herself. Already the smell of burning was in her nostrils.

"Holy Mother of God," Hachette shouted. "Victoire, you're on fire!"

I think I'm aware of that, she replied to herself, rolling in the dust and hoping the flames themselves weren't magical.

Hachette was at her side, beating the burning cloth with perhaps a bit too much enthusiasm. She decided not to complain; suddenly she felt very tired.

She opened her eyes to find Hachette kneeling beside her. Robert was at her other side, palms resting messily on her skirt. Which was, yes, badly scorched. *That's the end of this dress,* she thought. Neither of them was looking at her, though. Following Robert's gaze, she found herself likewise staring at the tiny tongues of sorcerous flame given off by the floating threads as God—or the Devil— drew them back from the world.

Whoever cast that prayer at me isn't going to be happy, she thought. "I think," she said, "it would be wise if we got ourselves out of here."

She could not get herself up off the cobbles. "Marie-Louise?" she called. Her voice seemed very faint to her.

Perhaps just a bit of a rest, then.

When the world returned to Victoire the first face she saw was that of Père Robillard. The priest's eyes were closed in concentration and she knew, by the absence of pain in her hands, that it was she he was concentrating on.

"Hachette," she muttered, her mouth feeling disgusting. "How are Hachette's hands?"

"He's fine," said Robert de Vimoutiers. "Your père and I took care of him first. Well, second, I suppose—after we'd smacked down another attempt to pray you on fire."

"What, in the name of anything sacred, are you doing here?" Victoire was suddenly conscious of the fact that everything she was wearing was blood-spattered—and that her face, from the way it felt and smelled, was blackened with soot. Other-worldly soot at that. It was absurd, that she should suddenly have a desire to change into better clothes.

"I am assisting you, mademoiselle," Père Robillard said in a quiet, acid voice.

Victoire felt her blush increase. "My apologies, père," she said. "I didn't mean you. I was speaking to—to that man there."

"You should be thanking him," the père said. "He has been most helpful."

"Could I ask you to repeat that to m'mother sometime?"

"Monsieur..." she said through gritted teeth. Then, realizing this was getting her nowhere, she turned to the priest.

"My père, I owe you a tremendous debt of thanks. I do not understand any of what has just happened, but I am not so out of my senses that I don't recognize what you've done."

"What don't you understand, child?"

There was no polite way to answer him. "Any of this. Why you would help me. I thought you despised me."

"And so you despised me in turn?" He shook his head, but she could read no emotion into the act. "It is my duty, mademoiselle Victoire, to love the sinner even as I object to the sin. You needed help; I was duty-bound to provide it.

"As, in fact, I have been trying to do for some weeks now."

She had been trying to sit up. Now she fell back, stunned. "Your visits to seamstresses and cloth-merchants were to *help* me?"

The priest sat back on his haunches as hands lifted her up into a sitting position. Some of those hands, she realized, belonged to Robert de Vimoutiers. Somehow she wasn't as angry about that as she ought to have been.

"Mademoiselle, what you are doing is both morally and legally wrong, but it has been clear to me for some time that your unhappiness about—well, about the current state of your business, I suppose—has been causing a great deal of anxiety and unpleasantness in your father's house. I decided that if I could help you to find your missing cloth it might restore the peace between you and your mother."

"You have been trying to help me find my cloth." *Why do I feel so stupid?* Victoire asked herself. "You weren't trying to destroy me."

"Destroy you? My girl, if anything I have been trying to *save* you."

Damn damn damn *it!* She felt tears filling her eyes.

"There's no need to be upset," Père Robillard said. "It is my duty as a man of God, child, to restore harmony between mother and daughter."

Victoire did not think it would be a good idea to tell the priest that the tears she'd shed were tears of frustration.

The one solid suspect I had, she thought, *and he turns out to think he's my ally.* "I don't suppose you found the cloth," she said after a long pause.

"You are certain you feel well, mademoiselle?"

"I am, Marie-Louise." Victoire brushed a stray strand of hair from in front of her eyes. "I'm just very tired. The kind of praying I've been doing today takes a lot out of one."

"I understand, mademoiselle. So would it not make more sense for us all to rest at the house until you've recovered your strength and Hachette's wounds have fully healed?"

"I'm fine," Hachette grumbled. His usual spirit was lacking though, and it didn't sound to Victoire as if even Hachette expected anyone to believe him. "I can rest on the floor the way I always do."

"I'm afraid," Robert de Vimoutiers said from behind them, "that your mistress is correct, young garçon. A day of bed rest will be better for you than a week on any floor."

"He could take my bed, then," Marie-Louise said. "I don't see why it's necessary to smuggle him into your parents' home."

"Well," said de Vimoutiers, "we can't very well smuggle him into *my* parents' home. M'mother would definitely not understand."

"There is room for all of us in the Hôtel de Berenguer," Victoire said, wishing de Vimoutiers had gone his own way but too tired to argue with him. "You will not be noticed up on the servants' floor. And I owe this to you, Marie-Louise, and to Hachette. Let's not argue about it."

She left de Vimoutiers in the courtyard while she escorted Hachette and Marie-Louise into the house through the kitchen. Once she had them safely upstairs, and Hachette in bed—and the servants sworn to secrecy—she went back to the courtyard, feeling as if her feet were encased in iron anchors. She wanted nothing more than to sleep for a full day, or possibly a week. But there was still a clue that had to be followed up, and at the moment Robert de Vimoutiers was the only person capable of helping her—however much she loathed the idea of it.

"How are your hands?" she asked him on her return to the courtyard. "I hope your gloves provided more protection than mine did."

"I wanted to replace them anyway," he said. She noted that he hadn't actually answered her question, but decided not to press. They had more important things to discuss.

"You told me," she said to him, "that you wanted to help." She walked past him to the ancient stone bench Papa had transported here from the ancestral chateau, and sat down, not looking back to see if he followed.

"And I meant what I said." He sat beside her, leaving a scandalously small amount of space between his legs and hers. "Command me, I beg of you." He smiled that idiot smile of his, but Victoire was too tired and too upset to be bothered by it. He kept his hands out of sight, she noted.

"If Père Robillard is not the person I thought he was," she told him, "then I can think of only one who could have attacked me with those cursed threads."

"Name him," de Vimoutiers said, "and I'll bring you his head on a platter." He thought for a moment. "That's from the Bible, isn't it?"

She suppressed a sigh. He was, she knew, doing his best to distract her from the seriousness of the situation. "It's not a him," she said. "It's Marguerite de Geoffroy."

He recoiled, and she didn't think he was jesting. "Isn't she a good friend of yours?" He frowned. "And why would a woman—oh, never mind. I was babbling again." He looked at her with some alarm, and she wondered what the expression on her face looked like. *I would like to remember that look, should I need it again to keep him in line.* The thought made her sit up. *Why would I need to keep him in line?* She shook her head. *Focus on the issue at hand,* she told herself. Robert de Vimoutiers was someone she'd recruited to help her out. That was all.

"She is a friend, yes—or at least I had thought she was." Victoire looked away from him, staring down onto the gravel path that ran through the centre of the courtyard. "But of all my customers, she is the only one to have found a new source of cloth—and Marie-Louise thinks there's a good chance the cloth Marguerite was wearing the last time I saw her came from the batch that was stolen from me."

She took a deep breath. "And—and this is not the first time someone has used prayer to set cotton threads attacking me. It happened outside the Tuilleries Palace a couple of weeks ago. Right after I'd had a conversation with Marguerite about stolen cloth."

She couldn't stay still. Getting to her feet she turned—and bumped into de Vimoutiers, who had hastened to his feet in response to her rising. She stepped back, awkwardly. "Monsieur de Vimoutiers, I would be happy to learn that Marguerite is not an enemy, but for now I don't know *anything.* I would be grateful, monsieur, if you—"

"Don't you think it's past time we started calling each other Robert and Victoire?" he asked. "You never answered me the last time I asked you this. But now, after all, we have shared blood in common. Granted it was mostly poor Hachette's blood, but I'm sure he won't begrudge that."

"Do you never take anything seriously?" *I want a bath,*

she thought. *A week-long bath, followed by a week-long sleep.*

"*Seriously* is overrated," he said, and for an instant there was no levity in his face or voice. That was a decidedly uncomfortable experience, and Victoire found herself grateful when he returned to his normal idiotic, animated self. "I do hope, my dear Victoire, that whatever my failings I will still be of use to you. What do you want me to do about madame de Geoffroy?"

"I don't really know," she confessed. *What really concerns me is* why *Marguerite had anything to do with the attack on me. Surely she couldn't think I would object if all she had done was find a new source of smuggled cloth.* "I have to know if she is trying to harm me. If you tell me she is, then I'll have to think about what to do next. But not before that."

"You're being evasive," he said. "Don't try that on me; I'm an expert. Is the baronne, or is she not, someone you think a serious threat to you?"

"Don't turn this into your own project," she told him. "All I am asking of you is a simple favour: investigate Marguerite de Geoffroy and see if she is in league with anyone truly dangerous—someone like Clopard, for instance." She pulled a piece of paper and the stub of a pencil from her skirt pocket and, writing Marguerite's direction on it, gave it to him.

"You sound like m' mother," he said. "If I didn't know better, I'd swear she had given you pointers on how to deal with me."

Exasperation boiled over. "Please," she told him. "This is not a Moliere comedy and we are not acting. Somebody is definitely trying to kill me and beggar my friends and I do not want to laugh about it. So, if you wouldn't mind, please keep your parlour-jest observations to yourself and let me be miserable if I wish!" She should have been embarrassed to be crying in front of this well-meaning fool, but embarrassment seemed to be wasted on him, and so she didn't try to stop.

Tears, at least, seemed to be able to shut him up when nothing else would, and for several long moments he simply walked beside her, radiating discomfort and with one arm twitching occasionally, as though it felt it ought to be around her shoulder but couldn't summon the energy and will to make the move.

Eventually he coughed and said, "So, once I've obtained some useful intelligence about madame de Geoffroy we can discuss next steps. By that time young Hachette should be back on his feet again and will be ready to chase down the man who shot him. And perhaps we can bait the villain—whomever it is—in his—or her—lair, or whatever it is one does when hunting game."

When she turned on him, he raised his hands and added, "But for now I think that what would be best if for you to have a long, hot bath and a good dinner and perhaps sleep the clock round." He took a step backward, and she couldn't tell whether the panic in his face was feigned or real. "Yes, that would definitely be the thing that I would prescribe. If I were your physician, or your, um, priest. Yes. Definitely. Lord, I'm babbling again."

"You are," she said, ignoring the red stripes crossing his palms that his gesture had revealed to her, and somehow the tears had stopped.

To the east Robert could see trees marking the spot where the city walls were being replaced by the Boulevard; south, a couple of short blocks to his right, were the impressive facades of the Place Imperial. This was a wealthy neighbourhood, one that he was pretty sure was above the touch of an ordinary baron like de Geoffroy.

The Hôtel de Geoffroy was on the small side, tucked in as it was against the Minimes convent on rue des Minimes, but from what Robert had been able to see of it from the corner it was a new—or newly renovated—and impressive house. Again, far more impressive than he'd thought de Geoffroy could afford, given the debts he'd accrued during his military career.

Lise had said something to him about this, hadn't she? He tried to remember. *Anyone who suddenly seems to have more money than he should,* she'd said. Well, something to that effect, anyway.

"Well," he said to the dog sniffing at a wall on the corner, "this seems to qualify as more money than he ought to have." But it wasn't the baron Victoire had asked him to investigate. "Surely the baronne isn't a Habsburg spy. What do you think?" The dog looked up at him, wagged its tail in a hopeful sort of way, then on realizing no food would be forthcoming, curled its lip at him and wandered off. "You're no help," he said to its hind-quarters.

Perhaps he'd spoken too loudly. Up the street a lackey appeared from the gate of the Hôtel de Geoffroy—and a singularly ill-favoured lackey, at that. The man stared at Robert for a moment, then darted back inside the gate. There was a brief burst of shouting from inside the grounds, then the shouting stopped abruptly.

"That is not very welcoming," Robert murmured. "Time I was moving on, I think." He did not run, but he made certain he was not sauntering either, because that shouting had strongly implied impending pursuit.

It very much appears that madame de Geoffroy is no

longer a friend of Victoire's, he said to himself. *I'm most sorry Victoire was right about that.*

A shadow flitted across his path; looking up he saw something fly past him, well over his head and headed south-east. *That's not a bird,* he realized. "Prayers with wings," he said aloud. "What *will* they think of next?"

He had planned to seek refuge with the marquise de Réalmont in Place Imperial, just two blocks from here. But that refuge lay in the direction the mysterious object was taking, and Robert now wanted to be as far away as possible from wherever the flying prayer was going. Slipping into a narrow lane between buildings fronting rue St-Louis, he cut across to the rue des Francs Bourgeois. If by some chance Fortune Vidal had returned to Paris with his bride, Robert could shelter with the jeweller while sending a message to Lise and Rafael. And if Vidal was still out of town, this route still took him away from de Geoffroy and toward the safety of home.

Fortune Vidal's shop was open, but monsieur Vidal himself was not yet returned. Robert did not feel comfortable imposing on the hospitality of a man who wasn't around to grant it, and so after leaving a brief note to Vidal he set out again, this time on a south-westerly course that would move him through the busier streets around the Hôtel de Ville and, eventually, the rue St-Honoré.

He did not reach his goal.

"Monsieur le chevalier de Vimoutiers?" It was a sergeant of the city archers who stopped him, and very polite he was. But the full squad arrayed behind him in the middle of the street did not look nearly so polite.

Without waiting for Robert to confirm his identity, the sergeant reached out and clapped a hand on Robert's shoulder. "I am charged to arrest you in the name of the emperor, monsieur. You will please come with us."

"Y'know," Robert told him, staring with hauteur at the sergeant's hand until it lifted from his shoulder, seemingly of its own volition, "I was just about to present myself to the authorities anyway. Would you like to keep me company as I do so?"

For a moment the sergeant looked puzzled. Then, apparently deciding that thinking wasn't going to get him anywhere, he grabbed Robert's shoulder again, spun him around and said, "You will please come with us."

"You have a few things to learn yet about polite discourse," Robert said.

He was still wrestling with the manifest unfairness of this treatment when he realized he was being escorted back along the rue des Francs Bourgeois. That would make sense if he were being taken to the Bastille and not to the Châtelet on the right bank north of the Île de la Cité, but what really mattered was that this route took him back past Fortune Vidal's jewellery shop.

As they approached the shop Robert tripped himself, stumbling deliberately into the shop-front and banging the large window. Luck was with him: Vidal's nephew was in the front of the shop with a customer, and looked up just as Robert was hauled back to his feet by the sergeant.

As the younger Vidal's eyes widened, Robert clasped his hands together in front of him in prayer, hoping the message they sent was *Help me* or something similar. Then, resisting the sergeant so that the man had to forcibly pull him away, Robert—locking his gaze to young Vidal's— slowly drew his right forefinger across his throat.

"Aren't you supposed to have a *lettre de cachet* when you

arrest a nobleman?" Robert asked the sergeant. "I demand to see that letter."

"All will be answered in due time," the sergeant said. He spat into the street. "Me, I just do what I'm told."

"Do you?" Robert asked. "If I told you to jump into the river where the sewers dump into it, would you do that?"

The sergeant did not favour him with an answer.

Chapter Thirteen

Walls Do Not a Prison Make, But Iron Does

"On whose orders have I been arrested?" Robert demanded. "And on what charge? Where is the *lettre de cachet*? I demand to see it, or you will have to face the wrath of the duchesse de Vimoutiers." *And if that doesn't put the fear of God into you, you're a duller-witted man even than I thought.*

The turnkey shrugged his shoulders and walked away, clearly unimpressed. *I should have demanded to see de La Reynie,* Robert decided. *Why do the best things to say always occur to me when it's too late?*

He had never been inside the Bastille before, but he knew people who had been, and he was pretty sure most cells were nicer than the one he'd been put in. For one thing, there was no window in this dank, wet, smelly chamber; what little light there was leaked in, under the door, from the torchlit corridor. Which made sense, given that he had been taken *down* several flights of stairs rather than up into the towers, where prisoners were normally kept. Plus, he was fairly certain that a cell occupied by a nobleman would have shown signs of having been whitewashed in the past decade. There probably would have been some furniture in it as well.

There was no question of the jailers not realizing his noble status, because he had no sooner entered the Bastille walls than he had been fitted with a thin iron collar and matching bands around his wrists and ankles. These weighed just enough to be uncomfortable without quite crippling him. They did, however, cripple his powers of prayer, making it impossible for him to magic his way out of here, or even to send a message—had he known how to generate that flying prayer-thing, which he didn't.

Very little of this adds up to anything official, he decided. So the question was, on whose authority had he been brought here, and how had that authority managed to convince the warden of the prison to ignore all of the rules governing aristocratic prisoners?

An obvious place to start was the lawyer, Chenal. But how could he have been involved, given the police themselves were looking for him and had been for several days? The only other enemy Robert could name was Clopard, and Clopard had also vanished—and anyway, no archer worthy of his tabard would have listened to anything Clopard had to say unless it had been said under torture.

Feeling deflated, Robert realized nobody would even know he was here. He hadn't told anyone at the family hôtel where he was going when he'd set out this morning to follow Victoire; and even Victoire knew nothing beyond the fact he'd promised to investigate the baronne de Geoffroy for her. Would Vidal's nephew correctly interpret his signs, and notify Victoire? If the young man failed him, how long would it take for Victoire to worry about Robert when he didn't report back to her? It was horribly possible she would simply decide that he'd fouled things up, and stop thinking about him.

He did not, he realized, want her to stop thinking about him.

The odds are, he told himself, *that you're going to have to get yourself out of here. Or at least start that ball rolling, by finding a way of letting Lise know you're here.*

He walked around the cell, which at least was big enough to be walked around.

On closer inspection the room turned out to be full of iron, almost to the point of making the collar and bands he wore irrelevant: heavy manacles, fixed to heavier chains, were bolted to massive iron plates that in turn were spiked into the stone walls. Robert was convinced he'd found bits of some poor bastard's bones in the rank straw beneath the manacles. The bars in the door were iron, and even heavier than the chains and manacles. And then there were the door's iron straps and hinges, and the massive, crude lock. You could have held the entire College of Cardinals in this room and their magic couldn't have defeated all that cold metal.

They had taken his purse, of course—and much good it would do them, empty as it was—and his épée and dagger when they had arrested him, so he had no tools with which to pretend to pick the lock on the door. Not that he'd have known what to do or where to go if he had been able to get himself through the door.

He began to pat himself down, wondering if he'd hidden something inside his clothes that might be of some use to him. He felt, and heard, a crinkling sound, and then something jabbed his chest. *Oho,* he thought. Turning his back to the door he fumbled inside his waistcoat to open his shirt. Inside the shirt and against his skin were the pencil-stub and the paper on which Victoire had written the directions to the Hôtel de Geoffroy.

After thinking a moment, Robert carefully tore the paper into eight pieces. He walked to the door, and its faint glow, and lay down on the cold floor where the light was best. Then, on each piece of paper, he wrote:

Arrested and held in non-noble cell. Contact duchesse de Bellevasse. Do not trust archers or any other police. You will be rewarded.

—*de Vimoutiers*

Now all he needed was a way to get his message out into the world.

"I think your new glamour should be a young man as handsome as you are pretty," said Catherine as she stirred some sugar into the drinking chocolate Victoire had smuggled upstairs for them. "It ought to be easier to maintain, don't you think?"

"You are such a romantic, Catherine," said Marie-Louise. "Beautiful young men get noticed, and mademoiselle Victoire doesn't want to draw attention to herself, remember?" She took the cup Catherine handed to her, then added, "Still, you can't really go the Hachette way again, can you, mademoiselle? Too many people seem to be familiar with his appearance now for anything similar to be safe."

Victoire nodded. "True. It was a good enough guise for its time, but I suspect that anything smacking of our dear Rat-boy is no longer a workable option, is it? I'm not sure I like the idea of being a young man of good address, though. Marie-Louise is right about that." She held out her hand.

"Well, if you can't be a handsome noble," Catherine said, passing chocolate to Victoire, "then you should aim for petit-bourgeoisie. Be a miller's son, or a weaver's. Not another street urchin."

"From somewhere nearby but not too close," Marie-Louise added. "In our part of the city, everybody knows everybody else."

"Thank you both," Victoire said, laughing. "You have done all my work for me; now all I have to do is write the new prayer and learn it."

"Oh, you're most welcome, mademoiselle," Catherine said, and she laughed too. Then she frowned, saying, "I don't understand why you have to go to that woman's house yourself. Can't one of us do this for you? Hachette would love to go, I'm sure."

"Don't you dare mention this to Hachette," Victoire warned them. "He's to rest until Père Robillard pronounces him healed. If Marguerite de Geoffroy truly is the one who has stolen our cloth, I will need a healthy Hachette to help me deal with her."

"I thought the chevalier was investigating the Geoffroy for you," Marie-Louise said.

"I thought that as well," Victoire said, feeling the laughter leak from her. "And yet here we sit, hours later, and has he sent us a word? He has not."

"Could something be wrong, then?"

"If his falling prey to the sudden urge to drink and gamble with his friends is something wrong, Marie-Louise, then yes, something could be wrong." *I shouldn't be taking this so personally,* she thought. *After all, I'm the one who told him not to make this a project of his own.*

"Mademoiselle," said Catherine in a quiet voice, "I think it's just possible you are doing the chevalier a disservice."

"The fact remains, Catherine," said Marie-Louise with supportive acerbity, "that the chevalier has not reported back to mademoiselle, and so we are none of us any wiser about the threat the Geoffroy might pose than we were this afternoon."

"And whether or not I am doing him a disservice, the fact also remains that I have to know, and know as quickly as I can, more about what Marguerite may be up to—and I do not know anything at the moment. Someone has tried to kill me, twice, today, and if that person is Marguerite then I have to be ready to take action against her."

Victoire stood up. "I am going down to my room, to use the table there for writing out the new prayer." She felt for the pencil, snarling to herself when she remembered giving it to Robert. "I will be back in a little while, and we can discuss plans while I practise the prayer."

The sun had set by the time Victoire was satisfied with the wording of her glamour's new prayer. She still hoped to venture out to investigate the Hôtel de Geoffroy despite the darkness, but that hope died when she returned to the small bed-chamber in which she'd placed Catherine and Marie-Louise.

"Hachette, what are you going here?" Victoire demanded. "You are supposed to be resting in bed." To Marie-Louise and Catherine she said, "You weren't supposed to say anything to him, remember?"

"We didn't," Marie-Louise said. "He showed up here on his own. Didn't you, Rat-boy?"

"Hey!" Then his eyebrows lifted. "Say anything to me about what?"

"Nothing, Hachette. I am going to be practising a new prayer that Catherine and Marie-Louise helped me with. I just didn't want you getting all excited. Père Robillard said you were to rest in bed."

"Bah," he said. "Rest is for old women. I am fine, mademoiselle Victoire. Your priest—and what a sour apple that one is—did a fine job of healing all of my hurts." He gave Victoire his biggest buck-toothed grin, waving his hands to show the pink, healthy palms. *Good lord*, Victoire thought. *He's even washed them.* "If he always prays that hard when he's healing, it's no wonder he eats like a fat bourgeois."

"In the countryside," said Catherine with a smile, "we'd have said he eats like a hog or a horse."

Victoire laughed, with Marie-Louise joining her. It was going to be very difficult, Victoire decided, to overcome the prejudices of several years' nurture, and begin thinking of the père in a less-hostile way. "Whatever his dietary habits, we should be thankful for his help, you know. And I still think you should be in bed."

"I'm well enough to watch you practise your prayer," Hachette said, his face set.

Victoire immediately abandoned all hope of getting out of the house tonight. "Very well," she told him. "But as soon as I see you getting tired, off to bed with you and no argument." Hachette scowled, but did not dispute her.

Victoire unfolded the sheet of paper she'd worked on. "I have taken your advice, and made this glamour to suggest the appearance of a young apprentice. A moderately good-looking apprentice," she added with a smile at Catherine. "My only concern is the archers don't get along well with apprentices. I don't want to attract any official attention."

"You shouldn't, mademoiselle," said Marie-Louise, "provided you're with us. Or at least not with other apprentice boys. It's the gangs of apprentices the archers watch out for."

"And that," added Catherine, "is because gangs of apprentices truly are dangerous."

"And gangs of students," added Hachette. "It's not just workers who behave badly, you know."

"Believe me, I know," said Marie-Louise. "I worked near the Latin Quarter once."

"I'd love to talk about that sometime," Victoire said. "I know nothing at all about the university, and I think that perhaps I ought." She bent over the paper. "But for now, I'm an apprentice."

"Let's make you a weaver's apprentice," Marie-Louise said. "I can teach you a bit about the work, and some of the slang weavers use."

"That's a wonderful idea, Marie-Louise. Thank you." Victoire closed her eyes for a moment, opening connections between herself and God. This wasn't going to be easy, she realized: she was still spiritually tired from the afternoon's exertions. But she had to try; if she was going to track down Marguerite tomorrow she had to get comfortable with the prayer tonight.

Opening her eyes, she began to read the prayer, whispering it because she wasn't yet familiar enough with the new components to be able to recite it silently, by heart. The transition began to shimmer into effect, but then it began to fight back, like muscles tightened from prolonged lack of use.

Hachette giggled, but Victoire was able to ignore that. She had a bit more trouble with the sound of Marie-Louise smacking the boy on the head, but after a moment's pause was able to continue through to the end. The stress of willing the prayer into effect was worse than the pain of lifting heavy bales of cloth, but after too much time she felt the transition complete its shimmer through her.

Exhaling, she felt her shoulders slump. *I'm so tired,* she thought. She kept the thought to herself, though, and opened her eyes.

To find the others staring at her in admiration. "Mademoiselle, you look *perfect,*" Catherine breathed. "Even the clothing is right."

"I'll make that easier to do," Victoire said, "by dressing the part rather than forcing the glamour to do it. That way I'll be able to keep it showing for longer." She looked at Marie-Louise. "What was he laughing about?"

"Oh, mademoiselle," Hachette said, whooping, "it was amazing! You looked like a boy, but you were still dressed as yourself. I never saw anything so funny!"

"What a good thing I have you with me, Hachette. This way I will never fall into the sin of false pride."

Victoire took a deep breath and let the glamour fade. "Again," she said and bent over the paper to read the prayer.

They fed him after some time had passed—the man who brought the food told him the sun was setting outside—and while the meal was pathetic Robert immediately realized some of it could be useful to him. The broth he drank down quickly—trying to taste as little as possible—but about half of the bread he tore into chunks. Into each chunk he inserted a rolled-up copy of his note, into a gap he clawed between the tooth-shattering crust and the gummy, gritty crumb. Better to turn the bread into a weapon than to injure himself trying to eat it, he decided. And anyway, the sort of person who'd pick up a piece of this bread from the street was probably going to be desperate enough that the promise of a reward from a stranger would be a tremendous incentive.

Tucking the bread-missiles into the cuffs and pockets of

his coat, Robert walked over to the door. Outside a torch glowed, with no fluttering of the flame to indicate the movement of even the smallest of breezes. There was no sound, either. So far as he could tell he was all alone in this dungeon—which would make it rather difficult to put the next part of his plan into action.

Throwing my message out into the corridor isn't going to do me much good, he decided. *And where else could I reach?* Again, he cursed the collar and bands that crippled him.

"Stop being such an ass," he told himself. Cousin Lise had often told him that she considered her absence of a proper Blessing to be—well, something of a blessing. *I was never able to take shortcuts,* she said once. *Having to do things the hard way has been good for me. Well, from time to time it has.*

Well, now was his chance to learn how to do things for himself. *The Lord helps those who help themselves,* he reminded himself. That had always seemed a pointless platitude before—what was the point, when prayer worked so well?—but now he found himself with a new respect for scripture. Or wherever it was he'd come across the saying.

Sooner or later something has to happen, he decided. *Either someone comes to take me before the emperor, or Maman turns the entire city upside-down to find me.* Unsure of which was the more likely, Robert lowered himself to the filthy straw in one corner of the floor of his cell.

Robert was awakened, from a sleep scarcely worthy of the name, by the sound of his cell door rattling open. "Get up," a man said. Robert, half-blinded by sleep and the light from torches behind the man in the doorway, did as ordered while trying to make out the man's face.

"To whom have I the pleasure of speaking?" he asked. He shrugged into his coat, which he'd been using as a pillow, then adjusted his waistcoat in order to distribute the remaining bread-messages to where they wouldn't be obvious. "And why are you here in the middle of the night?"

"Who I am is none of your business," the man said. "Why I'm here is that you're being moved."

"But I was just becoming comfortable here."

The man snorted. "I see your reputation for fatuousness is well-earned." He stepped back into the corridor and Robert caught a momentary glimpse of a narrow, long face wearing a priest-like expression. The man wore a very plain hat over what looked like his own hair. *Definitely a member of the prison staff,* he decided. *Nobody who could afford to dress himself would be seen dead looking like that.* Prudence made him keep this thought to himself.

"Has my family been notified?" he asked. "I would rather think m'mother would have arrived here by now."

"The people who need to know have been notified," the man said. "Now move. And keep your mouth shut, or you'll be bound and gagged." The man's voice was educated if not cultivated, and the tone held authority even if the timbre was thin and the pitch on the high side for the sort of man he appeared to be.

He might be a prison official, Robert decided, *but this is definitely not an official action. How much trouble am I in now?* Could this man be the chief of whom Clopard and Chenal spoke? For a mad moment Robert was tempted to ask what had happened to the lawyer. Instead he stepped into the corridor and followed the man away from the cell.

As he walked he took quick, furtive looks at the men who formed his escort. Again, it was difficult to make out much in the way of facial detail in the gloomy torchlight of this underground corridor. But he saw enough to know the men didn't wear the blue tabard of the main Paris police force. So if these really were policemen—and who else would have been allowed into the Bastille unsupervised?—they belonged to one of the mysterious forces of which he'd heard only rumours, even from Cousin Lise.

They took him back up the way they had taken him down, and one of the escort laughingly told the adjutant inside the entry hall, "Your *cachots* are empty again, fellow. Thanks for the loan." The men on watch at the prison entrance were very careful to look away when Robert was brought to the gate, and again he wondered at the unusual behaviour of the men taking him away. For a moment he considered dropping one of his messages on the way out. By the time he'd made up his mind to actually do this, though, he was already outside and crossing the moat separating the prison fortress from the eastern edge of Paris.

The streets echoed weirdly to the sound of the hobnailed boots of his escort. Robert wasn't much disturbed by this, however, as he had to admit to a fair amount of experience of walking these streets after curfew. When the party turned onto rue St-Antoine he casually slipped his right hand into the cuff of his left sleeve and wrapped his fingers around a piece of bread.

Without turning his head too much, he glanced at the men on either side. None seemed to be looking at him.

He dropped the piece of bread between his legs and onto the cobble-stones of the street.

Now he just had to pray the bread survived exposure to traffic for long enough to attract the attention of one of the thousands of hungry people in eastern Paris.

The strange party snaked its way through the side-streets

of the east side of the city, down rue Percée and rue de Norman to the rue de la Mortellerie. A second bread-message fell to the pavements outside the Petit St-Antoine hospital, a third as they passed rue des Barres, and a fourth fell into the place de Grève, near the Hôtel de Ville.

With his escorts seeming to pay him no attention at all, Robert was free to do something he'd never done when rushing home after a night of inebriated gambling: look closely at the nocturnal face of his city.

The moon was in its final quarter, and the streets and buildings were the colour of slate save for the few areas touched by lantern-light. The emperor had commanded every property owner to display a lantern outside his property so the streets would be illuminated, but like so many laws this one was nodded at without being much obeyed. So, the streets through which Robert passed were darkly menacing tunnels into which occasional shafts of gold intruded. What interested him the most was the way the stray bits of lantern-light were picked up by the glass of the windows from the opposite side of the street. They seemed to ripple, bronze washing against indigo, in a way that made him curious as to the cause.

"Why do you suppose the window-glass looks that way?" he asked, of nobody in particular.

"Shut up, you," said a voice from behind him. "Chief, can I belt him if he speaks again?"

"*Chief?*" Robert nearly stopped, before realizing his astonishment would not be taken as such by the escort. "What an interesting name for a policeman to use." *He should have said* Captain *or* Lieutenant *if these truly were policemen.* "So how is our dear friend Clopard? I haven't heard from him for quite a while."

"This is your last warning," the chief snapped. "Open

your mouth again and I'll stop it up with your boots. As for you," he said to the men around him, "shut your temple-damned mouths as well."

Shrugging his shoulders, Robert shut his mouth and resumed observation.

Through gaps in the buildings to his left he could see the Seine, could hear its splash and gurgle as it washed against the beach below the place de Grève, could definitely smell the river as it made its sewage-laden way to the sea; the smell of the effluent warred for supremacy with the stink of freshly spilled blood from the slaughter-houses just to the north. If you ignored the evidence of your nose, the moon and the stars made it look as if the river actually bore diamonds to the sea. Robert decided it would be wisest to keep his thoughts pointed in the direction of gold and diamonds rather than to worry pointlessly about upcoming events over which he had little to no control.

He dropped another message onto the quay Peltier.

Robert didn't realize where he was being taken until he was practically under the arch of its entry. The Grand Châtelet was not a place nobles visited. It was scarcely a place they acknowledged, unless they had the misfortune to be charged with treason. The building squatted atop the rue St-Denis like a miniature castle from a dark age, its mismatched turrets suggesting the broken fingers of a boxer thrust up from the street. No unearthly screams rose up from the base of the thing, but this was an unnecessary omission as Robert saw it; the Châtelet didn't need any more hell-on-earth scene dressing than it already possessed.

For good luck, Robert dropped his last messages onto the short stretch of St-Denis leading to the arched entryway.

And here I thought the dungeon of the Bastille was a

horrible place. Robert tried to breathe through his mouth, to keep the worst of the stinks away from his nostrils.

It didn't help.

At the bottom of the first flight of stairs below the ground he was made to stop while several members of his escort—his kidnappers, he supposed—consulted with one another. A couple of the men went back up the stairs, and the rest led him to the next stairway down. "How far down does this go?" he asked, beginning to perhaps worry just a bit. This building was awfully close to the river.

"Oh, you've scarce begun to see how far down you'll be going," one of the guards said with a bark of a laugh.

"What part of *Shut up* do you not understand, you idiots?" said the man who led them.

"What, still?" Robert asked, emerging from the stairs into a corridor whose walls glistened wetly in the torchlight. "I thought you were concerned about the sleep of the good people of Paris. Inside here I'm sure nobody cares if sleep is interrupted. Perhaps it makes for a happy change."

"I have just about had my fill of you," the chief said. "Why—why anyone would think you were a mastermind is a complete mystery to me."

"Perhaps you're just not as bright as Clopard." Robert pitched his voice more deeply, made himself louder. It would be a good thing if people here knew he'd been brought here, and more so as it was now very clear to him this man was trying to keep Robert's fate a secret from the world. "Are you bright enough to register my protest at this treatment? Nobles are not confined in the Châtelet, you know."

The chief's response was a curt signal with his right hand, and somebody behind Robert dealt him a blow to the back of the head that pitched him forward into the back of the man in front of him. When Robert came to his senses again he was on his knees and the man he'd been thrown into was scrambling, cursing, to his feet. Somebody picked up Robert under his arms and dragged him along the corridor. Eventually the party stopped, and Robert heard what sounded like a very large key trying to turn a very old lock.

He was thrown into a reeking cell, landing on his knees again. Cold water seeped through his stockings and the knees of his breeches. By this time he had cleared his head sufficiently to see, by the light of the torches in the doorway, that his cell was a large one, with a sprawling mound of what might once have been hay along the far wall. "Seems awfully spacious for one man," he said to the men in the doorway.

"You get special treatment," the chief said. "Normally there are fifty men in a cell of this sort." He waved his men away and darkness began to lap at the walls. "Enjoy your stay." He was still laughing when the key stopped grinding the lock shut.

Even for someone accustomed to the smell of the Seine and the slaughter-houses near Les Halles, the stink of this room was staggering. Feeling his way in the dark, Robert made a careful circuit of the room, if only to convince himself that there really was no part of it in which the smell was better, or worse, than in any other part. The straw was definitely rotting, and had been for some time, but vegetal decay was less disgusting than the smells from the corner of the cell that had been used as a latrine, and at least the hay was on the opposite part of the cell from that spot.

The floor was undressed stone, and wet. The walls were stone as well, crudely finished and also wet, though *damp* was probably a better word. Robert was sure he could hear the sounds of the river coming through the stones, though his head knew that the Grand Châtelet wasn't *that* close to the Seine. No doubt the damp was created by something even more unhealthy than the river.

I wonder how long I'll be in here.

He had just asked himself the question when the door opened again, and a torch-lit silhouette appeared in the doorway. "You might need these," the chief's dry, boyish voice was cut with vicious amusement; he tossed something dark and misshapen into the cell. "Don't feel too badly about it. This is likely the only food you'll get until I think to have you fed again."

Robert's spirit sagged and collapsed. He stepped toward the door just as it was closing, and was able to see in the diminishing light that the man had tossed a small bag of some sort onto the floor. Robert grabbed the bag and lifted it, but not before the water had seeped in.

The bag held the morsels of bread he had been dropping as they had brought him here. *I wasn't clever enough*, he thought.

Then he counted. There were only six pieces of bread in the bag.

Chapter Fourteen

Breaking In, Breaking Out

HACHETTE TUGGED AT Victoire's sleeve. "Slow down," he whispered. "Your glamour is starting to wobble, mademoiselle." He nodded in the direction of a side-street. "Should we duck down there so you can fix it?"

"Damn and double-damn," she said, allowing him to pull her from the rue du Roi de Sicile and into the shadows. "I thought I had this thing under control." Shaking his hand from her sleeve she said, "Thank you, Hachette. It's good to have you watching out for me."

"Hey," he said, "that's why you have me around." He smiled, showing slightly crooked teeth. "Are you sure we're going to be able to get inside this hôtel we're supposed to be checking out? What reason could we give at the front gate to get us in? Or even the back gate, if they have one."

"I'm a weaver's apprentice, remember? We'll tell the lackeys we have business with the baronne. They may not let us in at the front gate, but they aren't likely to refuse us at the back." *I hope.*

"I don't mind waiting outside, if it will make it easier for you," he said. "But what happens if you're inside their walls by yourself and your prayer gets befuddled?"

"I run like a rabbit?" she suggested. He laughed. "Please

don't worry about me," she said. "I am certain—well, fairly certain—that I have this prayer under control. I just have to be more confident in myself, that's all. Fear is a bad thing for prayers."

"You are the most un-scared mademoiselle I ever met," Hachette told her. "So you should do fine."

"Thank you, Rat-boy," she said, smiling at him and wondering, not for the first time, if she could ever domesticate him enough to be able to employ him in her aristocratic guise.

"Let's go," he said, trying to scowl and failing utterly, "before you call me Rat-boy again."

Her problem, she had to admit, was that it wasn't herself she was afraid for. It was one thing to believe, last night, that Robert had vanished into a fog of drink and gambling rather than perform the investigation she had asked for. It was another entirely to believe that he wouldn't have sent some sort of word by now. It was perilously close to midday for any somnolent aristo to still be abed, especially one who—he claimed—was interested in her for more than the socially polite reasons. *What has happened to him?* she demanded of herself for the hundredth time this morning.

"Slipping again," Hachette muttered.

Victoire snorted in disgust. "This isn't working," she said. Most likely the trouble was caused by the large muff she carried. It wasn't that the weather was cold enough to require it—though only in the frigid Americas of New France would today be considered warm—but the muff held the pistol and dagger she had decided would be necessary equipment for a visit to the Hôtel de Geoffroy.

"I want to take a break," she said. "I'll be myself until we're a bit closer to the Minimes convent." She stepped into the gap between two buildings, let her glamour lapse while Hachette guarded her, and then, emerging, walked north to the rue des Francs Bourgeois. She could always stop by Fortune Vidal's shop and see if he and his new bride had returned.

What she encountered at the shop was an alarmed boy— the nephew, she remembered—who bounced out of his chair the moment she entered the front of the shop. "Oh, God be praised," he said, his voice breaking. "I had no way of knowing your direction and so haven't been able to send you the news."

She felt cold. "What's wrong?" *Has Nicolette done something horrible?*

"It's your friend, monsieur de Vimoutiers," the boy said. "I saw him, late yesterday, being marched past here by a squad of archers."

"He was arrested? On what charge?"

"Mademoiselle, I do not know. I didn't dare ask, or even follow. The archers, they looked fierce and angry, and my uncle says we're never to do anything to draw their attention to us."

"Sound advice," she said. "But this makes little to no sense. If he had been arrested his mother would have been told." *And he would have sent me word.* "Something here is not right."

"They were going east," the boy said. "The archers and the chevalier."

"That could only mean the Bastille, then." Where else would archers take an arrested noble?

She did not want to go anywhere near the Bastille. It was at her request, though, that he had put himself into jeopardy in the first place. *All those times I refused his help,* she thought, *and he eased his way through everything he set out to do. And the first time I actually* ask *him to do something—*

The solution came to her. "We have to get word to his cousin," she told the boy. "Do you have a presentable messenger?" The thought of sending Hachette to speak to the duchesse de Bellevasse would have been comic had it not be so dangerous to contemplate. When the nephew nodded she said, "Then here is what you must send to her: her cousin, the chevalier de Vimoutiers, has been arrested on a spurious charge"—she hoped it was a spurious charge—"and taken to the Bastille. She should investigate immediately, if only to learn why his family wasn't notified."

That his family hadn't been notified was undoubted. Everything Victoire had heard about the duchesse de Vimoutiers made it impossible to believe that Robert would still be held anywhere within a quarter-hour of that woman learning the facts of the matter.

"Send someone with that message to the Hôtel de Bellevasse immediately," she ordered. *And I will set out to finish the job he was unable to.*

A shouted greeting accompanied the opening of the door behind her, and Victoire spun to see a beaming Fortune Vidal standing, arms outstretched, in the doorway. "Mademoiselle Victoire!" he called. "Truly I am well-named: what great good fortune to find you here to welcome me and my bride back to Paris."

"My felicitations, monsieur," she said, dropping into a quick curtsy. "This is the first chance I have had to give them." She tried to look around Vidal's bulky form. "Is madame Vidal with you?"

"Being helped from the carriage," he said. "How do you go, mademoiselle?"

"Things here have been better," she said, and as briefly as possible told him what she had just learned.

"Then," he said, his face setting, "you instructed my nephew wisely, and the message must be delivered immediately. Off with you!" he cried to his nephew, who squeaked and fled to the back of the shop.

"We will soon deal with this," Vidal told her. "Or, rather, her estimable cousin will. In the meantime, mademoiselle, will you take wine with me? I'm sure that you and madame have much to discuss. And she will no doubt have plenty to gossip with you about."

"I'm not sure I can spare the time just now," she began.

Then Jeanette entered the shop and Victoire's excuses died away.

"Mademoiselle," Vidal said, thrusting out his chest, "you are a woman of taste. You *must* tell me what you think of this day-dress I have had made for my love. It is, I believe, all the rage. I am so proud to be able to make of my Jeanette a model of fashion. Is it not wonderful?"

"Oh, it is," Victoire said, carefully, "Vidal, you absolutely *must* tell me where you got this."

The petticoat of Jeanette's new dress was a riot of happy blue elephants.

Robert was on the verge of beginning to think about possibly giving up hope of rescue when he heard Lise's voice echoing down the corridor outside his cell. "Unless you want to spend the rest of your miserable life in the galleys you will get that damned door open *now!*" she shouted. Robert wasn't sure he had ever heard her so angry. Not even when she was condemning the Prince d'Aude two years ago.

The flare of light when the cell door opened burned his eyes; the tears streamed down his cheeks until, by blinking rapidly, he was able to accept the gift of vision again. *How long have I been down here?* Part of him knew it had only been hours, but a different part was sure he'd been in the dark forever. "Get those metal—*things*—off him, you pigs," Lise snarled at someone." I swear, you are going to answer for this to the lieutenant-general."

"Madame, I promise you I knew nothing of this," a man said, his torch wavering. "There is no record of your cousin having been brought here. And why would he have been brought here in the first place? If he truly was arrested the chevalier should be in the Bastille. Whoever it was arrested him has to have known this as well." The man— presumably an officer of some sort—waved a subordinate past him. The subordinate carried tongs, a hammer and a vicious-looking chisel.

"I was there," Robert said. "In the Bastille." His voice seemed loud in his ears, surprising him a little. Just as his nose had learned to ignore the stink, his ears had accustomed themselves to the stony silence of this dungeon. "Just until it was late enough in the night that I could be moved here without attracting notice. And the person who brought me here wasn't the sergeant who arrested me." He coughed to loosen his throat, and held out one of the notes. "I do hope you're here because somebody brought you a copy of this."

"The most appalling old woman," Lise said, frowning. "How in the world did you persuade someone like her to approach my husband's people?"

"It was a blind throw of the dice," he told her, and explained the idea behind his gustatory appeal for help. "I hope the reward didn't cost you much."

"Less than we spend on bread for a day," Lise said, "and

under the circumstances well worth it. Robert, what in the arch of heaven is this about?"

"I think I know what has been happening," he said, turning to Lise, "but I can't explain it to you now. Here."

"Very wise, I think," Lise said. "So: let's get out of this place, quickly."

"I don't think I look very presentable at the moment," he told her. A glance downward showed his stockings weren't so much spattered as dyed the indifferent colour of filth and mud. "Not, I suppose, that I'll stand out too much in this neighbourhood."

"The courts are just on the other side of this prison," Lise told him. "You're going to stand out. But I'll take you home in a chair."

"Ordinarily I'd object, but today I accept, and gladly."

The metal bands removed from his neck, wrists and ankles, Robert followed Lise up the stone steps to the ground floor of the Châtelet. "We looked for you at the Bastille," Lise muttered to him. "The only record of you there showed you arrested late yesterday afternoon and released last night. No evidence of a *lettre de cachet.*"

"Somehow I am not surprised," Robert muttered back.

As she and her lackeys steered Robert to the prison's massive doors Lise turned and shouted, over her shoulder, "You will summon everyone who was on duty here before daybreak and hold them in readiness for an interrogation by lieutenant-general de La Reynie or his delegates. Do it now."

"Have you heard anything from Ma—from the duchesse my mother?" Robert asked as they stepped out into bright sunlight. "And is de La Reynie really going to come down here and put his underlings to the torture?"

"Nothing from your mother," Lise said with a sideways

glance at him. "Perhaps she's accustomed to your being absent from home without word. As for de La Reynie, he doesn't know about this yet, but when he reads my letter I will be very disappointed if he doesn't come himself or at least send his deputy."

"He will definitely be interested," Robert said, "if he is still curious as to the identity of that spy you were worried about a couple of weeks ago."

"Oho," said Lise. "So that's what this was about?"

"In part," Robert said.

"Your spy, I believe, is the baron de Geoffroy." Robert leaned back against the *chaise-longue* on which Lise had placed him. He took another sip of brandy—an especially good old Cognac—and snuggled himself more deeply into the Turkish dressing-gown Lise had given him following the impromptu bath that had been his first concern on reaching the Hôtel de Bellevasse. "Rafael's taste in clothing has improved, I see. No doubt your influence."

"Geoffroy?" Lise sat upright in her chair. "He wasn't even on our long list of suspects."

"He probably wasn't much of a spy," Robert suggested. "Thing is, if my guess is correct he wasn't the only member of his household getting richer at the expense of the emperor."

"His wife was a spy?"

"Not a spy. A smuggler."

"You're still going on about that cloth-smuggling business?" Lise snorted and swallowed all of the chocolate in her cup at one go.

"I am," Robert said. "I was arrested, I think, because I was getting too close to linking de Geoffroy—or one of them, at least—with an enterprise whose proprietor wanted it kept hidden."

"I can see how a spy might want his activities to stay a secret," Lise said. "No need to invent a new conspiracy when the same old one will do."

"And how, precisely, could the baron de Geoffroy arrange for my incarceration in a dungeon cell with no records being kept of the transaction?" Robert shifted to put his feet on the floor, and leaned toward Lise. "The man who removed me from the Bastille and locked me in that fetid pit under the Châtelet is a policeman of some sort," he said. "And I am willing to wager Rafael's fortune on that policeman being the head of the smuggling ring that has been alternately trying to seduce me and attack me since I first—since the beginning of the month."

"Since you first got involved with Victoire de Berenguer, you mean." Lise's face shifted into a smile that wasn't quite sympathetic. "You realize, I hope, that I can't help you help her. No matter how much you may want to."

"I do realize it," he said. "I'm sort of hoping I can persuade her to give up a life of crime." He smiled back, and in the same twisted fashion. "My problem is, I don't think I've ever felt so much like myself as I have lately. Does this mean I've discovered my criminal nature?"

"You idiot, it means you're in love with her. It's not crime that excites you, it's Victoire herself."

"Which doesn't, alas, get me any closer to persuading her to marry me and give up wickedness."

"You have to persuade her to marry you and embark on some entirely new form of wickedness."

He hoped she couldn't see the flush he'd felt at her words. He supposed she was trying to be encouraging, but he'd never been as comfortable with talk of—well, of that sort of wickedness—as was his appallingly outspoken cousin. "If it's all the same to you," he said, "I'll start with persuading her to give up her life of crime."

"Once we've dealt with this matter of your arrest," she said. "And my spy." She put her cup on a side table and god to her feet. "Tell me what clothing you'll want, and I'll send someone to your hôtel to collect it. As soon as you're dressed we'll go back to the Grand Châtelet and begin following this fascinating thread back to its origin."

With nothing to do but wait for the boy's return with his clothes—and, he didn't doubt, with Janvier his valet—Robert found himself increasingly fidgety, to the extent that Lise threatened to turn him over to her husband if Robert didn't calm down right away. Then a footman appeared in the salon and calm flew away like a bird in autumn.

"There's a young person at the gate, mademoiselle," the footman said, "who insists on speaking with monsieur le chevalier."

Lise lifted an eyebrow. "Another member of the gang trying to recruit you, cousin?"

"The person says his name is Hachette," the footman said.

"Bring him here," Robert said. "Now." He turned back to Lise, saw her glare, flushed. "With my lady's permission, of course."

Lise sighed. "Bring the boy."

"She was all set to break you out of prison, monsieur, when she saw the lady madame Vidal." Hachette did not, Robert noticed, seem even a little bit intimidated by the magnificence of the Hôtel de Bellevasse. *Wish I could be so blase.* "Then she bolted like she'd seen a ghost. Which it very nearly was, because it was our stolen cloth madame was wearing, or at least some of it."

"I definitely should not be hearing this," Lise said. "I'll be in the Yellow Salon if you need me, Robert." Hachette made as if to say something; Robert held up his hand to stop the boy until the door had closed behind his cousin.

"What is going on, Hachette? How did mademoiselle Victoire even learn I'd been arrested? I didn't get a chance to send her a message or tell anyone."

Hachette giggled. "You made a scene in front of monsieur Vidal's shop, monsieur. And I think you frightened the life out of that boy his nephew. Who is supposed to be on his way here only I know the city a lot better than any bourgeois and so I beat him here and that's why I got to tell you all about it."

"And yet somehow I still don't know what's happening."

"I think, monsieur le chevalier, all you really need to know is mademoiselle Victoire would have rescued you herself if she hadn't found out the location of the cloth. So, she sent me to fetch your cousin the police witch—sorry, monsieur, that's what the *canaille* call her—to get you out. Only you were already here so somebody else got you out of the Bastille. So, I'm just telling you she's gone to get our cloth back."

"Wait," Robert said. "She's gone *where* to get the cloth back?"

"Um." Hachette fidgeted, his wooden shoes twisting the carpet beneath them. "I don't know. She was in a hurry."

"She went *by herself?*"

Robert got to his feet. "Damn it, where is Janvier?" He opened the door, summoned the footman who had brought Hachette to him and told him, "Go and bring your mistress to me. Now."

"What are you going to do?" Hachette asked.

"First, I'm going to get dressed. Then you and I are going to pay a visit to monsieur and madame Vidal."

The closer she got to the cemetery, which was midway up the gentle slope of a hill, the more nervous Victoire began to feel about her decision to come here trusting only to her weaver's assistant guise, while that new glamour was still so unstable. She was in no doubt she was going to the right place—Vidal's description of the woman who'd sold him the cloth with the blue elephants was an almost exact match for Marguerite de Geoffroy—but she had not realized just how rural this location was. Vidal's directions had been carefully concise—*a row of old houses at a crossroads near the cemetery of Montparnasse*—but they had not included any sort of description of the houses' surroundings, and she hadn't thought to ask.

The presence of the weapons in her muff did not make her feel any less exposed. Once outside the city she had found a tree-planted lane that appeared to have begun nowhere, and had stayed on that lane until it ended in the middle of nowhere as well. Away from the lane and on one of the rural roads that crisscrossed the farmland outside Paris, she was easily visible to anyone who cared to look. There were too few people out today, and she was increasingly aware of how dramatically someone dressed and looking as she was stood out.

I should have hired a horse, she thought, *or at least dressed in boy's clothes if I was going to avoid the glamour.* She got very little comfort from the knowledge her realization had come too late, and that the mistake was entirely the fault of her impatience after seeing the blue elephants. There was no choice, really: she had to make the change, and better now than later.

A windblown copse of trees ahead was the only protection from prying eyes she could see, and she refused to turn back. There were still plenty of leaves on the branches, but overall the copse provided little in the way of shelter from watchers. *Not that I have much choice.* "Here I go," she said aloud.

This isn't going to be easy. Closing her eyes, she built in her mind the image of herself as the weaver-boy. *Surely it won't have to last for long,* she thought. *I'm under a quarter-hour from those houses.*

She struggled with the prayer. *You're breathing too quickly,* she told herself. *Nerves?* Fatigue was more likely, she decided: she was likely still worn from the prayers of last night and this morning.

Calming herself with deliberation and forcing her breathing to slow, she began to murmur the prayer, building in her mind the image of that weaver's apprentice and then painting that image over her self-image. Once satisfied with the way she felt, she reached out her mind to encompass the weaver's clothing as well. This was harder to do well. But she had actually held the breeches, shirt, coat, in her hands when developing this prayer, and so could add the touch-memory to the image she wove.

Once her mind was settled, and she could feel the new image firmly in place, she stepped back onto the road and resumed climbing the slope. *I wonder what that transformation looks like to anyone seeing it. Disgusting, most likely.*

Vidal had directed Victoire to the southern-most house in a row of very old buildings across the cemetery road on its eastern edge. She made herself walk past the house and all the way to the last one in the row before slowing down. A quick look around her persuaded her nobody was in view; none of the houses she had passed had their shutters opened, even those on the upstairs windows.

I wish I knew what was behind those doors, she thought as she turned back to the house on the end of the row. It was hard to imagine Marguerite spending any time at all in a place as run-down as this building. But she had to admit she knew very little about how most poor people lived, even after the time she'd spent with Marie-Louise, Catherine and Hachette. For all she could tell, each of these buildings had dozens of people inside them, living in a fashion she really didn't want to imagine.

Stop putting this off, she told herself. *You won't make it any easier or less risky.* Taking a deep breath, she walked up to the front door of the house.

The first thing she saw was that the door was locked. The next thing she saw was that the lock and the door both were new, and the door was set in a frame that, if not new, was at least solidly built. *I don't think I want to get in this way. Let's see if the back door's as strong,* she decided. The presence of that lock and door certainly argued strongly that someone—Marguerite or Clopard or Chenal—was using this house for some purpose even if they weren't living here.

She hoped it wasn't the latter.

The back door was solidly built, but not quite so solidly as its companion on the street. Its lock, while strong enough to deter the opportunistic, was neither new nor sturdy. She examined it, trying to imagine its workings. It was never easy to open a metal lock through prayer, so Victoire had taught herself some more mundane skills. Not that magic was completely useless; it was just a lot harder to pray effectively, especially if there was a lot of metal in the lock. She lifted her hat and, from her hair, pulled a set of picks and applied herself to the lock.

It took an embarrassingly greater time than she had wanted, but the lock eventually gave itself up to her ministrations, and when Victoire straightened, groaning from the pain in her lower back, she held the large metal pad in her hand. "Let's see what we have here, shall we?"

One wonders what is so appealing about this place, she thought as she entered. *It can't be the building itself, or the location. There are better buildings closer to the city gates, after all.*

Once inside she let the glamour lapse, gasping her relief from the stress of holding it. The house, when she explored it, showed very little sign of what Victoire would call habitation. In some respects, it was very much like a larger version of Catherine's house; but where that latter showed evidence of its inhabitants in each of its rooms, this house was bare of most of those signs. There were no beds; a couple of straw mattresses were in an ungainly heap in one corner of the kitchen, surmounted by crumpled blankets.

There is definitely more to this situation than I had thought, she told herself. *Though there is rather less to this house than I had hoped.*

For one thing, she realized even if her enemy wasn't precisely living here, someone was definitely sleeping and eating here—and they weren't doing it in solitude; that much was clear just from the mess in the kitchen. The realization there were multiple people using this house came as a sickening surprise; what faith could she have in the belief that nobody would disturb her while she searched?

Standing around and moping about it won't make you any more safe, she decided. *Search the place quickly and get out of it fast. Then you can worry about what to do next and how risky it can be.*

There ought to be a cellar beneath a house out in the countryside. She examined the whole of the ground floor before finding the cellar entrance in, of all places, the front entrance, at the foot of the stairs going up to the first floor. The door was new, and well-oiled, and it took little effort to lift it.

Getting down into the cellar turned out to require a considerable effort. There was a stepladder in place inside the trap, so the descent should have been easy enough— and would have been, had it not been for her skirts. The opening was easily wide enough to accommodate a big man, but to a woman in skirts it appeared no larger than the eye of a needle. She could only get onto the ladder by crumpling those skirts, and bunching them to force them through the narrow opening. Even when she'd got herself and her skirts fully through the opening, their bulk meant she had to descend slowly, one careful step at a time.

There's something odd about this, she thought, brightening her God-light to illuminate the corners of the cellar. It took a moment, but when she finally understood she whistled, low: the cellar was bigger than the house over top of it. The far end wasn't even visible to her with her God-light at its current intensity, and something warned her against making the cellar any brighter. Still, the implication was clear enough: *Are all of these houses connected? Just what is Marguerite doing here? And who is doing it with her?*

Despite the impressive evidence of both calculation and expense, she still had a hard time believing the baronne de Geoffroy was one of the inhabitants, even occasionally. It was nearly as difficult to believe that the lawyer, Chenal, would cross this threshold. *Why would any self-respecting bourgeois would put up with these conditions? Not if he had a comfortable place in town.*

If she could stay lucky it wouldn't matter. *There can be Turks sleeping here so long as nobody is in this house right now, and nobody comes here until I've finished.* She began a careful search of the parts of the cellar closest to her.

Unfortunately, the cellar she could see was empty of cloth. There were a few boxes in one corner, and when she lifted the lid of one of them she saw tufts and bits of thread suggesting that someone had indeed moved cloth to this place, hidden in boxes. *But where is that cloth now? And how does she—or he—move it around so easily?* There was something she was missing about this house, she knew. She just couldn't force her mind around it. *Should have got more sleep,* she told herself.

Along one wall she saw a ladder resting on its side. *Why another ladder?* There wasn't a second entrance to this cellar. Or was there? She brightened her God-light some more, trying to see how far this cellar went. *He comes down here and emerges from one of the other houses,* she thought, *and the cloth is stored under one of those other houses as well.* She began to walk toward the far end of the cellar, looking up for other, closed, entrances in the floors of the other houses.

She happened to be looking up when she caught her shoe in something that tugged like a rope-snare. She staggered, trying to regain her balance, and then suddenly the floor was rushing up to meet her and there was dirt in her mouth and her light was going out.

Chapter Fifteen

South of the City

"**I CAN ONLY** tell you what I told mademoiselle Victoire," Vidal said. He and his wife sat, looking worried and uncomfortable, in their home above the shop.

"That will surely be enough to help us find her," Robert told him, sipping from a glass of Vidal's excellent wine. *I wonder how much longer Vidal will continue to live here,* he wondered. *A rich man with a wife will want a large house.* There was doubtless more amusement to be obtained from this line of thought, but that was for another time. "If she has charged after the same people who tried to make me disappear, she's going to be in need of help soon. That means me, I suppose."

"And me!" Hachette's eyes blazed with righteous anger.

"Goes without saying," Robert told him. "Which is why I didn't. Say anything, that is."

"Are you always like this when you're excited, monsieur?" Vidal asked, trying to suppress a smile.

"Don't know. Never thought much about it before." *This is a new sensation for me—of course I never thought about it before.* He shifted in his chair; the sword he now wore was borrowed, his own épée still being missing, and the borrowed blade was longer, more awkward, and far more deadly. Of course, Lise would own multiple blades of this sort.

"If you would be so kind as to share your information?" he asked.

Vidal told him about the row of old houses near the Montparnasse cemetery, and about the noblewoman who had sold him the cloth, and Robert had no trouble believing Victoire would indeed have stormed the place with all the reckless audacity of Charles the Bold. It was clearly incumbent on himself to provide support.

Which meant he would be needing support himself.

"Monsieur, I am going to ask you to deliver a message for me to my cousin, the duchesse de Bellevasse." Ignoring the sharp intake of breath from Jeanette Vidal—it truly was strange the way nobles reacted to Lise's name—he requested paper, pen and ink; Vidal provided these without question.

Robert wrote slowly, taking care to make each word clear. *This is maybe one of the more important things you've ever written,* he told himself. *You don't want to muck it up.* He forced himself to finish the wine, in order to steady his nerves, before attempting to develop a plan for dealing with what might be serious trouble. Where Victoire had flown into danger with scarcely a thought, it seemed to him, it mattered hugely his note to Lise explain what he had decided to do and where he was going. Finishing the letter, rereading it and judging himself satisfied, he sealed it and addressed it to Lise. Then he handed it to Vidal.

"Please take this to the Hôtel de Bellevasse," he said. "I think it's probably best you not wait for an answer." *Best for you, at any rate.*

"My nephew will deliver it," Vidal said. He added, in a wry tone, "At least now he knows the way there."

"I also have a small task for you, Hachette." Before the boy could give voice to the protest that flared up in his eyes, Robert pointed a finger at him. "No, don't argue with me. This is important. If your mademoiselle really has discovered the location of her stolen cloth, how is she to get it safely away from there? Can you carry it all yourself?"

"You're just trying to keep me from coming with you!"

"Do you really think it will take you more than a few minutes to obtain a cart?" Robert smiled at him. "I thought you were the best there was."

"Saving Victoire is more important than any old cloth." Hachette made what he no doubt thought was a fierce face; however, the effect of his enormous front teeth projecting down over his lower lip was far from martial.

Robert stood and rested a hand on Hachette's shoulder. "For once in your life, boy, do what you're told. I promise you there will be lots of hitting and stabbing still to be done once you've found a cart. In fact, I promise that if I find the man who shot you I'll keep him alive for you, no matter how desperately he begs me to put him out of his misery. What's more, I won't even ask you to not to steal the cart you're going to get. Promise me you'll get the thing any way you can, and I'll let you follow me as fast as you're able."

Hachette's brow lifted. "Promise?"

"My word of honour as a nobleman of France."

"Oh, like that's worth something to me."

"Touché, you little rodent," Robert said, laughing. "All right, word of honour as a friend of Victoire."

"You remember that promise," Hachette shouted as he ran out the front door.

"Is it so bad as that, monsieur?" Jeanette asked. She seemed to be trying to shred the handkerchief she held in her lap; Robert thought it a tribute to Victoire that so many people seemed to care so much about her. "Is there some way in which I can help? Surely—"

"I was just about to ask you, madame. Do you know the house Victoire maintains on rue du Pet?" He hoped she wouldn't giggle at the name, because he was enough on edge that any sort of reaction from her would likely tip him into gales of laughter. Praise God all she did was nod, so Robert was able to maintain his *sang-froid* in saying, "Then would you mind very much paying a visit? I don't know if her friends Catherine and Marie-Louise know about all that's happened. I think that they should."

"I think we should all of us descend on this place at the cemetery," Jeanette said, showing fierce little teeth, "and confront this villain with all our might."

"All of us?" He couldn't prevent himself from smiling at her, remembering how little help she'd been when he and Victoire had rescued her from her cousin's hôtel.

"Well, not the boy," she said, smiling back and completely failing to understand him. "I don't think Hachette should be involved in anything dangerous. He's much too young."

"You needn't be worried about Hachette." Robert grinned at her, shifting the sword-belt to a more comfortable angle. "I know it was very careless of me, but I've quite forgotten to write him a pass to leave the city. I doubt he's going to be following me very quickly—and certainly not with a cart he'll likely be pulling by himself."

Jeanette was still smiling when he left the shop. It was perhaps unfortunate that the clothing Janvier had sent him was more appropriate to a meeting with the lieutenant-general of police than it was to breaking into a villain's sanctuary. But Robert was convinced there was no time for

247

anything but to make his way across the river and into the unfamiliar territory of the southern faubourgs.

Besides, it surely would look ludicrous to the point of unbelievability were anyone actually to witness him breaking into—well, into wherever Victoire had got herself.

The path he followed was one with which he had rapidly become familiar through his association with Victoire: across to the Île du Palais and from there to the Left Bank; through the Sorbonne on the rue St-Michel to the city gates, and then out of the city and onto the road south past Port-Royal monastery and the Observatory. Unlike his earlier excursions on this route, today he continued south for several leagues past his intended destination, skirting around the Montparnasse slopes to the far side of the hill; it was only when he was convinced nobody had followed him, and that he was invisible to anyone watching from the row of houses Victoire had vanished into, that he stopped, tucked the edge of his coat behind the borrowed sword, straightened his gloves, and retraced his steps until he was climbing the reverse of Montparnasse.

There were the ruins of three old towers at the top of the hill; no doubt they were the dens of men of the road or other bandits, but for now they were deserted, and so he set himself up in one that provided a clear view down the slope toward the city, and watched the isolated row of houses. Summer had definitely ended, but the weather was still mild enough he had to shed his cloak by the time he had proved the place empty to his satisfaction. A little stiffly at first, he set off down the hill toward the cemetery and the old houses.

He hadn't realized how nervous he was until the sight of a

figure leaving the house on one end of the row nearly made him shout with alarm. Then he had to fight to suppress a giggle at how frightened he had been.

Robert was surprised even after he'd absorbed the shock of seeing the man emerge from the house. For sure the man was Clopard, someone he'd expected to show up here eventually—but he had come out of the wrong house. Or perhaps Vidal had simply got the directions turned around; after all, he was a jeweller, not a geographer.

Clopard looked from side to side along the road but, to Robert's immense relief, did not look back before walking briskly in the direction of the city. Had the thief-master turned around, Robert would have been caught, pure and simple: there was no place to hide on this part of the hill.

Robert looked at the houses on the two ends of the row. *Which one, south or north? Or is it both?* But that didn't make much sense.

In the end he let proximity decide, and examined the house at the north end of the row—the one from which Clopard had come. The front door was new, well-built, and firmly locked. *Just the sort of thing a man would do,* Robert thought, *if he was trying to hide a fortune's worth of contraband.*

He walked around to the back of the house.

I wish I knew why I thought this might be appreciated, he thought as he used his dagger to pry open the back door. *It's not as if Victoire has ever found my efforts useful.* But he had to acknowledge a desire to accomplish something, anything. He wanted to be—well, worthy. And in a way different from any way he'd felt before. Stepping, with care, into the kitchen at the back of the house he paused a moment to wonder what his mother was going to say when he told her. Then he realized he'd have to tell Victoire first, and that made him stop thinking and concentrate on the house. He prayed his God-light into existence, at a discreet intensity.

There was a trap-door in the centre of the wooden floor. The wood of which it was made seemed new, and the door fit snugly into its frame. *Very recent construction,* he said to himself, beginning to think Victoire might have found her cloth at last. The door was not locked, and when he lifted it, he found a ladder in place just where it ought to have been. *If I leave this door open,* he thought, *some of the day's light will get through into the cellar and I won't have to wear myself out making my own light.* He regretted the sleep he had not been allowed last night.

Moving with deliberate care, he took himself down into the cellar.

Everything was darkness. It even *smelled* dark.

You're being melodramatic, Victoire told herself. *It smells stale, musty. The way dungeons are supposed to smell in romances.*

Her head hurt, a lot. She could not, she now realized, remember precisely how she had arrived here. Wherever *here* was. *Where was I this morning? Or is it still this morning? Not possible to tell down here,* she decided.

Time to get up. She put her palms down on a dirty, uneven floor, and pushed herself up to her knees.

Then, rather than vomit, she decided to lie down again. Clearly, more sleep was called for.

It was immediately apparent to Robert the cellar was not the treasure-cave he had expected. Something about the place was definitely unusual, though, once his eyes had become adjusted to the sad amount of natural light available.

"This seems to belong to a much bigger building, doesn't it?" he asked himself. His voice, even pitched low as it was, echoed weirdly back at him. "Somebody could certainly store a lot in here. Though there doesn't seem to be much around at the moment." He decided much as he liked the rumbling sound of the echo, it probably wasn't wise to continue talking to himself. *Not out loud, at any rate. Probably not healthy either.*

Then he saw something in the corner across from where he stood: Boxes. *Could it be?* He hurried to the corner, and clawed at the lid of the first box he came to. The lid hadn't been tacked down and came away easily. Robert had to kindle a small God-light in order to be able to see inside the barrel. He drew a deep breath.

Then he laughed, a little.

"So you are what all this fuss has been about," he murmured, gazing at the painted elephants. "Pleased to make your acquaintance." The elephants were purple-black rather than blue, but Robert attributed this to the poor quality of the light and did not concern himself about it further.

There was only one bolt of Victoire's cloth in the box, but that was more than any of Victoire or her associates had seen since high summer. *The rest of it must be around here somewhere.*

But where?

The remaining boxes were empty save for some threads that had caught on the wood as the cloth was put in or taken out. And there were no other containers he could see. *Am I going to have to walk the full length of this cellar?*

Something caught his foot. He kicked at it, and nearly fell over when the thing, whatever it was, refused to move.

He knelt down on one knee, keeping the trapped foot still. The toe of his boot, he realized, was hidden by something. That something turned out to be a heavy cloth, a cloth that had been weighed down by the boxes he had been exploring.

The cloth was covered with a thin layer of dirt.

Must have knocked some of the dirt away when I first came over here, and then I caught my boot in it when I tried to walk around it, he decided.

He tried to lift the cloth and found it most reluctant to budge. This, he concluded, was not because of the dirt on the cloth but because of the boxes weighing down the cloth. *Or anchoring it,* he thought, standing up and shifting a box off the cloth.

When he shifted a second box, there was a sudden rushing sound as most of the dirt fell from the cloth and into darkness.

When he shifted a third box the cloth itself fell away, revealing a large hole in the cellar floor—a hole easily four times the width of the trap-door above him. Robert realized he was standing nearly on the edge of this hole; one misstep while moving the boxes and he'd have gone head first into the hole and down—

—Into what?

In the mouth of the hole nearest him he saw the upper parts of what turned out to be a primitive ladder. The ladder went down into the unknown darkness. And so did Robert.

By the Good God, Robert thought once he'd raised his God-light to full strength. *This isn't a cellar. It's a cavern.*

An enormous cavern, it appeared. There must have been twenty feet from floor to ceiling, and he could not see any end to it in either direction. And the walls—the walls were so pale they glowed in the God-light.

Robert turned around. "Oh," he said. "Oh, my." His voice sounded tight in his ears.

It would appear I have found Victoire's missing cloth, he told himself. *Even if I haven't yet found Victoire.*

Sure enough, the far side of the cavern was built up with stacked bundles, and when Robert opened one he found cloth so marvellous he could only wonder that Victoire could have concerned herself with blue elephants. A second bundle had already been opened, and there—at last—were the rest of Victoire's blue elephants. "This," he said to himself, looking along the wall, "is a lot of cloth." Then he thought about what he was seeing, and about the amounts of cloth Victoire and her people had told him of, and realized what he was looking at. *There is more here than she could have brought back on four expeditions, much less the one. A lot more.* And as bright as he could make his light—which, admittedly, was no longer quite so bright— he couldn't really see where these bundles ended.

Stepping away from the bundles, he peered along the length of the cavern into the darkness. *It's not a cellar, no. But I'm beginning to think it's not a cavern, either.*

"Oh," he said again, feeling as he might had he been playing reversis and suddenly allowed to see everyone else's hand. *If this is a tunnel, and if such a tunnel goes back to the city and under the walls, then it suddenly makes sense why the people behind this were so concerned about competition from Victoire. They've been building up a much bigger business since—well, for some time now.*

In a way, though, it didn't make any sense they should

have concerned themselves with her—or with him. Chenal, or Clopard, or de Geoffroy—or even all three of them, which is what it now looked like, shouldn't have had to worry about a few bales of cloth brought in by a single young woman.

It's not just cloth, though. And it's not all Victoire's either. At first all he'd been able to think about was how happy Victoire would be when she got her cloth back. But now that he had had a chance to really see what was hidden down here he couldn't imagine it just being cloth in this tunnel. He couldn't even be certain that it was just *this* tunnel. What if there was a network of such tunnels underneath the city? It seemed ridiculous, but then the existence of this tunnel he stood in was ridiculous on the surface of things, and yet here he stood.

Who would have dug them, and why? *Who knows who, and who cares why? They're here.*

If there really was such a proliferation of tunnels, wouldn't the emperor's men know about it? Surely de La Reynie would. *And yet once again the evidence of this single tunnel, existing beyond the knowledge of de La Reynie— even beyond the knowledge of Cousin Lise, who seems to know everything—argues that it is possible.*

And even if there were no other tunnels, if this tunnel was full of a variety of smuggled goods....

Did Victoire really attract the jealousy of Clopard or Chenal? Or did she accidentally come to the attention of a smuggler far more serious about the business than she? Robert felt a chill come through his cloak and his coat and his skin and into his bones. *We may be in a lot of trouble here.*

"I think I have to find another way out of here," Robert

said, drawing his God-light closer to himself, the better to keep it shining as long as possible."

"I shouldn't advise such exploration," a sour voice said. "It's dangerously easy to become lost down here."

The voice was faintly familiar. Robert turned to find an unhappy man in lawyer's black at the foot of the ladder.

"The missing and much-missed Antoine Chenal, I presume?" he said.

I'm not alone down here.

Victoire took a deep breath and got to her knees. Voices echoed weirdly toward her from someplace up—or down—the tunnel she had apparently fallen into. Whoever it was talking in the darkness might be able to help her; her head still ached and she felt stiff and sore around her shoulders and backside.

No, no help down here. Slowly she remembered where she was. How she'd got here. The talker was likely to be someone without friendly feeling for her. In fact, it was probably that pig Clopard. No, there were two voices. Clopard and that lawyer, then—what was his name? *Wonderful,* she told herself. *I'm sick enough to want to die and the only people available to help me are those who'd much rather agree with me about that.*

She breathed in sharply. That wasn't an enemy's voice.

Robert has found this place? I have never been so happy to see him in my life. It cost her, but she struggled to her feet. She had just begun to move in the direction of Robert's voice when she realized she'd been right in her guess about at least one of the voices she'd heard.

She walked faster, as fast as she dared.

"Unbuckle your sword-belt, de Vimoutiers," the lawyer said, pointing a small but still deadly pistol in the general direction of Robert's heart. He set a large lantern onto the floor beside him.

"Must I?" Robert held up his hands. "I've only just been loaned this one, you see, and it's not mine to give away."

"Stop being such an ass; it won't get you anywhere. Take it off, slowly. Now, kick it toward me. That's good," he said as Robert complied. "Now, back away from the cloth and into the centre of this space."

"Not much of a man of the law, are you?" Robert said, keeping his voice slow and steady.

"On the contrary. I know the law very well, and so know precisely what I am doing." Chenal giggled and walked forward, slowly and carefully, until he had reached the discarded sword. Without looking away from Robert he hooked the belt with one foot and dragged it away until both he and the sword were well out of Robert's reach. "I won't say it's a pleasure to meet you again, de Vimoutiers, but it certainly is interesting."

"You have a much lower threshold than I have for *interesting*," Robert said. "Tell me, are you still working on the mistaken assumption that I have anything to do with any of this?"

"Oh, hardly mistaken, monsieur le chevalier. After all, you're here now, aren't you?"

"But not looking for you, I assure you. When you disappeared from the city I stopped thinking about you almost immediately," he lied. "The police, of course, did not. They have a good many questions for you. Which I'm sure they'll be in a position to ask very shortly."

"Shortly isn't going to help you, you high-born idiot. I'm going to be gone from here as soon as—well, you don't need to know that, do you? It's certainly not going to matter to you."

Robert knew he wasn't as good with a sword as either Lise or her husband Rafael, but he was pretty sure he could stick this miserable son of a bitch if he could only reach the blade he had just given up. His fingers twitched, anxious to wrap themselves around a hilt they couldn't touch. *Should have brought a pistol with me,* he told himself. *How long can I keep him from shooting?* "I still can't believe you were behind it all," he said to Chenal. "Where is your chief? I'm sure he'll be surprised to see me here, after all the trouble he went to yesterday."

"I have no idea what you're talking about," Chenal said. "And it doesn't matter. I'm the only person I'm worried about, and if it hadn't been for your arrival here I'd have been well away from here by now. And believe me, you're not going to be an inconvenience for much longer."

Robert was still trying to work out a way of distracting Chenal for long enough to reach his sword when the lawyer's nasty face broke into an even nastier grin. "Why, mademoiselle," he said. "How lovely of you to join us."

There was a bright flash of light and a horrendous noise, and Robert felt a small wind brush his cheek. The noise was loud enough he staggered backward and Chenal dropped his pistol and clapped his hands to his ears.

He missed me, Robert thought, relief flooding through him. Then he realized what Chenal had said just before firing the pistol. Spinning around, he saw Victoire standing, staring wide-eyed at him as a dark stain spread across her breast.

Then she crumpled to the floor of the cavern.

Chapter Sixteen

A Ghost of a Chance

HIS GOD-LIGHT REFUSED to appear in any useful quantity, and his head still ached. Worse, it sounded as if all the bells of Notre Dame had been stuffed inside his skull and set to ringing. But Robert ran to Victoire and had knelt beside her almost as soon as she collapsed.

"What has that bastard done to you?" he asked. It was very odd to not be able to hear his own voice. *I had really hoped this would never happen to me again,* he thought, remembering the prince d'Aude shooting him inside that old farmhouse two years ago. "Victoire, can you hear me?"

She opened her eyes and looked up at him. Then, after a moment's vagueness her focus sharpened and he knew she saw him. She smiled, and his heart twisted in a most unexpected way. She said something he could not hear. He got his arms under her shoulders and lifted her a bit so he could get her head cradled in his lap. Then he bent over to get his ear closer to her mouth.

"I said," she gasped, "By the Mother of God this hurts."

"I'll do what I can to ease the pain," he told her, "but I don't know if I can do much. I'm just not that strong."

"Anything you can do. Will be a help."

Robert fumbled through the memory-library of prayers

he had been taught or had taught himself. The prayers he knew best worked on the pains of a hangover, but he wasn't certain they would apply to the pain of a bullet wound. He tried it anyway; at least he knew it well, which was more than he could say for the healing prayer Père Robillard had taught him a few days ago. Tried to teach him.

She closed her eyes, and he thought he might have seen a smile. She didn't open her eyes again, though; that worried him. "Don't you do anything stupid, like die," he whispered to her. "It's taken me this entire month to figure out what you are to me, and I'm damned if I'm going to let you go before I've had a chance to—well, to explain myself. Lord, I'm babbling again."

Her eyes didn't open but she definitely smiled now. "Idiot," she said, and it sounded like the highest praise.

Sounds from behind him prompted Robert to set Victoire back onto the soft, chalky soil of the cavern floor. "My apologies," he told her, "but I feel as if I ought to deal with that horrible lawyer while he's still trying to reload his pistol."

When he turned around, though, he found Chenal walking toward him and Victoire, pistol in one hand and ramrod in the other. "Please don't bother getting up," Chenal said. "Not on my account." He giggled again.

"You're not nearly as funny as you think you are, you know," Robert told him, getting to his feet without waiting for permission.

"I told you to stay down," Chenal said, in a voice like a cold winter.

"No you didn't," Robert said, improvising and putting himself between the angry lawyer and Victoire. "Not the same thing."

"Now you're the one who's not funny," Chenal said. He

set the ramrod into the barrel of the pistol and jammed it down several times.

"Wasn't trying to be, believe me. Just trying to point out where you could have been more, um—what's a good word for *accurate*?"

"Feel free to ask God, should you ever meet him." Chenal cocked the pistol. "Not that I think it likely you will."

"My family knows where I am," Robert said. He was beginning to get the idea Chenal didn't intend to shoot Victoire with his next ball. *I suppose she's not as dangerous to him right now as I. Not that I'm amounting to much just at the moment.* It felt very strange, knowing one was about to be shot. When the prince d'Aude had shot him, several years and apparently a lifetime ago, Robert had been so taken by surprise that he didn't fully realize what had happened until Rafael had revived him. All he really remembered now was how loud it had been. "They're probably just about here already, if I know my cousin."

"I don't care about your cousin or anyone else in your family," Chenal said. "And by the time anyone finds you down here you'll likely be a pair of skeletons, and I'll be a long, happy way away from here."

"You really think you won't be tracked down?"

"I'm a lawyer, you idiot. I have taken steps to ensure that, whatever price is to be paid for my freedom and new riches, it is others who will pay it. Their greed will have undone them as surely as yours, and especially the young mademoiselle's, has undone the two of you."

His smirk broadened into a self-satisfied smile. That smile had just fixed on his face when a screeching filled Robert's ears and echoed through the tunnel. Robert had just enough time to think *What sort of prayer is this?* when the screech was supplanted by a cracking noise, as of river-ice breaking, and Chenal's chest shattered in a black spray. For a moment the lawyer stood, still smiling; then he fell, face first, onto the pale tunnel floor.

A screaming roar startled Victoire out of her happy reverie. The pain began to flicker back into life as she tried to make herself understand what had happened.

She realized what it must have been, and her heart felt as if it was collapsing in on itself. Then she felt arms tighten around her—he was apparently trying to shield her body with his own—and Victoire realized Robert, the blessed idiot, had not been shot. He might have been trying to say something, but once again Victoire could hear nothing in the aftermath of that ear-splitting noise, save for a rushing sound like that of falling water. The sound hurt her ears and she tried to lift her hands to press them against her ears, hoping this would reduce the pain. It didn't. In fact, just the effort of lifting her right hand sent spikes of pain through her breast.

Robert hasn't been shot, but I have, she remembered. And then:

Somebody has shot Chenal.

Or perhaps not. The echoes in her ears were not those of a gunshot, she realized, nor did they hurt her as much.

Well, whatever had happened, Chenal was definitely face-down on the cavern floor and not about to move anytime soon. She wondered if she had strength enough to summon a God-light, and no sooner had she formulated the thought than the cavern lit up with a yellow-green light that was not hers, and unlike any she had seen cast by Robert. *Who?* she wondered.

Then the man appeared, climbing down a ladder she

hadn't noticed before. She hadn't expected him, but at the same time she wasn't surprised.

"Monsieur le baron," she said to the baron de Geoffroy. "Where is Marguerite? Right behind you, I presume."

"Yes, and no," baron de Geoffroy said. "I am sorry to say my wife has not been as supportive as she ought to be."

"Perhaps she learned about your affair with the duchesse de Beaune," Victoire suggested.

"Oho," said Robert, over his shoulder. "Well, that certainly explains de Beaune's anger and disgust. Couldn't stomach a traitor as his wife's lover, then?"

"A complete waste of my time, that one," de Geoffroy said. "All women are a waste of time, I think. Except that Marguerite will be oh so useful to my friend and me." He gestured with a languid hand back up the ladder. "She is, ah, tied up in the cellar above us, where she will serve as a scapegoat when the authorities eventually find this place."

"Eventually," said Robert, "is a few minutes from now. I trust you are familiar with my cousin, the duchesse de Bellevasse?"

"De La Reynie's witch? She'd best not show up here by herself, de Vimoutiers. Most people might be afraid of her, but I know the truth of how limited her Blessing is."

"And her husband the duc?"

"Ask me again if he actually arrives."

"I can't believe," said Victoire, trying to sit up, "that you have even the smallest interest in my smuggling operation."

"Oh, he doesn't," Robert said. "Do you, de Geoffroy? But the man who does have that interest—your chief, I believe he likes to be called—knows all about your spying for the Holy Roman Empire, doesn't he? That's why you and your wife have been assisting him. However reluctantly. Not that I think there's been much reluctance in your case."

The baron snarled but said nothing. Victoire stared at Robert. "How did you—?"

"M'cousin Lise had me looking into the spying thing," he said. "And I'm pretty sure I met the chief last night when he tried to bury me in the dungeons of the Châtelet. I don't know who he is, but I'll recognize him when I see him. If you follow me."

"I am appalled," said a dry voice from the cellar above, "that you turn out to have been telling the truth all along, monsieur de Vimoutiers. Far from being the mastermind I thought, you really are as stupid and ignorant as you pretend to be."

"And here he is," Robert murmured to Victoire. "Right on time."

Victoire knew that voice. "No." She stared at the slender form descending the ladder in a halo of torchlight. "It can't be him."

"You weren't expecting a corrupt policeman?" Robert asked.

"He's not just a policeman. That, Robert, is Patrice Grenier, a senior inspector of his majesty's customs and excise."

"Well, that explains a few things." Robert turned to face Grenier. "At last we meet, inspector. You'll forgive me if I don't bow. Pretty sure you don't deserve it."

"You wouldn't think I deserved it if I'd met you under any circumstances, you aristocratic idiot." Inspector Grenier, reaching the bottom of the ladder, made a clinking sound as he did. He placed his torch in a bracket, then walked, still clinking, over to where the baron de Geoffroy stood, arms limp at his side. "How are you feeling, my dear baron?"

"Exhausted," de Geoffroy said. "Even for a soldier it's

not easy, killing a man that way. Especially one who's holding a pistol. All that metal," he said, gasping a little.

"Precisely why I asked you to do it that way," Grenier said. A thrust of his knee into the back of de Geoffroy's legs brought the baron to his knees; before the man could even voice a protest, Grenier had wrapped a steel band around his throat and locked it in place. "That ought to keep you from wasting your Blessing," he said, laughing, "until such time as we agree I need your services again."

"How dare you!" The baron tried to rise, reaching for Grenier's throat, but all he got for his trouble was another band around his left wrist. "You promised me!"

"And I intend to keep my promise," Grenier said, stepping back and drawing a pistol from his overcoat. "You've been scrupulous in your dealings with me so far, baron, and believe me I appreciate it. You may be the first aristocrat of my acquaintance who has kept his word.

"I just want to ensure that you don't succumb to temptation, the way poor Chenal did."

"If you're being truthful," said the baron, "then let us get out of here. Now, before that witch and her Devil-sworn husband arrive."

"If you say so, my dear baron. You have my permission to go up to the cellar and kiss your poor stupid wife good-bye. Then you can ensure that all of the supplies are packed onto the animals. It's a long way to the frontier and we won't be stopping in the sorts of inn your class of people favours."

"And the money?"

"Is travelling with me, of course. Never fear, de Geoffroy. Continue to keep your word and your share will be given to you when we part in—at our destination." He smiled at

Victoire. "No sense in saying anything that might get us into trouble."

As if you were going to leave us alive, Victoire thought.

She might well have said those words aloud, because no sooner had de Geoffroy disappeared up the ladder, Grenier drew a second pistol and turned to face them, pistols in both hands.

Robert had to lean into Victoire closely enough that their cheeks grazed. "He's resisting me somehow," she whispered to him. "I thought I had enough energy left for at least one spiritual punch in the face, but I can't get through. He's holding more metal than that pistol."

"Unless I'm very much mistaken," Robert whispered back, "he's stuffed his pockets, his cuffs and probably his boots with gold. Not only is all that metal going to make him rich in the company of the Habsburgs, it's completely protecting him from righteous prayer."

Then he remembered something he'd seen Victoire do the last time she had been confronted by a villain holding twin pistols. He turned his head a bit more lest Grenier see him smiling. "Victoire, my love," he whispered, "do you remember using God's wind to throw that *sabot* into the face of the blind gunman? And how well we worked together in healing Hachette?" He reached a hand down to the floor of the cavern, scraped a handful of dust, pebbles and stones into his palm and closed the fist around them.

"Let's do that again."

"A pistol would be more efficient," she whispered. "I have one. In my muff."

"I'm not a very good shot," he confessed. "And he has two pistols to your one."

"You think throwing stones at him will be better?"

"Certainly it will be easier to hit him. Besides, he won't be expecting it."

"That's because it's an idiot thing to do!"

"All the more reason to do it," he said. Shifting his face closer, he kissed her ear. "Shall we?"

"Idiot," she said, but he could feel her smile.

He summoned up a wind-prayer—and then he could actually *feel* her doing the same. It was almost arousing the way their Blessings merged, but he forced the thought out of his mind. For now. "Here we go," he muttered.

The sound of feet crunching on stone reached him as he turned to face Grenier. The inspector began to walk toward them. "It's time for me to go," Grenier said. "But I can't very well leave you alive now, can I?" In the torchlight his smile was a rictus.

Now. Robert triggered the prayer, tossing the handful of gravel up from his open palm. For an instant the torchlight flickered.

Then Grenier screamed, the cavern was once again filled with an explosive roar, and Robert found himself on his knees, pressing his hands into his ears.

He got to his feet, certain he didn't dare wait for the pain in his skull to fade. In the flickering light of the torch he saw Grenier on the cavern floor, face-up and his hands empty. He thought he heard, through the chimes in his ears, shouting from upstairs but a quick look up the ladder did not show anyone climbing down. Yet.

One of Grenier's pistols lay beside his left hand. It was still cocked. The other was a few feet away, hammer down. Evidently it had gone off when—oh.

Grenier's forehead was bloody, and from the very centre of it projected a jagged chunk of stone.

"Goliath," he said, "meet David."

"Oh, don't make me laugh," Victoire said from behind him. She gasped. "Dammit dammit *dammit!* That *hurts.*"

"I imagine you're in a lot of pain," Robert said. "I'm really sorry about that. If I could have stopped it I would."

"You have no *idea* of the pain I'm in."

"Um," he said, because he did know. He also knew that without treatment, and that very soon, Victoire was going to be in far more trouble than she was in pain.

"I don't think I have much prayer left in me," he told her in apology, "but I will do what I can for you, Victoire. Just as soon as I've done something about our friend here."

"You don't think Grenier is dead?"

"No, I don't. I don't think he's precisely *well,* but he's breathing and his lips are moving. I think I'll just tie his legs together before he recovers his wits. Such as they are." He found all the rope he could possibly desire beside some of the bundles and boxes against the cavern wall. Working quickly, he bound Grenier's ankles together, tying multiple knots such that a blade would be the only way of freeing him quickly.

"My eyes," Grenier mutter. "Burning."

"What a pity," Robert told him. "Take comfort, though: there's not really much to see down here anyway." Without taking any care, he stripped Grenier of his massive overcoat and bundled it, clinking, into a pillow.

He had just placed this under Victoire's head and begun to try to summon any sort of healing-prayer when a fresh burst of shouting flowed down from the cellar above.

"I sincerely trust," he told Victoire, "that this is help, finally arrived."

As if in answer to a prayer he hadn't uttered yet, a friendly voice called from above. "Robert, is that you? Where are you?"

"Lise!" Getting back to his feet, he ran to the base of the ladder. "I am so happy to hear your voice. I need help down here." He thought a moment. "Which is in some sort of cavern or tunnel underneath the cellar. You'll want to use a lot of light up there, because the entrance is just a hole in the floor, and if you're not careful you'll just walk into it." *Which is what must have happened to Victoire*, he realized. So, she was probably more seriously hurt than just by the bullet, as horrible as that seemed.

"I'm on my way down. Love," she said to someone else, "can I ask you to follow me when you're finished up here?"

The unmistakable voice of the duc de Bellevasse drawled, "It will be my pleasure, my love." *Oh, Lord*, thought Robert. *Rafael? We are in the soup now.*

A moment later his cousin was down in the cavern, hugging him in a way that violated several rules of sophisticated society behaviour. "What have you been up to?" she asked. "And what are you doing down here?"

"Later," he told her. "I need help with Victoire. She's been shot."

"Oh my God," Lise said once she'd looked around. "This place is all bodies." She stiffened, and Robert knew she had recognized Grenier. "Oh, my good God," she said, turning back to Robert. "Lieutenant-general de La Reynie is going to have to be told about this. Whatever it is."

He felt his shoulders slump. "I know." He had hoped, somehow, to delay this until Victoire had got her cloth out of this Aladdin's Cave of treasures. But her wound was too serious and just now money didn't matter. "In time though, please? I'm pretty much worn out; can you try your hand at healing her?"

"You know I have no Blessing of that sort." She turned, responding to sounds from above. "Here comes the Blessing you need."

"You do lead an interesting life these days, Robert," said the duc de Bellevasse once he'd reached the base of the ladder. To Lise he said, "the squad of archers is here now. They'll take care of de Geoffroy and his wife." He paused to take in the entirety of the cavern. "This is unexpected."

"I'll tell you all about it, Rafael, once you've taken care of mademoiselle de Berenguer over here." Rafael had a very powerful Blessing, and now that he was no longer trying to kill people or raise the dead with it, he was proving quite useful. Popular even. Robert paused. "Well, I'll tell you as much as I know, which I admit isn't a lot."

"It never is." Rafael bowed to Victoire. "Mademoiselle. It's good to see you again."

"Not in the best of circumstances, though," Victoire said. "The queen's audience chamber this is not."

"Once word of this escapade gets out, you'll have the entire court clamouring to hold parties down here." Rafael knelt at her side. "Mmmm. Not an especially clean wound, I'm afraid. Looks as if the ball went through bone. This is going to hurt, I'm afraid."

"Believe me, it already does."

Rafael laughed, not unkindly, and began to pray.

"How in the world did all this come to pass?" Lise whispered, pulling Robert back to the ladder. "When I left you this morning you'd spent a night in a dungeon and looked as if you wanted nothing more than to sleep for a week."

Robert gazed at the bundles of cloth. *What a pity,* he thought. "You were right about that. Except that I found out from—from a friend—that Victoire had come out here by herself. So, I sent word to you and came after her. What else could I do?"

When he turned back to Lise he found her staring at him, a tiny smile playing at the edges of her mouth. "What?" he asked.

"Later," she said. "What did you do to inspector Grenier?"

"Used some of God's wind to blow dust into his eyes. And, apparently, a stone into his forehead." Grenier had begun clawing at his eyes, whimpering. Robert searched himself for sympathy, found none, and was satisfied. "I confess I have no idea why he was doing any of this."

"Monsieur de La Reynie will learn it all," Lise said. "In time."

"We have to get her out of here," Rafael said, reappearing at Lise's side. "I've mended the bone and stopped the bleeding, but she's hurt more badly than she looks."

"She fell into this cavern," Robert told them. "I think she's hurt her head."

"That explains a few things," Rafael said. "Lise, please go back up and call a couple of lackeys down here. I don't want to move her, but we have to. We'll take her back to the hôtel, where I can summon our *chapelain*. He'll be able to complete the healing, or at least get her to the point where she'll be out of danger."

"We have to get this fool out of here as well," Lise said. "He goes to de La Reynie, along with de Geoffroy."

"Is he well enough to walk, do you think?" Rafael looked down at Grenier's feet. "My God, what sort of knotwork is that?"

In the end, a pair of muscular archers dragged Grenier up the ladder and draped him over the back of their sergeant's mule. Once the archers were on their way back to the city—leaving a pair to guard the house—Rafael helped Lise settle

Victoire into their carriage, then mounted his horse and set off to alert the *chapelain* of their coming. Robert walked around to the other side of the carriage—and saw, of all people, young Hachette, hiding around the corner of one of the old houses. Evidently the boy was more clever than he looked. When he saw Robert looking at him, Hachette smiled broadly. Then he pointed to the house and mimed carrying something heavy.

Robert smiled back, relieved. He nodded.

Victoire awoke in the softest bed she had ever been in. She had been dreaming of great pain, but the dream had ended and now she felt blissfully indolent, as though she were waking the morning after an especially successful party.

She yawned and stretched her arms—and yelped at a sudden, deep pain above her right breast. *Not a dream, then?*

The door to the bedroom opened—and Robert stepped inside.

"Monsieur! I am hardly in a state to receive guests."

Robert said nothing, just moved to one side of the doorway. A young woman, tall and slim, followed him in; Victoire recognized her, and the dark, lithe man who trailed her, as the duchesse and duc de Bellevasse, whom everyone in Paris knew.

"I seem to be confused," Victoire said. "Where, precisely, am I?"

"You are in the Hôtel de Bellevasse," the duc told her. "We brought you here after you were shot."

I remember. Memory was unpleasant. "Do I owe my recovery to you, monsieur?"

"Indirectly, I suppose. It was my *chapelain* who did the work, but I pay him."

"Please thank him for me." She was having trouble thinking; all that came to her mind was the knowledge her cloth was gone again, and this time there would be no getting it back. "I apologize for the grotesque inconvenience I must have caused you," she said, trying to keep her voice level.

"No apology is necessary," Lise told her.

"I think my wife sees in you a kindred spirit," the duc said, with a dark smile.

"Now that you're awake, though," Robert said. "you have some visitors to attend to, I'm afraid."

"Visitors?" Then she realized what he had meant, and smiled despite herself. She heard Hachette's voice, and laughed.

"We'll leave you alone with your friends," duchesse Lise said to Victoire. "You just have to ask for anything you need." And then Hachette burst into the room, followed immediately by Marie-Louise and Catherine.

"Mademoiselle, you're all cleaned up! Last time I saw you, you looked like a ghost!" Hachette whooped with laughter.

"That's because she was covered in plaster dust," Robert said as Lise, following Rafael out of the room, closed the door behind her. "I have learned that she fell down into a plaster mine."

"Plaster?" Hachette asked.

"*Plaster of Paris* they call it out in the wide world," Catherine said. "I knew, I suppose, that our forefathers mined for plaster here. But how——?"

"I'm told people mined here for stone and plaster a

thousand years ago," Robert said. "So, who knows how many tunnels are under the city, or where they go."

"I know where some of them go," Hachette said. He grinned broadly.

Victoire stared at him. "Hachette, what did you do?" She had the strong impression she had missed something obvious.

Robert said, "Hachette seems to have been more efficient than I'd thought. I was sure I'd arranged to keep him trapped in the city yesterday when I set out to find you, but when Lise and Rafael and I brought you out of Grenier's old house I saw Hachette hiding and watching.

"And then it appears he went down into the cavern. The mine, I suppose I should call it. And then he invited some friends to join him. Between them, he and half the young thieves of Paris, seem to have, under the very noses of the archers, moved all of your cloth into the city through those tunnels, and then sneaked it into your house."

"Mademoiselle, if we hadn't taken it, the emperor would just have burned it or spent it on wars or something," Hachette said.

"Instead of which, you will get the money you deserve," Marie-Louise told her. "And possibly more, because for some reason there is a shortage of painted cloth in the city."

Victoire was still trying to absorb this news when she realized Robert had behaved oddly throughout the entire meeting with Hachette, Catherine and Marie-Louise. He had spoken in a flat voice, like a priest teaching Catechism.

Worse: he hadn't properly smiled at her the entire time. Not once.

The next two days sped past so quickly and so efficiently

that Victoire scarcely had time to think about what she was doing or what was happening to her. Lise de Bellevasse, her hostess, had turned out to be a warm and engaging woman who seemed as fond of her cousin Robert as she was amused by him. She had gone out of her way to make Victoire comfortable when it would have been much easier to resent the intrusion into her home of someone with next to no social capital to spend.

Catherine and Marie-Louise had managed to sell all of the cloth within twenty-four hours—and for far more than Victoire had ever fantasized it could be worth. She was now possessed, Marie-Louise had told her, of a fortune of over four thousand livres—and this after generous payments to each of the women and Hachette. She could pay off the most pressing of her debts and live quite comfortably for several years on the proceeds of this unexpected good fortune.

There were only two things wrong with her life now.

"Oh dear," said the duchesse de Bellevasse, walking into the salon in which Victoire reclined, taking in the early-autumn afternoon sun. "I had thought you were feeling better today."

"There is nothing wrong with me," Victoire told her. "Well, with my body, at any rate.

"Only—Lise, what am I to *do*, now?"

"You want something to do? Ah," the duchesse said, understanding dawning on her face. "I know precisely what you mean. After the excitement of your life so far—"

"An excitement I know I am sworn to abandon," Victoire pointed out. "I had thought all I really wanted was to be able to afford to lead my old life, to return to court and be the happy girl I believed myself to be. Now I see that's not enough. Not after what I've lived. I know this sounds silly to you, Lise. But you have your work and your—your husband. And I—"

"Have some unfinished business with my cousin Robert," Lise said, smiling.

And there's the second thing that's wrong.

Victoire had been dreading this moment. Lise, however, was not someone who could be soothed with a non-committal answer, not on this subject. "I cannot persuade him to see me," she said. "Ever since you and he brought me here he has avoided being alone with me."

"What?" Victoire was surprised: Lise really did look startled at this.

"I realize I'm not the most attractive prospect, but I did think he cared for me." She took a deep breath. "I know that I care for him."

"You may, from time to time," Lise said in a dry voice, "have heard one or another of his family refer to Robert as an idiot. I believe he's outdone himself this time, though."

"Could you get the two of us together? I have no doubt of my powers of persuasion, but I have to get him in the same room in order to get to work on him."

Lise laughed. "I believe you are fully recovered from your injury now. Shall we stalk him together?"

"This is a very good Cognac, Rafael." Robert inhaled the scent again, relishing the spicy sweetness and wishing his parents had developed Rafael's taste in brandies. "I envy you." Robert settled back into his chair, crossing his legs at the ankles and letting the heat of the fire in Rafael's library penetrate the soles of his boots.

"I thought you deserved a bit of a treat," Rafael said, walking to the fire from the liquor cabinet. "It seems to me you ought to be supremely happy now—but instead you're the gloomiest I've ever seen you."

Robert shrugged, suspicious of the direction this conversation was taking. "I surprise myself, Rafael. I find myself without direction. Bored. Suspiciously flat."

"You're about to have more money than you've ever possessed at any one time," Rafael told him. "Lise gives me to understand there will be some sort of finder's fee or reward from the government, for the recovery of the loot Grenier had been hiding in the old mines. I imagine it will be shared between you and mademoiselle de Berenguer."

Rafael's dark smile would frighten small children and cardinals, Robert decided. "Which brings me to the reason I asked you to visit."

"And here I thought you enjoyed my company."

Rafael favoured him with the same satanic smile, and Robert had to suppress an urge to shiver. "No offence, Robert, but your peculiar approach to the social graces has never held much appeal for me. It's enough that my wife finds you amusing and calls you cousin, don't you think?" He leaned forward, and now the look he fixed on Robert was something Robert had never seen before. "Lise has informed me your mother hasn't spoken to you about mademoiselle de Berenguer. I don't expect your father even to know about this yet, but someone in your family ought to have said something by now. So, we have decided, Lise and I, that the duty falls to me."

Carefully, Robert set down his glass. "You might have spared yourself the bother. There is nothing to say." It was a cowardly thing to admit, but Robert had hoped this issue would just vanish, since he'd thought himself to a standstill about it.

Rafael glared at him. "You'd best explain that remark."

"I was about to. You really ought to be better at understanding people, Rafael." Robert got to his feet. "I can't marry her. Surely you understand this. Even if she wanted me, which I doubt—"

"Lise says she does."

"She does?" Hope flared up, was starved for air, died. "No matter. I can't provide for a wife." He laughed, but the laughter sounded flat in his ears. "I never really thought about it before, but you'd be surprised at how much I've been thinking about it the past couple of days. And there's no answer."

"To what question?"

"Only a man with as much money and property as you have, Rafael, would have to ask me. I'm a younger son. I won't be inheriting any property. Might get a bit of money from Maman, but she's hale and hearty and will probably outlive me. I've got no interest in the priesthood and no aptitude for the army." He kicked a spark back under the grate. "A friend of mine said pretty much the same thing to me a while ago, you know, and I thought he sounded an idiot. But the sad truth is, he was absolutely right. Men like me have no business whatever marrying women like mademoiselle—like Victoire."

"Because she has no dowry? I didn't think you quite so mercenary, Robert."

Robert turned away so that Rafael shouldn't see his anger. "I know that I wouldn't have a chance against you," he said as carefully as he could, "but you might agree that I could call you out for that comment, yes?"

There was death, or something very near to it, in Rafael's eyes. But after a moment he gave a shaky laugh and said, "All this time I have assumed, Robert, that you were a happy, easy-going idiot. I now see my mistake. You're very nearly as stupidly stubborn as your cousin. What a relief I only have to be married to one of you." He pulled the bell-cord.

"Are we to fight, then?" Robert asked. A sword-wound would at least take his mind off his more metaphysical hurts.

"Yes," Rafael told him. "With your mother."

"I never forbade you to marry, Robert." The duchesse de Vimoutiers bore an expression of utter dismay at the suggestion she would have even considered such a prohibition, an expression only slightly compromised, in Victoire's judgment, by the icy look in her eyes. "In fact, if we are gathered here—in my best salon, by the way—to hear truths, then I must confess I have long since thought it past time you married."

Victoire saw the proud expression on the duchesse's face falter, and realized that the older woman had realized too late the opening she had created. "So, you will not object," Lise de Bellevasse said, smiling as she charged into that opening, "to Robert marrying the woman of his choice?"

His choice, Victoire thought. When had he made the choice? *And when,* she asked herself, *did you realize he wasn't quite the happy fool people think he is?* Under the very worst of conditions he had somehow made himself indispensable to her well-being, and never offered even a hint of what he was doing. Or why he was doing it. *How deep does he go?* she wondered. She felt a happy lurch, a sense that she was about to float away, at the realization that she might actually be granted the opportunity to see for herself what lay beneath that happy veneer of his. *I just have to talk him into it.*

"I'm not sure," the duchesse said, extemporizing in

the calm unruffled way Victoire's father had used to deal with courtiers. "The de Berenguer family is so old, and honoured, after all. And Robert is, well, a younger son and perhaps not so distinguished as his father and I had hoped for."

"You never showed her your scar, did you, Robert?" Lise asked, pointedly. "Have you in fact ever showed it to anyone? Or even talked about how you came by it?" The questions were ludicrous, the very worst sort of non-sequitur—until Victoire saw the way they'd made Robert squirm, even as Lise's intense, dangerous-looking husband, smiled in stern approval.

"Somehow I've never got around to it," Robert said. "And I don't think this is the time to start."

"This is, in fact, the perfect time to start," the duc de Bellevasse said. He turned to the duchesse de Vimoutiers. "Madame, I take it from your somewhat startled expression that you have no idea what my wife has been talking about. I apologize, in advance, if the subject we are about to raise disturbs you. But if you are somehow labouring under the impression that your son is not worthy of marriage to any of the great houses, I must inform you that you are wrong. The scar to which my dear wife so abruptly made reference is the remnant of a wound suffered in the course of saving several lives during the Prince d'Audemar's unfortunate attempt to overthrow the emperor."

Victoire was startled by the duchesse's response: the woman's face flushed deeply and her eyes darkened. At the same time Victoire realized the duc had been making a reference to the Affair of the d'Audemars, the duchesse's eyes opened wider and she said, "Hold a moment. He saved *lives?* Whose lives?"

"Couldn't be sure," Robert said, shrugging, "who the

prince might have shot if I didn't, well, force him to shoot me first."

From the modest but earnest shriek the duchesse uttered, Victoire knew the older woman had been as startled by this revelation as she had been. A memory flooded back into her mind. "So when you were so upset by poor Hachette's wound," she said to him, "you were speaking from experience." *And God alone knows what you thought when I was shot.*

"Just wish I'd been able to help you better than I did," he said. He still wasn't looking at her.

"Show me." It startled Victoire to realize the voice had been hers.

"What?" This from several people and not just Robert.

"I'd like to see it. To see why you think that it doesn't matter that you are brave enough to put yourself in harm's way. To see why you don't seem to think that you are worthy of—of me. Does your wound look anything like mine, Robert?"

"Probably not," Rafael said with a snort. "He made my mother leave a ridiculously ugly scar so that he could impress susceptible women with it."

Robert winced. "Thank you, Rafael, for taking my side."

Victoire got to her feet. *What has come over you?* she asked herself. "You," she said to Robert. "Come with me."

"What? Where?"

Italy might be nice. I have always liked Milan.

"Outside. With all due respect to the rest of you, we don't need your help resolving this. We just have to talk, head to head."

"Don't bother calling for help, Robert," Rafael said, not quite laughing. "I promise you nobody will hear you."

"Has anyone ever told you, you don't act very ladylike?" Robert felt his face flush; Victoire's matched the way his felt but he felt sure she wasn't really angry. Not yet, at any rate. He decided he was grateful she had dragged him out into the hall and well away from the look of shock his mother's face.

"I'm unconventional," she said. "Isn't that what you want in a wife?"

"Good Lord, how would you know what I want in a wife? I've only just started thinking about it myself."

"You want me," she told him. "You have been following me and getting in my way and just generally imposing yourself on me for months now. What other reason could there be for this behaviour? Why can't you just accept it, and admit it to me?"

"You're worse than Lise," he replied, not answering her question. "What sort of husband would I make you?"

"The sort of husband I want," she said. "The sort I *need*. Robert, I don't know why you feel you have to play the fool with everyone, but I promise you, it's not necessary with me. I know you. I know the man who outsmarted one of the greatest thieves in Paris with a cheap trinket. I know the man who stole Jeanette Desmarais out from under the noses of the duc and duchesse de Beaune. I know the man who worked out that the baron de Geoffroy was not only Nicolette de Beaune's new lover, he was a spy. I know the man who somehow manages to be there to help me even when I don't realize I need help. That's the Robert de Vimoutiers I want. And I'm pretty sure that's the man who wants me, too."

He smiled, but the weight in his heart wasn't lessening

any. "You really don't know what you'd be getting, Victoire. I've no money, and no prospects. No future."

"I've had an idea about that—"

"No. Don't even start. I don't think I could allow any wife of mine to be continually risking her life by breaking the law."

"Not what I was going to propose," she said, trying to glare at him but for some reason failing. "Anyway, I promised your cousin Lise I wouldn't break the law any more." Now she broke out into a broad grin. "Not the emperor's law, at any rate."

"What?"

"Tell me, Robert. When you burst into my house offering to accompany me across the mountains into Italy in the midst of winter, what were you thinking?"

"You already pointed out my lack of wisdom," he said. "No need to do it again."

"Stop being so defensive. I truly want to know if I'm right in what I think was your goal."

He paused, thought back. He'd been quite excited about it, hadn't he? "I was looking forward to the excitement of it, I think."

"*Yes!*" She was practically bouncing on her toes; she grabbed his shoulders and pulled him down and into an astonishing kiss.

"*That* is the kind of wife I could make you," she said when she let him go.

"I think," he found himself saying, "that I now understand what women mean when they say they are getting the vapours."

"What would you say," Victoire asked him, "if I asked you to come with me to the Holy Roman Empire? Not to smuggle cloth but to find out who it was who set de Geoffroy to spy on the emperor."

He had to choke back his instinctive dismissal. This was something different. "Spies?" he asked, after what felt like a very long pause. "Us?"

"Who better? Do you honestly think," she told him, "that the man who outsmarted Clopard and Nicolette de Beaune, and the woman who helped him beat Chenal and Grenier, can't pull the hats down over the eyes of a bunch of inbred Habsburgs? Do you have so little faith in us, Robert?"

She tugged at the neckline of her gown, revealing the round pink spot where her wound was still healing. "You may not remember this, but I do: When we met you asked me if I didn't believe in fate. Well, we were shot in the same place, my beautiful idiot. Our Blessings mesh perfectly. How can I think we're not fated to be together?

"And how can you think that?"

He surprised himself then. Bending quickly, he kissed the wound, feeling the sensation ripple up through his moustache. She giggled for a moment, then breathed in sharply, suddenly. "Fated," she said.

Something in Robert's chest broke and he found himself laughing. "You have convinced me," he said. "I may well be an idiot, but I'm not stupid." Somehow his arms were around her. "I would love to be a spy with you."

"We will play a grotesquely vulgar, wealthy young couple," she told him. "I even know how we will finance this deception."

"I know you did well in selling your cloth," he said, "but I also know you didn't do *that* well."

"But what you might have forgotten," she said, laughing, "was whose overcoat it was you used to pillow my head in that cavern of a mine, after Chenal shot me."

"I hadn't forgotten. I just hadn't thought about it. It was Grenier's coat."

"Yes. And it was *full* of gold. Gold coins. Gold bars, even gold lace. I found it when your cousin Lise sent it back to me this morning. With her apologies because it didn't seem to her I would ever be able to get the bloodstains out." She laughed, but with a sort of eagerness he was beginning to recognize. And love.

"You were absolutely right," he told her, as he led her back toward the salon, and the future.

"We're fated."

About the Author

MICHAEL SKEET IS an award-winning Canadian writer and broadcaster. Born in Calgary, Alberta, he began writing for radio before finishing college. He has sold short stories in the science fiction, dark fantasy and horror fields in addition to extensive publishing credits as a film and music critic. A two-time winner of Canada's Aurora Award for excellence in Science Fiction and Fantasy, Skeet lives in Toronto with his wife, Lorna Toolis.

Books by Five Rivers

NON-FICTION

Big Buttes Book: Annotated Dyets Dry Dinner, (1599), by Henry Buttes,
   with Elizabethan Recipes, by Michelle Enzinas
Al Capone: Chicago's King of Crime, by Nate Hendley
Crystal Death: North America's Most Dangerous Drug, by Nate Hendley
Dutch Schultz: Brazen Beer Baron of New York, by Nate Hendley
The Boy on the Bicycle: A Forgotten Case of Wrongful Conviction in
   Toronto, by Nate Hendley
John Lennon: Music, Myth and Madness, by Nate Hendley
Motivate to Create: a guide for writers, by Nate Hendley
Steven Truscott, Decades of Injustice by Nate Hendley
King Kwong: Larry Kwong, the China Clipper Who Broke the NHL
   Colour Barrier, by Paula Johanson
Shakespeare for Slackers: by Aaron Kite, et al
   Romeo and Juliet
   Hamlet
   Macbeth
The Organic Home Gardener, by Patrick Lima and John Scanlan
Shakespeare for Readers' Theatre: Hamlet, Romeo & Juliet, Midsummer
   Night's Dream, by John Poulson
Shakespeare for Reader's Theatre, Book 2: Shakespeare's Greatest
   Villains, The Merry Wives of Windsor; Othello, the Moor of Venice;
   Richard III; King Lear, by John Poulsen
Beyond Media Literacy: New Paradigms in Media Education, by Colin
   Scheyen
Stonehouse Cooks, by Lorina Stephens

FICTION

Black Wine, by Candas Jane Dorsey
Eocene Station, by Dave Duncan
Immunity to Strange Tales, by Susan J. Forest
The Legend of Sarah, by Leslie Gadallah
The Empire of Kaz, by Leslie Gadallah
   Cat's Pawn
   Cat's Gambit
Growing Up Bronx, by H.A. Hargreaves
North by 2000+, a collection of short, speculative fiction, by H.A.
   Hargreaves
A Subtle Thing, by Alicia Hendley
The Tattooed Witch Trilogy, by Susan MacGregor
   The Tattooed Witch
   The Tattooed Seer
   The Tattooed Queen

A Time and a Place, by Joe Mahoney
The Rune Blades of Celi, by Ann Marston
  Kingmaker's Sword, Book 1
  Western King, Book 2
  Broken Blade, Book 3
  Cloudbearer's Shadow, Book 4
  King of Shadows, Book 5
  Sword and Shadow, Book 6
A Still and Bitter Grave, by Ann Marston
Indigo Time, by Sally McBride
Wasps at the Speed of Sound, by Derryl Murphy
A Quiet Place, by J.W. Schnarr
Things Falling Apart, by J.W. Schnarr
A Poisoned Prayer, by Michael Skeet
A Tangled Weave, by Michael Skeet
And the Angels Sang: a collection of short speculative fiction, by Lorina
  Stephens
Caliban, by Lorina Stephens
From Mountains of Ice, by Lorina Stephens
Memories, Mother and a Christmas Addiction, by Lorina Stephens
Shadow Song, by Lorina Stephens
The Mermaid's Tale, by D. G. Valdron

YA FICTION

Eye of Strife, by Dave Duncan
Ivor of Glenbroch, by Dave Duncan
  The Runner and the Wizard
  The Runner and the Saint
  The Runner and the Kelpie
Avians, by Timothy Gwyn
Type, by Alicia Hendley
Type 2, by Alicia Hendley
Tower in the Crooked Wood, by Paula Johanson
A Touch of Poison, by Aaron Kite
The Great Sky, by D.G. Laderoute
Out of Time, by D.G. Laderoute
Diamonds in Black Sand, by Ann Marston

WWW.FIVERIVERSPUBLISHING.COM

A POISONED PRAYER

ISBN 9781988274119
eISBN 9781988274126
by Michael Skeet
Trade Paperback 6 x 9
May 1, 2018

En garde! Paris, in the 1680s. Dashing swordsmen compete for the favours of licentious women, and magic—God's Blessing—is strong enough that prayers really are answered.

Into the City of Light comes Lise de Trouvaille, a young noblewoman of modest means and no apparent Blessing, searching for an advantageous marriage. But the first eligible man she meets—during a werewolf attack, no less—is exactly the wrong person. Rafael, duc de Bellevasse, is at once too good for her and too bad (he is both the scion of one of the great families of France and a scoundrel presumed to be in league with the Devil, paying huge sums for death-magic spells).

Knowing they are wrong for each other, Lise and Rafael find themselves drawn into plots and conspiracies combining a peasant uprising with the glittering aristocracy surrounding the imperial court. Each has a reason for wanting to solve a series of murders. And each has more than one reason for wanting to avoid the attentions of Nicolas de La Reynie, lieutenant-general of the Paris police and a man

who knows, more than most, that something is going badly wrong in Paris.

I didn't want to put this book down.
Goodreads

A great historical mystery with a strong woman brandishing a rapier!
Amazon

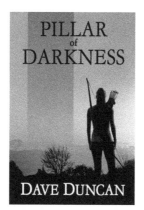

Pillar of Darkness
ISBN 9781988274577
eISBN 9781988274584
by Dave Duncan
Trade Paperback 6 x 9
January 1, 2019

Two hundred miles wide and higher than the moon, Sungoback has stood over central Africa for thirty years, a pillar of light by night and of darkness by day. Science cannot explain it; it destroys technology. What secret lies at its centre: aliens, eternal life, distant past, or far future? Most who venture inside Sungoback are never seen again. Why would anybody dare?

They all have their reasons. This book tells of a party of nine very dissimilar people, who venture into Sungoback together—their motives, their sufferings, and—eventually—their fates.

CPSIA information can be obtained
at www.ICGtesting.com
Printed in the USA
BVHW031459030719
552601BV00001B/23/P